Cross Country with Grandma

Karen Testa was born in Ohio, USA and grew up in Richmond, Virginia. She currently works in England and lives in Hampstead where she and her husband share their flat with one aloof house cat.

Also by Karen Testa

HAPPY LIKE BARNACLES

Cross Country with Grandma

Karen Testa

New York London Toronto Sydney Tokyo Singapore

First published in Great Britain by Touchstone, 1995
An imprint of Simon & Schuster Ltd
A Paramount Communications Company

Simon & Schuster Ltd
West Garden Place
Kendal Street
London W2 2AQ

Simon & Schuster of Australia Pty Ltd
Sydney

A CIP catalogue record for this book is available from the
British Library

ISBN 0 671 718452

Typeset in Goudy Old Style
by The Wordshop, Bury, Lancashire
Printed and bound in Great Britain by
Harper Collins, *Manufacturing*

Dedication

For Peter
and for Marcella Christina Dailey and
Marjorie Audrey Kilmer
Each to each

Acknowledgements

The medical information in this book owes its existence to Courson Cunningham MD and Janice K Dailey BSRN, both of whom were exceptionally generous with their time and knowledge; any errors are the fault of the author in translating fact to fiction. To Lia Jeans goes heartfelt gratitude for her endless patience, her willingness to read and read again, and her commitment to fair critique. And thank you Alex Gourlay, Hugh Hamilton Meikle, Gabby Naher and Sara Fisher, for your honesty, which I appreciate both when things work, and even more when they don't.

Herring Bay, Maryland

The envelope I hold in my hand will break my heart. I know it will, I recognise the return address. This envelope was posted, probably three days ago, from the farthest point West on my own personal horizon, and I stand holding it here, on the East Coast where I have belonged for twenty-nine years. Over my head lilac blossoms bounce in winds which blow freshly off the Chesapeake Bay. Just beyond my bare toes a pile of asphalt holds in place the post of our mailbox, and the sun has heated that black pile until the tar, glistening, serves up an odour to fight with the lilacs. The envelope is thin. In sharp contrast to the current whims of society, the thinness of this envelope means failure; a fat envelope would surely have indicated success. But it would have agitated me as much as this thin envelope.

As they slide along the edges, my thumb and index finger can sense each other through the paper; this envelope is less than thin, it's emaciated. I bet it contains one single sheet of paper – a rejection letter – close-typed and worded so beautifully, so hopefully, and in such admiringly regretful language that it will be, all by itself, a consolation prize. Rejections from big, honoured universities, and particularly from the medical schools attached to them, are invariably works of art worthy of the institutions themselves. An acceptance letter, on the other hand, would be fleshy with details, thick, adipose congratulations and instructions. And still my heart would break because I would have to leave my East Coast home and go West.

It is one of the symptoms of my sickness that I don't think of deserts, oil, and disagreements when someone mentions the Middle East. Instead, the images which arise are of my family, of steamed blue crabs, and broad rivers which empty into the Chesapeake Bay and bear succulent names: the Rappahanock, the Potomac, the Patuxent. For me, Maryland, Washington DC, and Virginia are the Middle East, and the term represents everything I know and cherish in this whole enormous country. And within even this small group of States my love is most fiercely concentrated upon the coastline which stretches and curls, separating the Middle East from the Atlantic Ocean.

I am a doctor and can make my own diagnosis. I suffer, happily and incurably, from *mylocusphilia* – love of my own place. At varied points along this middle coast which collects Northerners who drift down like snowflakes and Southerners who bubble up like hot springs, I was born and raised and schooled.

Nearly thirty years ago, long before this area became a fashionable enclave for the affluent, my parents bought our house on Herring Bay, a back bay of the Chesapeake. For the first eighteen years of my life Herring Bay was my whole world. I grew up playing with the daughters of watermen and was the greatest tomboy of them all. My life moved with the cycle of the water's warmth; I swam until August when the jellyfish moved in, then, my limbs stung red from tentacles, I climbed aboard one of the bathtubby skiffs which our community deemed suitable for children. Not for us the zippy catamarans of resort towns, we didn't even envy those; the boats we rowed or jury-rigged for sailing were first steps for children who might one day captain commercial crab boats. Reluctantly, in October, we beached our little fleet and rode out the winter on land. But by early April my friends and I came back to the water, last year's polka-dot cotton bikinis showing skin, fragile and pale, like the soft shell crabs for which we fished.

I always looked like a Bay girl, tall and tanned and strong with crab cuts on my fingers and lights in my dark hair. Even my temper took after the Chesapeake Bay, renowned for sudden storms and erratic lightning flashes. But I am grown now, and calmer. At eighteen, I left Herring Bay for college in North Carolina, followed by a year in Virginia Beach, then medical school in Charlottesville. For the past three years I have been a resident intern in Washington DC. It doesn't take a flow chart to follow the draw of my blood – always east. Into this middle coast I have sent down roots so deep that, if ever I were transported, my rootball would require an entire flat-bed truck for itself. Relocation would have to be delicate and carefully planned and, despite every precaution, it could be fatal in the end. *Mylocusphilia* can kill. People fight for their places.

In every sense of the expression, this envelope concerns my fight for my place. Seven years ago, during my year in Virginia Beach, a friend whom I thought I would have forever died of pancreatic cancer. He kept his disease a secret for nine months – long enough to produce a human – and in this gestation period generated an idea about how to die that became an epiphany for me. Until my friend Nathan Cawley died, my life followed its programme on an auto-pilot course which had been determined when I first saw *To Kill a Mockingbird.* At twelve years of age I decided to become a lawyer *à la* Gregory Peck, and from that day until the day Nathan told me he was dying, I followed a pre-set path to law school. Aiming for the University of Virginia, I tailored everything to that: my stellar grades, my fervent participation on the high school debating team; even my college I chose because its graduates seemed to feed big name Middle Eastern law schools with regularity. After attaining my law degree I planned on settling in comfortably with a Washington DC firm while living in a condominium overlooking the Potomac; I would never need travel more than one hundred miles inward from my beloved Middle Eastern Coast. Then Nathan died.

Until the night he told me – me, the first of his five close friends and housemates to learn of his disease – I did not realise how my life could change. Nathan sat in our magnificent kitchen with a cat on his lap, a cat who ate smoked oysters and burped terrible, tinned, sea-scented burps, and without preface he said, 'I'm dying.' The reverberation of those words never has ceased humming through me. I stand by my mailbox with an envelope that my fingers have opened without instruction, and even now I hear Nathan. When I decided to study medicine, specifically oncology – the treatment of cancer – I altered the course of my life so that one day I would not have to listen to those words inside my head.

Someone on the West Coast folded this letter in thirds. That someone is a Californian, and he probably paused between making the first and second creases to take a sip of herbal tea, a special blend whipped up by his aromatherapist for urging his negative ions into positivity, soothing his fraught nerves, and softening his ear-wax. But that someone works for a fine medical institution where I could learn miracles. 'If you get the chance to go,' said the doctor who serves as my mentor, 'how could you not? You would have immense opportunities, mind-boggling . . . you are lucky even to be considered!'

He's correct.

I became a doctor because my drive to do so was deep. I am not a natural physician. My grades at medical school were passable, not exceptional, my mind disciplined to literature and logic, not chemistry and biology. From the beginning, though, I've known that I wanted to specialise in oncology, and my advisor, who is fascinated by my drive, has helped me as much as he could. Neither one of us expected that I would be accepted for my oncology fellowship at one of the big East Coast cancer treatment centres, and neither one of us was surprised when I wasn't. But then came a sudden opening at a major university hospital out West, in a department run by my advisor's brother-in-law. My advisor was dangerously enthusiastic, and assumed I would be too.

'What on earth are you *thinking*?' he asked, puzzled and irritated by the troubled expression with which I greeted his opportunity for me.

Try explaining *mylocusphilia* to someone who doesn't believe in human root systems. Just in the time I've stood here, holding this letter, I've sent down into this Middle Eastern soil one enormous tap root and a whole umbrella network of grabbing tendrils. It's a form of protection, lashing myself down before the harvest. Every breath of this rainforest-humid air works like fertiliser on my roots; every time I watch the sun rise over the Bay the image nourishes me. Where does the sun rise in California? I have no quarrel with a sun which sets in the Pacific, because everyone knows that the great solar blob in the sky rises in the East and sets in the West. But at what point East of California does the sun *rise*? Does it come out of Nevada, for God's sake? My sun rises in the Atlantic and goes down below an office block on the west side of Washington DC.

Not for very much longer. The first sentence on the first third of my letter reads, 'We are pleased to inform you . . .' On the third third of my letter I learn that I have to hurry, because I am needed for work on the first of July, and already the date on my watch says June fifteenth. The letter slides back into the envelope, and the envelope slides back into the mailbox where it lies on its back looking lonely and apologetic. Facing the water I walk past the house and down the slope of our back garden. In the shade of Attila the oak tree, so called because the back yard is shaped like Asia, and Attila bestrides the area as a colossus, my mother and grandmother sip tea. Before they see me, I see them and overhear their words. Here at the edge of the Bay voices carry.

'You must have used small, sweet, liver-spotted bananas, Maude. Perhaps those dwarf bananas from the Windward Isles? You can always tell when they're ready for baking because they darken and shrivel.' Mom sounds thoughtful. 'Like simian penises, really. At any rate, this is an excellent batch of banana bread – one of your best efforts,' says my mother.

Though her back is to me, I know Grandma's face looks pinched and pink and pleased, but all she says is, 'It's just an old-fashioned recipe, Liz. I make it 'zactly the same every day, 'spite using different fruits.'

Tea parties are my family's habit, freely engaged in whenever our work schedules permit. Today looks like our archetypal family tea – fruit bread and Earl Grey out on the grass with spring sunshine like lemon zest and Mom and Grandma gently sparring. Theirs is the sort of low-key feud which I imagine would occupy two hermit crabs who fancy the same new shell. To further the feud metaphor, let me suggest that neither crab would think it particularly sporting to go off on a solitary search for a more suitable shell.

Grandma's tea loaves slice beautifully, as they are wet

with fruit and firm from bran. For the half-mile walk between our house and hers, she wraps the day's loaf in waxed paper and settles it, brick-like, in the bottom of her pocketbook. A fruit bread, Grandma declares, is good for the digestion. Into each loaf goes a pound of either bananas, dates, apples, apricots, raisins, prunes, peaches, or blueberries, but never lemons, thank God. Grandma once made a lemon loaf which puckered my entire head.

'Are you all right?' Mom asks, glancing up and taking in my distress. 'Pour some tea for her, will you, Maude? Honey, has the mail come today?'

Almost simultaneously, Grandma pipes up with, 'I haven't seen such a long face in donkey's years. Who rained on your parade?' Because she is busy peering at me, she pours most of the tea on the table.

Around my head a whole conversation eddies, but I fear opening my mouth because I think I might cry.

'You didn't get your position out in California,' guesses my mother. 'Oh, honey, don't worry.'

I shake my head and concentrate on acting my age. Remember that you are twenty-nine, I tell myself. I smooth my skirt under my thighs and pull my spine into a straight line.

'Sheesh!' Grandma whips a hankie out of her bosom and mops the table before pouring me another cup. I can feel her staring fiercely out of her thick glasses. 'You're constipated, aren't you?'

'Oh for heaven's sake, Maude,' says my mother softly, as a tiny bleat comes from the bundle in her lap. My mother is an assistant curator at the National Zoo, and, with hundreds of animal births, spring is her busiest time of year. On her lap, nestled into a woolly ski cap, Mom holds and bottle-feeds a miniature Nubian goat. It has bright, tiny, black eyes and a faintly furry nose. Being a dwarf goat to start with, premature birth has made the kid even smaller.

I smile despite the pit in my stomach. 'When will it be big enough to make cheese?'

My mother does not reply. Grinning, relieved at my response, she unwraps the lower portions of the kid and exhibits enough of its anatomy to prove that *chèvre* will not be forthcoming. Grandma leans in for a closer look.

'Big balls for such a little fella,' she says.

After I laugh I find that I can speak without tearing up. 'On the first of July I start work in California . . .' My mother's eyebrows flee into her hairline and Grandma claps her hands.

'My dear young doctor,' Mom smiles at me, 'that is not at all what I expected you to say!'

Grandma is staring at me again. She has new tri-focal lenses in her spectacles, and perhaps this is what lends a disconcerting intensity to her gaze. 'How you gonna get there?' she asks.

Her question has unexpectedly fierce undertones which match her eyes. When I look at her from this angle, the three levels of her lenses divide each eyeball into three steps, and the result is fearsome.

'I don't have a clue.'

'How's about you and me drive out there?' Grandma leans into my face and favours me with a gaze similar to, but more searching than, that which she bestowed upon the goat gonads.

Mom laughs, then tries to make it sound like a cough.

'Hush up, Liz!' Grandma turns the stare on her.

'Perhaps with a week together in the car, my daughter could teach you my Christian name,' Mom replies, smiling sweetly.

Grandma continually irks my mother, whose name is Elizabeth, by calling her Beth, Betty, Liz, Liza, Lizette, and worst of all, Bets. Even my father calls Mom by an unadulterated 'Elizabeth', and why my grandmother has never learned to do so my mother pretends not to understand. I suspect Grandma of harassment, particularly at holidays, when she uses 'Liz' irritation as a companion to other forms of nettling. I remember such Grandma-isms as, 'What a delicious turkey you've baked, Liz. But why on earth did you go to all the trouble? We could have bought something ready baked and it would have been just as good.' Or, as she said one year when my mother had used ten months' worth of lunch breaks to embroider Grandma a Christmas stocking, 'This is nice, Betty. Someday you should see the really lovely crewel work my other daughter-in-law does. She finishes off her knots so beautiful you just can't tell one side from the other.'

My mother is the person who shares my father's life most intimately, the person who laughs with him and cooks for him. Grandma can't bear this, and particularly that Dad prefers Mom's cooking, and so Grandma staggers under a bizarre burden. She hates, baits, and fears my mother. And yet, my grandmother loves Mom too, because

Grandma adores her son and wants him happy.

'Thank you for the offer, Grandma, but I don't want to go West at all, much less take a week to drive. And there's not much time. I'll take a non-stop flight to San Francisco and relocate in one fell swoop.' I feel that I sound brave.

'That's not how to do it.' Grandma shakes her head vigorously. 'You were Momma's-little-angel and Daddy's-little-girl when you were five, and it's the same set-up these twenty-four years on. You should take a week with me to get accustomed to the West, and I'm the perfect one to guide you. I've been there.'

'You're a Mid-Westerner, Maude, from Indiana. What do you know about California? You've never been West of Chicago.' It is a double sneer. My mother speaks with the unconscious superiority of one who has dwelled always on the Eastern seaboard, along with all her ancestors. She makes it sound as though the earth's crust has only recently cooled West of Washington DC.

'Well for corn's sake, Liz, don't rattle your trap about what you know nothing. Thomas and the boys and me all went West in the summer of 1949. I was thirty-nine years old and I'd never been more than fifty miles from Evansville before that, so you can figure I wasn't keen to go. But I'd got no choice in the matter. Thomas had fixed up an old butcher's delivery truck for travelling . . . I'll never forget the stink in those wooden floorboards. Same smell as if you'd slit a sow's belly and stuck your schnoz right in. Of course, Thomas loved it. He said the smell made him hungry. We went all the way out to Sacramento in that truck, then down to San Diego and back again to Evansville, Indiana six years later. In the same truck we left in, naturally. So don't tell me, Liz, that I know nothing about goin' West.' Grandma looks out over the water.

Mom and I stare at each other. Then I turn to Grandma. As I watch her now, I see a tiny, eighty-five year old woman of alarming energy. She enjoys phenomenal health and a life so full that there never seems time to inquire about a previous existence. When she moved to Washington twenty-three years ago, she decided to work four days a week, eight hours a day babysitting neighbourhood children. Grandma continues this schedule. In addition she has a vast network of friends who insist on seven-day rituals: the weekly bridge game, the poker night, the Sunday Lunch bunch, the Monday, Wednesday, and Friday Dawn Treaders who walk three miles before seven a.m. . . honestly, I find my own hospital schedule lighter, and I'm an exhausted trainee doctor.

Nearly three quarters of my grandmother's life is a mystery, and I am not the only one to have that mystery revealed suddenly; the revelation about Grandma's six years in California has stunned my mother just as much as it has me. Grandma never volunteers her past, just as my father never discusses his childhood. Because the present is crammed and demanding, it overwhelms the past, and I am startled to note the omission only now. What do I know of my grandparent, alias Maude Orpwood Suche, the mother of my father? The things that I know are the things one learns from legends. I know, for instance, that

Grandma emerged into this world after fifty-one hours of labour in the middle of a thunderstorm so cataclysmic that the midwife passed out from terror. And at the moment of Grandma's arrival, a tree limb stabbed through the bedroom ceiling, paralysing everyone with fright. My grandmother's own mother had to cut the umbilical cord on her newborn child. The midwife came in handy later, however.

Shortly after Grandma's birth it was discovered that she had an extra finger, like a secondary pinkie on her right hand. The midwife knew just what to do: tightly she tied a length of white cotton thread around the base of the supernumerary digit, and, on the sixth day after Grandma's birth, the finger fell off. Though she carries no evidence of deformity, to this day Grandma swears she can feel a fingernail growing out of the side of her hand. As a child I often commandeered her right arm, all the better to peer at the coarse and crackly skin around her fingers and thumb. Searching for that sixth stump, I held on until Grandma required her hand to follow her elsewhere.

About my grandmother I know, too, that sixty-three years ago she married Thomas François Suche. But no legends have been created for him. I remember him simply as a Pocket. A Pocket made of red and black checked wool and lined with breath mints, loose bills, sugar cubes, and keys. Hanging loose and inviting on a coat of the same material, the Pocket was all I could see of my grandfather. He was a tall man, and I was short for five years, the age I'd reached when he died.

The Pocket seldom appeared in the same environs as

Grandma, but that never seemed odd. Grown-ups come and go, and the rationale behind their movements is as impregnable to children as it is accepted. Grandfather, whenever I saw him, was just the Pocket, and his sugar cubes made my grandmother's cows smack their lips and chew a hundred times.

'Time for this old gal to skedaddle,' Grandma says, rising and collecting her handbag and the last slice of banana tea loaf. 'I've made my offer, and now I'm going home.' Suddenly her index finger stabs in my direction. 'You think about it,' Grandma commands. 'Seven days across the United States and we would split all the travellin' costs.' The rest of Grandma's hand joins her index finger to flap at us a characteristic horizontal goodbye.

'Baaaaad idea,' Mom says, but nothing more. The kid on her lap sleeps. In silence we sit overlooking the Bay while the sounds of my Middle East fill the air: the wind in Attila's leaves, the lap of water, squawks of an osprey hawk who is feeding her young out on a channel marker . . . last weekend I swam out close enough to count the chicks and smell the fish bones around their massive nest.

I squeeze my eyes shut and imprint the scene on my inner eyelids, for one day soon when the reality lies east behind me.

Because of what I learned at the mailbox this afternoon, I have only five more days as Doctor in Residence at my downtown Washington DC hospital. For three years I have worked here, and I love the place. I love the murals, painted by art students at Georgetown University. I love the familiar feel of the elevator buttons, and the fact that if I'm not in a hurry, I can ride up to Obstetrics, walk past the nursery observation window, then catch a service elevator up to Oncology. I love that the cafeteria ladies stock Twining's Irish Breakfast tea bags just for me. This hospital is my place.

The other doctors offer congratulations on my transfer, and I react with false enthusiasm which fools all my well wishers. Fortunately, though, it is a busy night, with little time for talk. In between a visit to Emma Paterson, a patient I admitted ten days ago with progressive liver failure, and a fast trip two levels down to the ICU floor, my beeper goes off. It is nearly ten p.m. When I go to a phone, an 'urgent' call is transferred through to me.

'Listen,' Grandma's voice instructs. 'I won't keep you too long. I only got a minute, 'cause the gals and I are playing bridge and I'm dummy. What I got to know is, are you scheduled to work tomorrow morning?'

'No, I'm not, but I'll be working anyway. I have to cover for a friend from seven a.m. until two p.m. Now that the other doctors know I'm leaving, they're calling in past favours with a vengeance. I'm free in the afternoon, however.'

'Well then, tomorrow afternoon at three o'clock could you take me to the grocery store?'

'Grandma! You put an urgent call through to the hospital for this?'

'Hush, now. Don't you blow my eardrums out, you're s'posed to be a healer. This call is a lot more important than you think, and it won't last much longer – the gals are getting their knickers in a twist 'cause it's my deal. *Have you booked a plane ticket yet?*'

'Grandma, in the six hours since I last saw you I have not made a single preparation for getting out to California. I'm still in shock.'

'Good. Don't you do *anything* 'til we have our chat at the grocery store. Whoops, gotta go.'

I hang up and try to envisage the real intent behind this phone call. Grandma cannot possible be worried that I have already reserved a flight. What travel agent would sell me a ticket this late at night, even if I had the time to book it? Then my beeper goes off for a real emergency.

Or maybe not. The Oxford English Dictionary defines an emergency as a sudden juncture demanding immediate action. When I run back upstairs, a nurse meets me and walks us briskly along in the direction of Mrs Paterson's private room. The nurse tells me she was sitting with Emma when she realised that the patient's breathing was becoming more laboured, so she called Respiratory and beeped me. Two men are setting up oxygen as we walk in, and the nurse and I keep out of their way while efficient fingers slip an oxygen mask over Mrs Paterson's face.

'Do you want her transferred to ICU?' the nurse asks quietly, handing me Emma's clipboard. We both look down on the patient as automatically I feel for a pulse.

Mrs Paterson has immaculate brown hair streaked with grey, and she wears a pretty flannel nightgown with red ribbon woven into the lace around the neck. When I was little I loved nighties like this, which drive me crazy now because the long swath of fabric twists around my knees as I sleep. Mrs Paterson does not move; her life is waning. Which is not, technically, an emergency, because I have no immediate action to take. Nothing I will ever learn anywhere could possibly help this woman who came to the hospital less than two months ago with what she thought were bad cramps, and was in reality a primary tumour in the tail of the pancreas, metastasised to her stomach and liver. The first time I looked at Emma Paterson's abdominal x-rays, I nearly vomited at the thought of what I had to tell her.

'Do we have a provision for a Living Will?'

'No,' says the nurse, sighing. Over the past ten days she has spent a lot of time in this room. Both she and I have grown to like Emma Paterson very much, a favourite patient. 'Her family is not supportive.'

'All right, then I'll need to speak to them. Could you please call them to the hospital?' The nurse nods as I speak, and barely has she left before I find myself weeping for Mrs Paterson. Every few weeks I lose a patient. The doctor who is my advisor warns that I will cease to be effective if I don't learn to distance myself from this work. I cannot, however, imagine facing the shell of Mrs Paterson with equanimity. Tears make the back of my hand glisten and then the voice comes, as it always does. Inside my head Nathan's voice sounds softly and peaceably: 'I'm dying.' Damn you, Nathan. I couldn't help you when I knew no medicine, and I can't help Mrs Paterson now that I do. I am about to leave everything I love because I feel that I must become the best oncologist on earth, and even after I have added West Coast medical knowledge to my store, my efforts will often be ineffectual. What is the point?

I pat Emma Paterson's shoulder and turn away. Later on tonight I will speak to her family, giving them the options. And if their love is tempered by mercy, then I will come back to her clipboard and write *no code* – no resuscitation.

Goodbye Mrs Paterson, and goodbye familiar hospital. Goodbye East Coast home. The big question of why all these goodbyes are necessary is too much for me to face, so I'll concentrate on less traumatic puzzles. Why does Grandma care so much about how I travel to California? And why does she want to come too?

Between the grapes and the honeydew melons, Grandma and I stand in the fruit aisle at The Giant Food Store. She seems to have forgotten that she has vital things to tell me. We move on to bananas. Picking up one bunch after another, Grandma nudges her fingers through thickets of stems to examine each fruit individually. 'These have more age spots than I do,' she says, frowning. 'Whatever happened to bananas that start out yellow?'

'Perhaps perfection is impossible through tri-focals. Take off your glasses, Grandma, and everything looks nicer.' I squint down at her, filtering her face through my eyelashes, and I find that yes, Grandma does indeed look nicer when I view her less clearly. She had her hair trimmed this morning, and it is so short that she looks prepped for boot camp. Earlier, when I queried Grandma on her hairstyle, she said that it was short and simple for travelling . . . 'Have you considered nectarines instead of bananas?'

'I got to have bananas,' says Grandma firmly. 'Maybe some nectarines for when we go cross country, though. You like nectarines?'

I don't reply. Taking hold of the shopping cart's handle, Grandma zooms over to the carrots and eyes them critically. 'Every day I eat three of these,' she says, 'and that's why I see so well.'

'The lenses on your glasses, Grandma, are half an inch thick.'

'You don't got to tell *me* that. What I mean is that most folks my age have runny eyes, just like waterfalls either side of their schnoz. Cataracts, they call that.'

'You have your definitions mixed,' I inform her, but she ignores me. The shopping cart is now layered across the bottom with one complete coat of fresh fruit in plastic bags. Grandma nudges me off the handle, where I am leaning, and scoots off to peer at the canned vegetables. After working at the hospital night through morning and morning through early afternoon, I don't have the energy to keep up with Grandma, but I am in no danger of losing her. Once her spurt of adrenaline has carried her to the appropriate place, she will settle down and begin reading the labels on myriad cans of creamed corn.

I decide to take the plunge. 'Grandma, I am going to book a one-way airline ticket to San Francisco this afternoon. You are more than welcome to fly out there with me. I'll be busy trying to settle in – find a place to live and all that – but you could do some wandering while I'm busy, and we could have dinner each night. I just don't have the time to drive out to California. In fifteen days I start work!'

'You're gonna be one homesick little chicken,' Grandma tells me via a can of Jolly Green Giant Corn Niblets. 'Take my advice. You got to go West in stages. 'Cause your brain, even a big doctor brain like yours, can't accept five hours on a plane, then, BOOM! A new life starts. So we'll drive out there, you and me.'

'No we won't. Not unless you can give me a compelling reason for doing so.' I shake my head. Grandma appears not to have heard a word I've said, and her insistence and her lack of any logical explanation are beginning to irritate me.

'Well, well,' says Grandma. She stops there and reaches into the sleeve of her sweater to remove the resident soggy tissue. Then she embarks on a colossal nose blowing interlude. Grandma possesses an extraordinary nose which is large and handsome enough to be the pride and joy of her face. In fact, her nose makes up a considerable proportion of Grandma's entire body. Near the pinnacle of her five foot and one quarter inch tall frame, Grandma's beak is on a level with my sternum and it sticks out farther than my breasts.

Pinching her nostrils together with her tissue, Grandma looks thoughtful. She starts to replace her tissue in her sleeve, then thinks of a better place – her budge. That intimate position between her breasts where Grandma tucks money, handkerchiefs, and notes to herself.

'I got to show you something,' Grandma tells me. The canned vegetable aisle is empty around us, and her hand hovers over her breasts. 'For mosta the last twenty-four years, ten months and fifteen days, what I'm about to show you's been stuck in the back of my safety-deposit box. Believe it or not, I'd forgot all about it.' Something shiny arises from the neck of her blouse.

'Jesus Christ, Grandma!' The smooth silver weight she presses into my hand is a gun. I look around wildly to see if we are observed. 'Jesus Christ!' A gun. It lies on my palm about four inches long, deadly and strangely beautiful. Someone put a tremendous amount of work into this weapon; beautiful script engraved along the barrel reads *Li'l Maude*, and on the dark wooden handle, mother-of-pearl has been inlaid to look like waves. 'I don't believe this! You've got a *gun*!'

'Give it back,' Grandma says, then slides the pistol out of sight as easily as a gunslinger finds his holster.

'What in God's name are you doing with that? It's named after you, isn't it! *Li'l Maude*. A personalised pistol, Grandma?'

'It was a gift,' she says, sounding testy. And then, knowing I will follow, she begins pushing the shopping cart to the domain of the frozen peas. 'A fella called Nerf made *Li'l Maude* for me as a wedding present. Nerf Fleishman. That name's not passed my lips in fifty years – but no matter, he was the dearest friend I ever had. You know that name, don't you – '

'Grandma,' I put my hand on the side of her shopping cart and hold it stationary, 'you mean Fleishman, as in major weapons manufacture? Like Colt, Winchester, and Fleishman?' I look down at her in amazement. 'You know the family?'

'I do. Fleishman is a real big company now, but they still run it out of Evansville, Indiana. My friend Nerf Fleishman didn't start Fleishman, but he designed all the most popular guns: rifles, shotguns, pistols and the like. Sometimes he'd let me test-fire 'em. But it was his father, Nerf 'Nester' Senior, who got round to usin' those designs and settin' up the company. He gave up his farm to do it.'

'Where is Nerf Fleishman now?'

'Dead.' Grandma says this quietly, making of it a syllable suited to the frozen food aisle.

A son dying before his father and a father carrying on the business provided by his son. It seems out of the natural order to me, but before I can grasp that, my mind swings back to the hospital. Two years ago I spent a rotation in ER and there I treated some of the most horrific wounds I have ever encountered, most of them a result of the favoured hand-gun in our nation's capital. By the end of my rotation I could distinguish the work of the Fleishman 345 Magnum semi-automatic pistol from any other weapon. I became familiar, too, with the hallmarks of the Fleishman Special Forces rifle and a revolver called the Fleishman Fury. As a doctor I hate guns of all kinds. The knowledge that my grandmother packs Fleishman fire-power in her breast is mind blowing. And sickening and fascinating.

'Is it loaded, Grandma?' The thought has only just occurred to me, and I wonder which way the barrel is pointed, and how close Grandma is to a radical mastectomy.

'Laws, but you're dumb. I used to carry her everywhere, for a longer time than you've been alive!' Grandma looks impatient with my reaction to *Li'l Maude*. 'Take up the slack in your jaw and stop catchin' flies. Listen to me.'

Pushing the shopping cart at arm's length, Grandma marches to the meat section. All the while she speaks quickly, with a voice modulated many notches below her usual stentorian tones. 'When I looked in my safe deposit box the other day, all I really wanted was a quick gander at my will and testament. But I started openin' some cardboard boxes I'd stuck in there, lookin' out little things for you kids to remember me by – you know, not valuable stuff, just knick-knacks. Then I came upon *Li'l Maude*. I hadn't seen her for years. *Li'l Maude* is all the parts of me I put away when I left the Mid-West. For me that's Evansville, Indiana, if you want to put a finger on it exactly.

'You know,' Grandma continues, 'I got a nice little life now. I got manicured nails. And I got my babysitting for work and my card games for play. But I've only lived like this for twenty-three years, and do you know how long twenty-three years is to an eighty-five year old woman? It's not squat. Not more'n a drop in the bucket. Seeing *Li'l Maude* started me remembering things that riled me considerable. Things about your grandfather, things about me. You can't ignore your past, and that's what I been doin', because there's no place for my past here. So . . . I got to go West again.'

Grandma picks up a piece of pork tenderloin, squeezing

and discarding it with unconscious discernment. 'I'm askin' you as a favour for me, but I'm thinking it'll help you, too. I got to make peace with my past, and you got to come to face your future. Let's drive West and see what happens. What do you say?'

'Give me until tomorrow morning to think about it, please. I promise I'll consider this and I'll give you a call.'

Grandma nods, then twirls to grab one of the store's assistants. 'Young man,' she says, linking arms with him and leading him in the direction of frozen vegetables, 'I want to ask you about the peas you're sellin'. Last year's fresh garden peas. Now, are they flash frozen? Because you lose all the vitamins if they're not flash frozen.'

'Grandma,' I call after her, 'can I find anything for you?'

'No.' She fires the response over her shoulder, and it is a meaningful monosyllable. It means, 'No, how on earth would a granddaughter, especially a granddaughter who keeps her brains back at the hospital, know how to pick pork chops which will be suitably priced *and* capable of combining meltingly with home-made rosy applesauce?' It also means, 'No, how would a granddaughter know *not* to buy the pastel toilet tissue which has dyes in it to make your privates itch?' Just no.

I don't understand how Grandma can say that she has lost touch with the past. The past surrounds her; it is her vault of treasures. Ever since I can remember, Grandma has paraded me past her possessions. 'Your second cousin Gordon's Aunt Isabel tatted that for me on my christening day,' she says, pointing to a thin band of lace sewn on to a thread-bare tablecloth. 'That's antique lace.' Or, 'Look at this beautiful carriage for dollies. Your Great Grandfather Bertram Ingold made it for me out of pipe cleaners. It's an antique.' Antique. I grew up thinking the word means something you love because it's old; I learned Grandma's definition.

Grandma's past dominates not just her possessions, but her mind as well. Her thoughts are antiques, and any idea which has not orbited in her mental galaxy for at least half a century is suspect for its ridiculous youth. For Grandma the Republican and Democratic Parties are antiques, but not the President, particularly not any President younger than her sons. And Grandma's views on divorce and the sanctity of marriage ignore fifty years of changing times.

Food merits antique status. In particular, pickles can be antiques, but only if they are Aunt Henrietta's Crystalline Cukes, from the recipe so old no one can remember who first invented them. Grandma says that Henrietta made the tastiest pickles of her generation, so she got to add her name, but the origins of the recipe precede my Great Aunt Henrietta by nearly a hundred years. In her own garden Grandma grows antique cucumbers from seeds which are descendants of the vegetables she grew when she was newly married.

'I planted that first garden. It kept our bellies full during the Depression,' Grandma tells me, with love and pride in her tones. And from hearing her, I know the Depression is an antique, too.

My grandmother has only known my mother for thirty-five years, a period of time which renders Mom thoroughly contemptible. My mother is not part of Grandma's past. Perhaps, though, in fifteen years, when their fierce friendship dates back a full five decades, Mom will have the Order of the Antique conferred upon her. By that time Grandma may be dead.

Maybe it is her age which gives such urgency upon this trip, and maybe not. Maybe I've got it all wrong, but I don't think so. Whatever reason lies behind my grandmother's urgency, my intuition asserts that something odd is about to happen. I am beginning to believe that Grandma's decision to go West occurred independently of my decision to apply for an oncology fellowship in California. Though my letter of acceptance must have seemed like Fate's endorsement, I think Grandma was determined already. When she saw *Li'l Maude* again, for the first time in almost twenty-five years, I think she decided right then and there that she must go West. Banks provide private cubicles for customers to examine their safe deposit boxes; I can imagine Grandma in one. In my mind's eye I see her rummaging through her possessions until her fingers touch a chamois-wrapped bundle. The bundle lies at the very back of a long steel box, and Grandma tilts the box forward so that the gun slides to her. She rolls the bundle over and over, unshrouding it. Then *Li'l Maude* explodes into her present.

Grandma says she has not seen the gun in nearly twenty-five years, and I believe her. But I do not believe that she had forgotten about the gun until recently. Ignored *Li'l Maude*, perhaps. But not forgotten her. I believe Grandma went to the bank deliberately looking for

Li'l Maude. Maybe she also sought the woman who once possessed such a gun, possessed it full-time and strategically settled in her budge. Why seek that woman now? Right now? Why relive the trip she took with my grandfather and her sons forty-six years ago? Even if I arrive in California by airplane, I believe that somehow, Grandma will go West by car. And I think she'll do it soon.

On the fourteenth day before I commence the practice of medicine in California, the telephone rings. It is only seven-thirty a.m. but I am surprised that the calls which link my father to his far-flung business dealings have waited this long. Dad stretches for the phone. 'Good morning,' he says into the receiver. A moment's silence, then he says with a subtle change in tone and texture, 'No, I do not have a sinus flare-up.' More silence. 'Fine. I'll put her on. She's right here, shoving a doughnut into her mouth.' My father pushes the hold button on our business-like kitchen phone.

'It's Grandma,' he says. 'Clear your mouth, then tell her you'll call her back on the other line. And tell her to put her teeth in, for God's sake. I can't understand a damn word she's garbling.' Dad thrusts the receiver at me.

'Grandma?' I say. I am talking into an empty phone. Though I punch the hold button again, she is definitely gone. Dialling her number, I listen to it ring fifteen times before she picks up.

'Your fadda hung u' on me,' she says, sounding aggrieved.

'I don't think so. He put you on hold, then you hung up on him.'

'Oh,' she says. Grandma's monosyllables are more eloquent than whole paragraphs. This particular monosyllable is a short, chopped noise between 'ow' and 'oh' which says 'I ha'nt got time fo' new fan'led technogy, you foo'.' It is Grandma snapping her lips, as dismissive as snapping her fingers. 'You ma' a decisi'n yet?'

No. 'How about I call you back after you put your dentures in, all right?'

'Yeth.'

I can picture Grandma trundling around her house in the interval before my next call. She will be wearing a pink cotton nightdress which falls to her knees, and, despite the warmth of her rooms and the humidity of the morning, a heavy flannel dressing gown patterned like a traditional red and white bandanna. For three years this garment has held first place in Grandma's affections. Originally it was a present from my father to my mother, then when Mom eventually loaded it into a bag for the Salvation Army, my grandmother seized the opportunity for a dramatic rescue scene.

'Liz! For pity's sake, Liz! You can't mean to throw this beautiful robe away! Why there's years of wear left in it.'

'Really! *I* think it looks like something the Marlboro Man would whip out of his pocket when he needs to sneeze. How about *you* wear it.'

So Grandma does, every morning. And quite often she brings it to our house when she comes for dinner. 'Just a pretty litte wrap to guard me from the chill, Bets.'

Because Grandma has barely risen from bed, she will not be wearing her glasses yet, and the numerous folds of skin under her eyes will show clearly, as will the pits flanking her nose – in the past seventy-five years the pads of Grandma's heavy glasses have made their mark deeply. The eyes requiring such thick glasses show whites which are the blue of skimmed milk, whites which merge with her pale, pale irises. While she walks to her bureau, to retrieve her teeth from the glass in which they rest, Grandma will be slathering Pond's Cold Cream on to her cheeks. The skin there is so loose and flexible that, if I were watching, I might think she was rearranging her face.

Virulent breath will cloud the air around her head, because while performing her morning breathing exercises Grandma expels hundreds of cubic feet of fetid air. The ritual goes like this: one deep breath sucked in through the nostrils then held for fifteen seconds to reap the oxygen's goodness; then two puffs out through the mouth. The exercises turn her scalp pink, lending a rosy aura to the thin white fluff which is Grandma's hair.

Normally she rises at seven-thirty and before nine-thirty watches two hours of breakfast television and drinks two cups of instant coffee. Grandma's morning repast involves a banana, one multi-vitamin tablet, one capsule of selenium and two odourless capsules of concentrated garlic.

I wait nearly ninety minutes before calling Grandma back, giving her time to digest the day. 'Hello, Grandma.'

'I been sittin' here, getting old as Methuselah, waitin' for you to call me back. I got to hurry, 'cause I'm due at Jenny Platfoot's to look after her little Nicholas. What's your answer? Are we goin' West together?'

'My reply, Grandma, is more complicated than a simple yes or no, so perhaps you could come to dinner tonight and we can discuss it. I have to be at work this morning by ten but I'm off at six p.m. How about you come here around seven o'clock?'

'Dadgummit, all I ask's a yes or no.'

'No, Grandma, not right now.'

'You mean you're not coming?' The intense disappointment in her voice makes the phone lead-heavy in my hand.

'No, I mean I can't answer you right now.'

Seven years ago I approached decisions much less rationally than I do today, and I believe that my medical training is responsible for the change in me. A few months after Nathan died, I took my violent, frustrated energy and showed up at an MCAT test centre where a pleasant man told me I could sit the medical aptitude exams as a standby. I did, and the next day I applied to medical school at the University of Virginia. Though I had missed the deadline for admissions by many months, I was offered a place when another student dropped out. Open slot, fall right in. It was as though destiny underscored the appropriateness of my decision to practise medicine. But it was not a rational process, and I have never told anyone exactly *how* and *why* I became a doctor. If my fellow resident doctors ever learned that I hear a dead man's voice in my head, they would have me committed. Nathan's voice is, and probably always will be, the constant irrationality in my life. One lapse of rationale is enough; my decision to travel with

Grandma must make sense. Unless, of course, events simply arrange themselves in unavoidable affirmation.

On the way to the hospital I buy a road atlas of the United States and, on a break, I study it. By my calculations the distance from Washington DC to Palo Alto, California measures 2,886 miles.

My God, that's a long way.

Seven years ago I would have said, 'Wow. Let's do it. Let's pack a cooler with a week's worth of food and do all our cooking underneath the hood of the car. Beef Carbonade *à la* Carburettor. Steamed Sea Bass with Spring Onions on the air filter.' But I was a *mylocusphiliac* even then, so I would have travelled on the condition that I could drive out to California, then back to my Middle East, 5,772 miles.

I am listening to a patient's heart. This is Peter Fenway, a mildly renowned DC legislator in for monitoring and observation after undergoing yesterday the first of ten scheduled radiation treatments. During a routine post-radiation check of his vitals, a nurse discovered that his heart was beating far slower than it did before the treatment. Then his pulse rate speeded up to 130. One of today's tasks is to account for such dramatic arrythmia. I am listening, listening, listening.

'2,886,' I tell him, and his eyes widen.

'Not my pulse rate, surely,' he says.

Feeling foolish, I smile at him. 'No, Mr Fenway, it's not. Sorry to startle you.' Grandma's notion of travelling cross country is intruding on my thoughts. Suddenly, standing over Peter Fenway, I realise that I have become so involved with her need to go West that I've forgotten to be prematurely homesick. The roots I've sent down into this Middle Eastern soil are wiggling looser all the time. I have not even noticed.

'Mr Fenway, I'm going to ask you to breathe slowly and deeply. Try to relax.' Mentally I dress my brain in a lab coat.

2,886 miles.

Mom and I are making dinner.

In front of me sits a glass bowl of steaming split-skinned tomatoes, and it is my job to flay them. Each time I slide the membrane off of one, another appears. 'Damnit, Mom, how many of these are we going to *do*? These are hot!'

Serenely she goes on dipping tomatoes into boiling water, watching them bob for ten seconds, then tonging them into my bowl where the hot tomato skin parts suddenly, peeling back like a fault line. 'Would you like to switch jobs with me?'

Having made my complaint and been acknowledged, I shake my head. My fingers turn an even hotter pink, and the pile of tomato skins, lying limp and filmy-useless, grows. 'Mom,' I say, and then close my mouth. What I want to do is ask if she knows about Grandma's pistol. 'Mom,' I say again, 'if I mention the name Fleishman, as in Fleishman the gun manufacturer, what does that mean to you?'

'Humane killers.'

'Excuse me?' Guns so powerful a person expires before feeling pain?

'Fleishman makes a very effective bolt action humane

killer. Makes or made, I don't know which, because the zoo doesn't use bolt-action mercy guns. But years ago back in vet school I had to fire one into an arthritic pony. Precisely into its temple, an absolutely indelible experience. Why do you ask?'

Now I am slicing open naked tomatoes while Mom scoops out the innards. I have about two seconds to decide whether to tell on *Li'l Maude*. 'Because I found out today that Grandma knows the man who founded Fleishman, and she called his son – the guy who designed all the important guns – the dearest friend she ever had. Does that seem strange to you? It's like having a Rockefeller or a Rothschild for a best friend and never telling anyone. The son's name was Nerf Fleishman . . .' I wait, holding my breath. I want her to know more about this than I do, and I want her to tell me.

'No,' Mom says, smiling a little. 'Not Nerf. I would have remembered that name, certainly. I knew your grandmother knows a family called Fleishman back in Evansville, but I had no idea they were the Fleishmans of *Fleishman.* It must be a large family, all dying off now. She buys several sympathy cards every year. I always mail them for her, and they go to names like Emmeline and Clara, and one to someone called Nester – I remember that name specifically. And something else. Actually, it was very strange.' My mother is chopping the tomato flesh into rough chunks, and then she stops. 'This will only take a minute,' she says, tilting her head away from the tomatoes. 'Come up to the spare bedroom with me. We can finish this later. I want to show you something odd.'

It is an inlaid wooden box with the dark sheen of good chocolate. A very expensive piece of craftsmanship, the kind that should hold a fabulous present, probably jewels. And it rattles as my mother lifts it out of the drawer where she settled it for safe keeping. 'Your grandmother brought this to me. I didn't know what it was when she brought it – it was in a cardboard mailing case with a typed label addressed to Maude *Orpwood*, not Maude Orpwood Suche. It came from a firm of lawyers in Evansville, Indiana, and they obviously didn't know her married name.

'Anyway, your grandmother brought it to me and asked that I keep it for her. I was to open it and keep it until she asked for it. And she requested that I never mention it to her, either.' Mom looks thoughtful. 'It's kind of a *clichéd* concept, the secret box, the oath of silence. But Maude was very dignified when she asked, and she asked gracefully, for her. So I agreed. It's been four years easily, and you were at medical school or I would have showed you then. But I forgot, and Maude has never asked to see what the package contained.' My mother shakes her head and passes the box to me. 'I don't understand it. But you brought up the name Fleishman, so perhaps you'll know what this is.'

I discover when I lift the lid that the rattle comes from rocks. Not diamonds, just rocks. They look like granite. And on top of them are two letters, one of which is a cover note from the firm of Evansville lawyers who handled the estate of Mrs Nester Fleishman, who died in 1991 at the age of one hundred and two. According to the instructions of her will, the letter goes on to say, this package was being sent to Maude Orpwood of Deale, Maryland – formerly of Orpwood Farm, Evansville, Indiana. The lawyers state that they regret they are unable to offer any explanation of the contents of the box, but their client Mrs Nester Fleishman remained of sound mind until her demise and she regarded the sending of this package as the first priority after her death.

The second letter is from Mrs Nester Fleishman herself, and it is addressed to my grandmother without greeting. *You will be alive to read this* says the letter. *Orpwoods are a long-lived group. My son is dead fifty years this month. I wanted to let you know that I've never forgotten, and I'll never forgive. These rocks are from the quarry pool, to help you remember.*

'I don't know, Mom.' The letter from the law firm is typed, and the letter from Mrs Fleishman handwritten. Mrs Nester Fleishman used a broad nibbed fountain pen with thick black ink on creamy paper, and she pressed hard enough that the back of her letter feels like engraving. 'This woman hated Grandma.'

'I'm sure you're right,' my mother says quietly. 'Dump the rocks out on the bed – don't worry, there's no dirt, I imagine those rocks were cleaned and kept for years – and look at the inside of the box. I have no idea what it means.'

Inside the box, beneath the rocks, is a velvet lining moulded precisely for coddling a small hand-gun. I know instantly that this was made by Nerf Fleishman, for the presentation of *Li'l Maude* to my grandmother, but I can't tell my mother, not when Grandma has kept her pistol a secret for so long. If I were going to talk about this with Mom, I know now that I would have said something while we flayed tomatoes. She looks at me curiously and is about to speak when I speak first. 'I don't know what's going on, Mom, and I don't think *asking* Grandma will do any good.'

'Dear God, please let her finish soon.' It is my mother's private prayer, whispered almost silently under the words rolling interminably out of Grandma's mouth. Mom is careful that only I, seated to her left, hear her.

Grandma's pre-dinner prayers of grace are stirring, all-encompassing affairs during which the food grows cold. First she blesses everyone present, giving a short description of each person's salient characteristics in case God is confused as to which individual at our dinner table Grandma refers. Tonight she says, smirking under her eyelashes at my mother, 'Thank you, God, for Liz, who works so hard for all Your furry beasts and yet still finds some time for her family and my son.' Then Grandma moves on to heap blessings on the heads of various cousins, aunts, and a legion of dead people I have never known, half of whom I'm certain Grandma has never known either. This is The Grace Game, for two players ages fifty-six through eighty-five. Whoever stops the game, loses.

My mother reaches her limit midway through the second minute. 'Amen,' she says, pulling her hand out of Grandma's pink paw.

'Amen,' says Grandma, pious and triumphant. Then

she starts digging through the pile of pasta in her bowl. 'Isn't there any meat in this?'

'Not a bit,' says Dad, shovelling into his food. 'Just asparagus, cheese, and tomato. I love it. It's one of my favourite foods.'

'Well, I suppose it's not bad.' Instantly she is determined to enjoy her plate every bit as much as my father enjoys his. "Course the best noodles I ever had was at your Aunt Nettie's place. Her speciality was a dish of broad egg noodles, chopped hot dogs, and barbecue sauce. Now *there* was a woman who could cook a fine noodle.'

Parry, aaaaand thrust. An unkind blow, I feel, on Grandma's part. As the victor in The Grace Game she can afford to show some magnanimity. But she chews her pasta and regales us with the tale of Aunt Nettie's wonderful pasta anyway, and as she chews, she pretends, as she does sometimes when she has dinner with Mom, that she has never learned the delicate, necessary etiquette of speaking with a bite of food in her mouth, yet not sharing the composition of that bite with her fellow diners. As she talks, Grandma spits red, white, and green.

I laugh, but Mom is severe. 'It would be nice if you could chew with your mouth closed.'

'I do,' snaps Grandma, and her lips flap shut as though hermetically sealed.

Collecting bits of food that Grandma has expirated, Dad lines up an asparagus tip, a clump of cheese, and a tomato seed on his thumb. 'The Italian flag,' he says and smiles.

'Oh, for Pete's sakes,' says Grandma, finishing her pasta in silence.

We are not going by the rules: Grandma broke them first, and then Mom fed the undercurrents by issuing Grandma a real reprimand; Dad shored up Mom's flanks, and now our dinner is a tense one. The only way to feud bloodlessly and entertainingly as a family is to play by the rules: one shot, then retreat and no dodging for the return salvo. Grandma broke the rules, and I know why.

'Don't take it out on Mom because you're mad at me, Grandma. And don't be mad at me because I couldn't give you a straight answer on travelling West by car. You know I'm in a hurry, so can you be ready to go in four days?'

She puts down her fork. 'Yes.'

'And can you arrange your own way home? I have to stay in California for two years.'

'Yes,' Grandma says. 'I got a single ticket, one-way from San Francisco to Washington DC, reserved already. Just been waitin' on you.'

Mom and Dad exchange glances, and I gaze between them both until my eyes turn slick with moisture. Down in my pasta bowl where my swimming sight focuses is an asparagus tip which looks like a pine cone. When I was younger I dipped pine cones in scented wax to make fancy fire-starters for my parents. And in warm weather the sharp cones still bury themselves in our grassy lawn, all the better to leave splinters in bare feet. On this asparagus tip the whole of my Middle East comes to roost, every bit of the Middle East which has played a different part in each one of my ages. I can't bear that I have just made the plans for leaving home. Quick, Grandma, before my tears turn my face into a salt lick, distract me, as you did before. Wave *Li'l Maude* at Mom and Dad, or hint at why this trip is so urgent for you.

Tell me why we're going West.

Deale, Maryland

Pulling into Grandma's driveway I stop the car just inches shy of the marigold border which delineates her grass from the paved drive. While I park she stands on the porch and looks down at me. Beside Grandma, on the three brick steps which lead up to her front door, sit two plump suitcases and her handbag. The sizes of her luggage are nicely graduated, with the bigger suitcase on the lowest step, a middle-sized suitcase on the second step, and her capacious pocketbook on the highest step. Grandma ruins the pattern; she stands on the level surface of the porch and she is considerably larger than her handbag. But she looks so pleased and eager that I forgive her easily. My watch says five-thirty a.m. on June twenty-second.

'You're just in time,' Grandma says, sounding thoroughly satisfied, and I think she means more than what she says. Not only have I arrived to collect her exactly at the appointed hour, but I am helping Grandma keep a self-scheduled appointment with her past and she likes being punctual. Almost as much as she enjoys keeping secrets.

By what route will we travel West? What kind of trip are we taking? I don't know. When Grandma appropriated my United States road atlas she told me not to worry about our itinerary. And I don't know if today we embark upon the one-star bare bones tour or the two-star luxury jaunt, but I have packed for both. For the first type of trip I have a tent, equipment for cooking at campsites, toilet paper and a small spade, water purification tablets, and an emergency credit card. For the second kind of trip I have smart attire, a guide book for steering us to exquisite gourmet sites across America, and four brand new, never-before-burdened credit cards.

Secrecy creates distractions. Because I can't fathom what lies ahead, I have less time to worry about what lies behind me – the sun rising from the Chesapeake Bay, for instance. And surprisingly, my rationale has submitted gracefully to all but one of the uncertainties surrounding this trip. What you cannot disregard, says my rationale, is that your passenger is eighty-five years old. The physician in me claims this is a risk, while the granddaughter in me says that Maude Orpwood Suche will live forever. For evidence, the granddaughter cites the physician an incident earlier this spring.

'Liz,' Grandma cried out over her teacup one day in March, 'I can't breathe any more!' Grandma took another sip of Earl Grey as my mother tried to determine how alarmed she should be. The older woman looked in no immediate danger of asphyxia, and besides, my mother had been expecting an outburst from Grandma for some time; most of Grandma's friends are sickening or dying off, and, without exception, they are younger than she is.

Conversation over the card tables must be macabre; even the censored snippets which Grandma relates to Mom and me have ghoulish facets. 'Violet Dilworth died at lunch-time on Tuesday,' she said one day. 'Poor soul got a paper cut, and it pussed all up an' poisoned her. Hope I'm made from sturdier stuff.' Soon after we heard of colossal bunions which confine women to wheelchairs. And then Grandma telephoned Mom at work to talk about her dear friend, Pidgy Freeman, who was seeing a 'bladder expert' to find out why she leaks when she sneezes.

'I got nothin' to contribute when all my cronies talk about their ills,' Grandma said, sounding gloomy. 'And, dadgummit, they talk on sickness *all the time.*'

When I heard this I responded in the wrong, cheerful tone of voice, and I said precisely the wrong thing. 'Face it, Grandma. You're terminally healthy, and you may as well enjoy it.'

So Grandma went away to chafe long and hard over the inadequacies of her anatomy, and by mid-March she had consulted with her body and discovered a shortness of breath. 'Really, Liz, I can barely breathe. Sometimes after I eat I turn blue. You don't look too concerned, so I guess the old saying about the tailor's family goin' bare-assed and the doctor's grandmother goin' unattended is true. Eh?'

I ran a massive battery of tests on Grandma, whose most recent visit to the doctor was when her youngest son was born, fifty-four years ago.

'Dad is fifty-six years old, Grandma. Not fifty-four. It's

been even longer than you think since you last saw a doctor.' I drew 10cc of blood from Grandma's wrist as I spoke, and she did not reply.

After a chest x-ray, an EKG, complete blood work, and urinalysis, I concluded that Grandma was ten pounds too heavy for her girdle. If she stopped wearing one, or took the revolutionary step of buying a new one, I promised that her breathing problems would disappear. And they did.

So the evidence stands, the granddaughter in me informs the doctor who inhabits the same body. Grandma has the heart and lungs of a twenty-five year old marathon runner and the cholesterol level of a lemon. But if you must, the granddaughter says, hoping to appease the doctor, then travel with a first aid kit the likes of which the world has never seen, and settle it within easy reach behind the driver's seat. *I've planned that already,* replies the doctor. *I suggest ampules of nitroglycerine for chest pains, and antibiotics for high fevers, and serum for bee stings. I'll have saline/sugar packs in case of dehydration. Someday, though, no matter what I do, we will hear Nathan. 'I'm dying,' he'll say, softly and peaceably, and he'll be talking about Grandma.*

I don't think so, replies the granddaughter. But if and when it happens, we'll tell her about how Nathan died. And if she achieves such grace, then she really will live forever.

'Are you ready, Grandma?'

'You bet,' she says. As we load the car with her suitcases, Grandma shakes her head. 'You know what the hardest part of gettin' ready to go's been? Cancelling all my babysittin' jobs for a week. Now wouldn't you think that an eight-five year old gal could get away from work without a problem? T'ain't so. I'll bet I've had a tougher time than you had leavin' the hospital. Why, Jenny and Nicholas offered to pay me a dollar more an hour, and Allan and Bitsy were very upset, and Marge, who's pregnant and big as a barn, wanted to know how she's supposed to handle things if the new baby comes while I'm gone.' She sighs and settles into the front seat with her pocketbook in the foot well.

I can never keep track of all Grandma's customers; she is in great demand to look after people's children, and her pride in being everyone's favourite babysitter is enormous. She talks about each child and its parents as though I should be familiar with them all, but I have given up trying to sort out Bitsy's baby from Ellen's toddler, from some anonymous someone's kindergartener, Andrew. To add to the confusion she also cares for several cosseted dogs who are considered as offspring by their owners. The 'clever Christopher' with the 'beautiful hair' to whom Grandma often refers might be a dog.

'What did you tell all these parents who complained about you leaving for a week?'

'Well, I want to keep the work, don't I, so I generally acted kinda pathetic and just quivered out, "Don't grudge me the holiday, dear. I'm eighty-five years old and I'm prob'ly at death's door." Sayin' that shut most folks up, and I got some big tips so as I could buy myself somethin' nice on this trip.'

I laugh and shut Grandma's door for her. As I walk round the car an exclamation sounds from within.

'Jeezle peezle!' Tugging determinedly at the strap which my car automatically pulls snug across a passenger's chest, Grandma repeats herself, 'Jeezle peezle! I'm hurting. What d'ya call this thing? I've never seen such a seat belt! You got to adjust it, 'cause it's so tight *Li'l Maude* is diggin a hole in my nipple.'

Without a word I adjust the strap. Then I sit back in my seat and stare straight ahead as the silence lengthens. Suddenly I am not enjoying this at all. I can't hide it from myself any longer. I am leaving my Middle East *and* I'm embarking on seven days hard drive with a pistol-packing octagenarian who won't tell me what she has to prove. I don't even know, and I'm not sure I *want* to know, whether her small shiny weapon is loaded. But I don't want it in the car.

'You got a real peculiar look on your face, what with your lips all pinched up tight. You look just like Liz,' Grandma says at last. 'What for? Surely you figured out that *Li'l Maude* has to go West.'

'Actually, no I hadn't. And this may sound like a stupid prudish question, Grandma, but do you have a current licence to carry a concealed weapon?'

''Course not. In all the world, outside'a you and me, there've been just two people who know about my pistol. And they're both dead – one of 'em breathin' through daisies, darn his hide, and the other one breathin' hot fumes in Hell, if you believe the Scriptures and what they say on taking your own life. Who's goin' to know or be hurt by this tiny pretty thing between my boobs? I don't carry it for killing, if that's what you're all tetchy about, even though *Li'l Maude* was made to be beautiful *and* a killer.'

'Is your pistol loaded?'

'No she isn't, and she never has been. Nerf Fleishman, who made this gun for me – '

'I *know* Nerf Fleishman made your weapon. I *don't* know why he made it, or why you've never talked about him.'

'Don't interrupt. Nerf made just four silver bullets to go in her, and because *Li'l Maude*'s got tricky innards, once these four bullets get used, there'll be no others.'

'I thought silver bullets were only for vampires.'

'Well, I suppose that's what Nerf was thinkin', too. But I put this gun away almost twenty-five years ago, that's the important thing. The year before Thomas died I wrapped it in an oiled rag and put it away. Didn't even look at it 'fore I lay it in that safe deposit box. I wrapped *Li'l Maude* up as though I'd never see her again, and, when I'd done that, it marked the last decision I had to make in the matter of your grandfather. For better or for worse I made that decision, and 'cause God is kind, I didn't have to live with it very long.'

'What decision, Grandma?'

Raising a hand to pat her chest, she looks over at me and sees my eagerness for her answer. It used to embarrass me intensely when she did this in public, patting her breasts as if to ascertain, unconsciously, that they're still firmly fixed atop her breastbone. Some of my patients on the oncology ward touch their hair in a similar fashion, and the gesture no longer annoys me. Then Grandma says, 'I'm reckonin' on you deciding never to come home again. Do you figger this as a permanent thing, your move out to the West Coast?'

'No.' Because it is in the code of my creation, I, too, can exclaim in meaningful monosyllables. This no says, 'what a damned bitchy thing to say, Grandma. You told Mom and me about leaving your childhood home in Evansville, Indiana, and travelling out to California with Thomas Suche, and you sounded pretty upset when you said it. At thirty-nine years old, you were heartbroken with homesickness. So you should understand that I don't want even to imagine never coming back here, you antique unfeeling cow.'

'You don't like my question, do you?' she asks.

'It seems insensitive to me, Grandma. I had almost fooled my roots into thinking of the next two years as a transfer, not a transplanting. You've riled my rootball.'

'Well, I'm sorry. I sorta lashed out without considerin', 'cause I didn't much like *your* question.'

'What question?'

'You asked what decision I had to make almost twenty-five years ago, and I just don't feel like answerin' that right now. It's early, I haven't had my coffee, and I haven't thought about it in donkey's years. Let's you and me make a rule for this trip – if ever you feel like askin' me a question, you talk to your gut first and listen to what it says about whether or not it's a good time to ask. OK?'

'Certainly.'

'Now, let's get goin'.'

'You have the map, Grandma. All I know is we're going West.'

'You got that right, Doctor. Head like you're goin' to Charlottesville, back to the Univers'ty of Virginia Medical School.'

Our departure morning is a fresh one, white-washed with the promise of sun so bright that it will catch at the edges of our eyes. Driving up to meet the Interstate 95 loop around Washington, we travel in the jet-like suction flow behind a big truck. The truck, tattooed with a moving company's name, is roaring along, and the speed makes my car hum.

Over the hum I hear the short report of snaps and buckles being prised open on Grandma's pocketbook. Somewhere from within, Grandma takes out a wad of raggedy-edged papers. The papers are rolled up like [illegible]

[illegible] envelopes?' With one hand she nudges me before slipping the rubber band off the papers. Grandma wears a collection of rubber bands on her wrists like bracelets.

Smiling slightly I ask, 'For what reason would I save envelopes?'

'Why, to make notepaper, of course. You can get four little notes out of a business envelope. All these bright young things talking about recyclin' – I was recyclin' before it got fashionable, before there was even a *name* for it. Your Grandfather Thomas just called it penny-pinchin', and it put him in a temper, but I say why pay good money for a notepad when I can make my own?'

'I never buy notepads. I never have to; doctors see so many little notepads thrust at them that they think pads multiply like bacteria. Drug companies send them out to us for advertising purposes, and the notepads say things like "Zofran".'

'What's that supposed to mean?' Grandma asks, smoothing out the top sheet of her home-made pad.

'Zofran is a drug I often prescribe. It counteracts the nausea which patients feel after chemotherapy.' Falling silent, I consult my 'gut' to see whether I can question Grandma about the writing on her notepad. Out of the corner of my eye I can see her minute runic writing, and I want to know what it says. Grandma saves me from having to ask.

'I got some requests for our trip,' she tells me, tapping one long polished talon on the paper. 'I didn't tell you these before we started, 'cause I didn't want to put you off, you bein' in such a hurry and all. The first request is that we never go more'n a hundred miles between bathroom stops.' Grandma waits on my nod before continuing. 'And thirty minutes after I drink my morning coffee, I *got* to go to the toilet, so even if it's less than a hundred miles we got to stop. Or else we'll both be sorry.' She looks down to read rule number three from her list.

'I prob'ly don't even need to read this one, but I will anyway: *Li'l Maude* is private. No mentionin' her in public, not ever.'

'You're right, Grandma. You didn't need to tell me that. I've no intention of getting us both arrested.'

'Good. And the last rule's the most important. Don't

ever question why I say we got to go by a certain route, why we got to go to a certain place. Don't you worry about gettin' out to California on time, 'cause you'll get there with four days to spare – I've planned it all out. Or at any rate I've planned *most* of it. Some things I got to judge by how I feel, if you get my drift. But just don't ask, you hear?'

This time I don't nod, because I'm puzzled and slightly uncertain about what I'm agreeing to. Grandma, however, does not wait for an acquiescence.

'That's it for the rules. Short and sweet, so if it's all right by you, I'm gonna take a little snooze now. I got up awful early for an old gal like me. Wake me up when we get to coffee, and you can play music if you got to, but just please don't play it loud.'

Twisting under the seat belt, Grandma turns away from me, and, shortly, begins to snore. Each time she breathes out there appears a cheeseburger-sized patch of fog on her side window. The moisture has time to evaporate in the long intervals between each breath, and I find myself listening very carefully to make certain her respiration remains constant. Soon I am holding my breath in time to the silence between snores. Geneticists theorise that nature makes babies adorable to entice adults into protecting them. Here I am developing my own genetic theory, about how nature has old people sleep in such a way that those unfortunates listening to them will hang on their next breath; you look after what you worry over. Eventually I have to turn on the radio for distraction, because both the doctor and the granddaughter in me are dizzy with awaiting Grandma's next breath.

Albemarle County, Virginia

One eye follows on the road, but just like a dog, my nose is up at the crack in my window. I don't possess Grandma's still keen olfactory organ, but I don't think even she could find the scent I seek. After heading deeper and deeper into the heart of Virginia, we have finally come to the point where I can no longer smell or sense the Chesapeake Bay or any of its tributaries, and I am disheartened nearly to dizziness. And as we pass Culpeper, the only city between Washington DC and Charlottesville, Virginia which the atlas deems worthy of bold letters, the ground begins to swell. The road, too, swells – just as though we are travelling up the curling underside of a wave while it gathers speed and rolls for the shore. If I follow this geographical metaphor farther, I locate the Blue Ridge Mountains as crest of the land wave which crashes on to the shore of my Middle East. By travelling West, Grandma and I are riding against the tide; I can feel the drag on my body.

Beside me Grandma never stirs. Her snoring, however,

has kept pace with the music; so far I have had to turn my tunes from a whisper level, up to the decibels of quiet speech, and now to the volume of normal conversation. Almost magically, Grandma adjusts her snores each time so that they are loud enough to overwhelm the music. It is baffling.

'Grandma,' I finally say. 'Grandma . . . wake up. We've reached the outskirts of Charlottesville, and I need you to tell me where to go.'

She comes to life slowly, her head swivelling around until I come into view. 'Hmph. Coffee. I got to have some coffee. Is that a McDonald's I see up ahead? That's where we got to go. McDonald's.' She brings the atlas into the restaurant with her.

At the counter I ask for hot tea, a request which provokes an upheaval among the workforce.

'My granddaughter's a difficult one,' Grandma says archly. She addresses a chubby boy wearing a blue and white uniform, and she bobs her head in my direction.

'Yes, Ma'am,' the counter boy says obligingly.

As I walk away to wash my hands, I hear Grandma asking the boy why he isn't in school, and I know that by the time I have hit the button on the electric hand dryer in the washroom, Grandma will have sucked him dry of his entire life's story.

It must have been short. I return to find Grandma seated in a booth and completely occupied with stirring four sugars into a heavy paper cup of coffee. Peeking out of the side pocket of her handbag is another sugar packet, and the bulge beneath that one is the size of a package of cigarettes. Grandma has made a comprehensive raid on the McDonald's sugar stores.

'What a nice boy,' Grandma says, pointing at the counter person who helped us.

'I hope you didn't tell him that he needs to lose weight. Sometimes you tell people truths that they might not necessarily want to hear.'

'It ain't so all powered awful if a fella's got a little meat on him – I like that in a man – so of course I didn't tell him that he's just a tad on the heavy side. I know how to talk to people!' Grandma puffs with indigation. 'But what I *did* tell him is that if he sleeps every night with a rubber band around his ears, they'll stick out less and he'll be more successful in his career.'

Spluttering into my tea, I blow the top inch of liquid all over the table.

'It's the truth,' says Grandma with dignity. From her bosom she fishes out a tissue and begins wiping the table. 'Laws but you're a mess.'

'Please tell me you're not going to replace that tea-soggy hankie back in between your breasts. I hope I'm not breaking the rules when I ask this question, Grandma, but *might something in there rust?*'

Looking sharply at me, she whispers, 'Hush! *Li'l Maude* is silver. Maybe not silver all the way through, 'cause I reckon that'd make her body too soft to be much use, but she's coated real thick with pure silver. Silver don't rust!' Nonetheless, Grandma folds a dry, clean napkin into a square and dips it into invisibility beneath her blouse. For good measure, she sticks another clean napkin into the sleeve of her sweater. 'There,' she says with satisfaction.

Picking up the atlas, I open it to the page labelled 'Virginia' and set it in front of Grandma. 'Where?' I ask, liking the spartan rhyme.

'Well, we got a ten-thirty a.m. reservation in White Sulphur Springs, and I figure the best way to get there is to find Route 64 West out of Charlottesville, then just stay on that straight through to the border of West Virginia, where we find White Sulphur Springs. You got that? I bet it's on the tip of your tongue to ask me what's in White Sulphur Springs, but don't, just don't. Now,' says Grandma, folding her hands and leaning back, 'we can drive or we can stay, but I'm gonna have to flicker in half an hour. Like I told you, I got a real headstrong bladder about the size of a pea.'

'In the medical profession we use words like *frequency* and *urgency*. And we don't say pee or flicker, we say *void*, unless, of course, we're feeling pompous or defensive, and then we say *micturate*.' I slide out of the booth. 'We'll stop again in half an hour, if that's all right with you.'

'Well, sure. But t'ain't just me, ya know, with this problem. When I go toodlin' on bus trips with my senior citizens' groups, the men who drive the buses plan the route so as we find facilities exactly thirty minutes up the road from where we eat.'

'That certainly gives me a standard of excellence for which to strive, Grandma.'

'Doctor, don't get smart with me.'

I walk out to the car at top speed, but Grandma beats me to the bumper. 'Now we do our exercises,' she says.

Starting out with deep knee bends, she moves on to extending her arms above her head, then patting various parts of herself on the way down to bending at the waist and dangling her fingers above her feet. All the while she hums something which sounds like, 'Head and shoulders – gasp – knees and toes, knees and – gasp – toes.' To finish off the exercises she circles the car three times at a fast trot.

'Whew,' she says, pulling a napkin out of her sleeve to wipe her forehead. 'I do these same exercises each time I go on a bus trip, and everybody does them with me.'

Imagining Grandma as she herds all her cronies three times fast around the bus, I begin to laugh.

'Next stop you oughtta do my exercises, too,' Grandma urges.

'Did you take exercise breaks the first time you went out to California?' The question pops out before I have time to ask my intuition whether or not the timing is appropriate.

'No,' says Grandma and settles down into her seat. Hers is a noncommittal, middle-of-the-road monosyllable, and I wait for either a rebuke or an elaboration. 'Come on, let's get movin'.'

'No, I didn't take my exercise breaks. In 1949 nobody took any exercise at all, and even if they had, I was too busy on my first trip out West, too busy sitting in the back of that butcher's van, smellin' hot pork and pickin' sawdust out of my clothes.'

Just outside of Waynesboro, Virginia, the road inclines steeply, and my ears refuse to pop. From our higher vantage point we can see over miles of peaceful green valleys and blooming mountain laurels. These are the foothills of a not terribly high but exceptionally beautiful mountain range. Sometimes sudden dips in the road make Grandma cover her mouth and clutch at her stomach. 'Ooooooh,' she says, but it is the only noise she makes for miles.

'Turn left, here, on to Skyline Drive,' Grandma says without preamble. 'I want to see the Devil's Knob.'

'The Devil's *Knob*?'

'Sure. About three miles down this road. 3,851 feet tall. Did you know I got a real thing about mountains? Mountains do somethin' to me right here.' Grandma pokes her abdomen and sighs deeply, then begins to read from the map. 'These are the Blue Ridge Mountains and the Shenandoahs, then come the Appalachians and the Allegheny Mountains. Accordin' to the atlas, the Appalachian Trail is in the Shenandoah Mountains, not the Appalachians. Now why d'ya suppose that is? Look.'

'I'm sorry, Grandma, I can't take my attention off the road right now.' It's winding and narrow, and as my car labours upwards, the automatic transmission falls from seventy to fifty miles per hour even with the accelerator pressed to the floor. At 3,000 feet above sea level my poor car sounds a wreck. What will happen in the Rockies of Colorado? While I am wondering, Grandma sits up a little straighter, peering hard at a sign I barely even notice, and she leans forward. Though I am peripherally aware of her actions, they don't really register, and then suddenly she sucks in her breath shudderingly hard.

Grandma's next words hit me like an electric shock.

'Stop!' she shrieks. 'There!' And her arm snakes out to jab one fingernail at the glass.

On reflex I swerve from the inner lane across one other lane and into a crescent-shaped pull-over. The pickup truck travelling just behind me honks loudly, repeatedly, having to swerve to avoid collision. When I kill the engine the only sound I hear is the pounding of a heart in my eardrums. It was incredibly good luck that the truck did not hit us. Staring at the steering wheel, I sit stunned, but beside me the passenger seat is empty. Even before we came to a complete stop Grandma catapulted from the car, all the better to see the Devil's Knob.

Rimming the outer edge of the parking crescent, a thick stone wall prevents cars from pulling too far forward into . . . what? A little shakily, I walk to the edge and see a sheer drop of what looks like a thousand feet. 'Holy shit.'

Grandma rams me in the side with her elbow. 'You can't say that here! It's blasphemy!' All around us, in the most majestic silence imaginable, mountains rise. But Grandma's jab was a painful one, and I am furious.

'Don't ever, *ever* shout at me when I am driving, because we very nearly died! If that truck hadn't swerved we'd be a huge blaze of pyrotechnics right now, all so that you could see a damned mountain! Did you just not *think* or do you feel indestructible? Forget about rising up out of ashes, Grandma, because phoenixes happen only in *fairytales*!' I glare at her while my temper spends itself. Grandma stares back, then without a reply turns to look at a National Park Service bulletin board which explains what we are meant to be looking at from this spot.

What am I doing?

I should have flown out to California. I don't have the time or the heart for this drive and I don't have the energy necessary for making the three-hour return trip to Washington DC, then booking an airline ticket, then having to say goodbye to my home all over again. Which is what I am going to have to do, because surely Grandma's feelings are too hurt for her to want to go with me anywhere. What on earth do I say to her? While I am trying to decide, I hear Grandma marching over, grinding gravel into powder beneath the heels of her sneakers.

'Three thousand eight hundred and fifty-one feet tall,' she says. 'The Devil's Knob.'

'That's a big knob.' Then I blurt it out. 'Listen to me, please, Grandma. I'm awfully sorry for shouting at you like that. I accused you of acting without thought, and then I did precisely the same thing. Not smart.'

She regards me silently.

'You know,' Grandma says at last, 'it's been fourteen, no, fifteen years since I last drove. Do you know how I learned to drive a car? I learned to drive a car after havin' taught myself how to drive a *truck* – an eighteen-gear Kenilworth Conventional hooked up to a tractor trailer chock-full of young steer. I was forty-seven years old, and scared to death, but there was no one else to do it, and that beef just *had* to get into Evansville proper for the three-monthly market. Did you know I could drive a vehicle with a twenty-ton axle? Betcha didn't. After the first few times I even got to like drivin' such a giant. And when I went to learn the car, that seemed easy after toolin' round in an elephant.' Looking off at early summer in the Blue Ridge Mountains, Grandma continues, 'I guess what I want to say is that I should have known better than to surprise you when you're drivin'. I should've thought before I hollered at you to stop. In your position I prob'ly would have screeched a little myself.' Grandma reaches up to pat me on the shoulder, then the pat turns into a gentle push, steering me back to the car.

'Come on, let's get goin'. I'll tell you somethin' you should know about me and the mountains.'

Love, Virginia

Here is what Grandma told me about mountains. It took her over an hour to explain, because she spent more time in her memory than she did in my car. I would give an extra day in my Middle East to know the whole of her mountain memory, to see the things she saw in her silences. I know so little about the her that existed before I did.

'I was thirty-nine years old before I set eyes on anything taller than the steeple of the First Presbyterian Church in Evansville, Indiana. Thirty-nine years is an awful long time to go without ever seein' anythin' much grander than yourself. When Thomas and the boys and me left home to go West, we travelled two days before I looked on anything but flat land. Illinois, Iowa, and Nebraska were so flat – I got cookie sheets with more curves – that when we came to Colorado, I was just expectin' more of the same. Flat, flat flat.

'"The power of earth burps" – that's how Thomas explained our first mountain. It took my breath away. I don't mean Thomas's dumb explanation, nat'rally, but that mountain itself. And when we got to Denver, the "Mile High City", I was so excited the boys and me were just dancin' in the back of that butcher's van. I can't explain the way I acted any more'n to say that once you see somethin' so awesome, so surely moulded by the mighty hand of God, you think your life is goin' to change. I felt that nothing'd ever be the same again, and I felt it right down to the pit of my stomach.

'Of course, nothing changed. But I never have lost my faith in mountains. Each time I see one, my stomach jumps like it's tryin' to soar, and I feel real humble and hopeful.'

White Sulphur Springs, West Virginia

I have a bad head, tea stains on my blouse, and cut-off shorts.

'I'm surprised Liz let you out of the house lookin' as you do,' Grandma says, gazing at me with disfavour while drawing breath to expand upon her theme. 'Your mother puts nicer things than what you're wearin' into the good-will bag. I always tell Liz, of course, that the very best thing to do with old clothes is to make rags for cleanin' windows, then you never got to buy paper towels. But she don't listen to me. These duds you got on'd be good for polishin' the john. This what you wear at the hospital?'

'A labcoat covers many sins, Grandma. *You* look very nice today, but then again you knew that we have a reservation at someplace special. I did not.'

'But I always dress this nice,' Grandma reminds me, and it's true. Today she looks her usual intensely colour-coordinated self, the only concession to travelling being that she features a high percentage of polyester because it refuses to wrinkle. Today's colour scheme is hydrangea blue.

Below the waist Grandma wears a knee-length hydrangea-blue golf skirt and white ankle socks. Astonishingly, her sneakers are the exact same shade of blue as her skirt, a sartorial spectacle which rendered me mute when I joined her early this morning. The sneakers sport pristine white laces which match both her socks and the background of her blouse, a sleeveless garment scattered with a print of tiny hydrangea-blue daisies. Draped from Grandma's shoulders is a lacy, white, crocheted sweater, and around her neck hangs a strand of hydrangea-blue and cat's nose-pink glass beads. On her earlobes she wears more cat's nose-pink in the form of clip-on blobs. These appear, on closer inspection, to be a young artist's interpretation of soul of rosebud. Being rather lighter, but the same general species of pink, Grandma's scalp contrasts nicely with her earrings.

'My gut tells me to ask you where we are going, Grandma, and how I'm supposed to get there.'

'You'll see signs in just a sec,' Grandma says. 'We're goin' to The Greenbrier.'

'You must be joking! For breakfast?'

'Yes.' Grandma sounds unaccountably serious. 'It oughtta be dinner, but that don't match up to your schedule. Now, pull over right herre at this gas station so you can find yourself a decent outfit. Trot on into the restroom and come out lookin' like you're accustomed to human society, because I got other things to think about than you embarrassin' me.'

The Greenbrier! I am too pleased to wonder why it 'oughtta be dinner' and what other things Grandma has to think about, because The Greenbrier is a Middle Eastern Mecca. For years I have heard people talk about this incredibly exclusive hotel and resort community. It is an institution because it is a temple to hedonism, and, most particularly, because it is a place to pamper the stomach.

In White Sulphur Springs we travel the length of the town's main street while Grandma directs me to the hotel. When we finally reach it, even The Greenbrier's entry road is magnificent, leading through lushly landscaped grounds backed up to old-growth forest. Though I look for signs to the main restaurant, there are none visible. Almost certainly this is the kind of place where if you need directions, you have not arrived at the proper destination. But Grandma is unworried by our status as first-timers, and she seems happy to wander the grounds.

'I hope somebody I know sees me here,' she says, as we crawl down a road lined with guest bungalows. She sits up tall in her seat and twirls her head in every direction. 'Look!' she whispers loudly, a sound to carry across canyons. 'Look! There's one of those Royce Rollers. That's a very expensive car! Why do you suppose no one's out and about? It ain't that I don't see anyone I know, I just don't see anyone!'

She sounds so disappointed that I hurry to console her, and, unwittingly, deal her vanity a bruising blow. 'Don't feel bad, Grandma. You probably wouldn't know anyone here anyway.'

'Whadda *you* know? Why, Chip and Ginger stay here

all the time, and Dr Fizer and his lovely wife . . . and I swear Nancy comes up here to meet some man, 'cause she's always havin' me to mind her beautiful little Shelley on weekends. Better she stay home with that child than go off to rut with some fella. But . . .' Grandma pauses, taking in our surroundings. 'If you are havin' a rendezvous, isn't this the most romantic spot? I wonder if they sell postcards. We're here on business, you and me, but it can't do no harm for the gals to know I've been here.'

Serious business? At The Greenbrier? We pass a fountain set in a stone gazebo with colourful shrubs around it, and on impulse I stop the car. 'Just in case you don't see someone you know who can tell all the people you both know that they know you were here, would you like me to take your picture at this very distinctive fountain? Then you'll have proof.'

The fountain looks out of use and slightly shabby, but Grandma does not hesitate to drink from it. 'Ugh! Tastes like a fart.'

'I believe it's mineral water. People used to come here for its healing properties.'

'Well, don't plan on a picture of me drinking stink water. You just take my camera and stand over there. Make sure you get that plaque in the picture, it says Greenbrier, don't it?' Posing herself nonchalantly on the fountain, Grandma thrusts her nose into the air and arranges her lips in an arrogant smile. She tries to keep her mouth motionless as she asks, 'How's my hair look?'

'To be scrupulously honest, Grandma, I think you had it cut too short this time, but, as you might say, "If the

Lord had truly wanted me to look like a sheep dog, He would have provided the hair". Say *Parmigiano Reggiano.*' I put my eye to the viewfinder and snap, capturing her for filmy eternity.

Its roll completed, the camera whirrs as it automatically rewinds the film. Solemnly, Grandma removes and stows the spent film before reloading the camera. 'I got to be ready to get pictures in the hotel restaurant. I want this whole trip on film, 'cause this is the last time I'm going West, and once I learn what I need to know, I got to be able to recollect how I learned it.'

We wind around until we reach a building too imposing to merely sleep in. Figuring that this is the restaurant, I park the car and in we go.

'Two for breakfast?' asks the *maître d'*. 'Do you have a reservation?'

'Yes. The name's Mrs Maude Suche.'

After consulting his book, the *maître d'* requests that we follow him. Though I pause momentarily, waiting to walk in behind Grandma, she gestures urgently that I should go first, so I do. She trails behind me by about ten yards, ranging the grand reception areas like a bird dog. By the time we reach our table, she has managed to snitch two books of matches, a pen and a thin sheaf of Greenbrier notepaper which formerly sat upon a writing desk.

'I have to go to the ladies' room,' she announces, and the *maître d'* leads her away.

Grandma is walking strangely, notes the doctor in me with concern. *Not really a limp, as such, but perhaps arthritis in the hip joints*? Don't be a dolt, responds the granddaughter, she's strutting because she's at The Greenbrier. Both sides of me note the direction of her movements; the physician watches so that she will know where to go if Grandma has not returned in five minutes, while the granddaughter simply wants to know where to pee. Once Grandma disappears from view, my attention turns to our surroundings.

The breakfast room here at The Greenbrier is immense, with paintings in gold frames on the walls, and windows which frame gardens prettier than the pictures. An intensely patterned floral carpet covers the floor, and above it tables sprout like elegant mushrooms. Though I sit too far away from the next table to overhear any individual's conversation, the sound of voices fills the air with a general muted graciousness. These are Southern voices, mainly. I can discern the ease and length of the vowels, and I want to fill my head with this sound so that I can never miss it: certainly no one in California will sound like this. Here in White Sulphur Springs, just 225 miles from my home, I feel a pang of homesickness which unsettles my roots, wrapped as they are for travelling in a kind of protective mental burlap. I can hear them calling plaintively, can feel my roots wriggling around as they seek familiar soil.

'A homemade wild blueberry muffin, Madam?' asks a waiter proffering a laden tray. 'I also have raspberry bread, croissants, and oatmeal walnut bread. Please help yourself.' He extends tongs to me, and I smile at him with such warmth that he is startled. Thank you, muffin man, for averting an attack of *mylocusphilia*.

In addition to ample and admirable napery, a small

lamp, and various condiments, our table hosts preserves and jellies in the colours of stained glass windows. I help myself, taking particular pleasure in mandarin orange marmalade on wild blueberry muffin, topped with a curl of cold butter. During Grandma's absence I also have time to decide on my breakfast – a grilled fresh mountain trout accompained by tomato conserve and herbed potato pancakes. The idea of fish for breakfast has always pleased me, but until now I thought the only way I could obtain it was to go camping by a stream.

'You should see the bathrooms,' says Grandma after the *maître d'* has tucked her back under the table and glided away. 'I got three bars of Greenbrier soap, a little bottle of Greenbrier lotion, and one roll of toilet paper.'

'Toilet paper? And all of the above is currently in your pocketbook?' I stare at the lap on which her purse perches, trying to see if I detect any distension in the sides of her handbag. 'You didn't need to snitch toilet paper – I brought a roll for makeshift arrangements should we decide to do a night of camping.'

'Oh my, no. This roll's just for a souvenir, or in case we run outta napkins. I'd never use it on my rump. The Greenbrier's toilet paper might kill you. It's the real fancy soft stuff, and I read that soft toilet paper gives people diseases because it's more absorbent and folks get number two on their fingers when they don't realise it. I don't allow no family I work for to use soft toilet paper.' Grandma's face assumes the repose of the virtuous, then, almost instantly, rearranges to look peevish. 'I tell your mother this, but she don't listen, of course. Liz says my son won't use scratchy toilet paper. Now, I tell you! Nobody of my Blood's got a sensitive tookus. That's just Liz talkin'.'

Grandma does not sound as vehement as she might if she were sitting under the shade of Attila the Oak and sipping tea with my mother. Evidently warriors find it difficult to fight one-sided battles enthusiastically. Our table grows silent as Grandma settles down to read the menu, and I, savouring the sound of each entrée, re-examine my choices.

Faced with gastrointestinal paradise, Grandma sighs her befuddlement. 'Well, I fancy something I can't make at home, and I'm partial to waffles and I don't have a waffle iron, so I reckon I might have buckwheat waffles, real maple syrup, applesauce, and a slab of country ham. But, then again, the crab omelette sounds good. Oh, I just don't know.' Grandma balances her menu indecisiveness with a breathtaking contrast of tactical strategy: even as she is dithering, her hand rises up from her lap to snatch five packets of Greenbrier sugar and another matchbook. I see her eye the salt and pepper shakers speculatively.

'Grandma,' I hiss, 'what are you trying to do, set up a souvenir shop?' Though I shake my head at her, she smiles her unrepentance. Saved by the approach of a waiter who wishes to know our choices, the salt and pepper sit smugly on the table while Grandma conducts her inquisition.

'Well, I like the buckwheat waffles, I think. But about the country ham, is it that awful salty stuff? You know, the stuff Southerners like? Me, I'm a Mid-Westerner, I like a little ham with my salt.'

After the waiter assures her that the ham is excellent, a

piece of premium Greenbrier-cured low salt and low fat prime pork, Grandma changes her mind and orders the crab omelette.

'Thank you very much,' she tells the waiter by way of dismissal, and her nose tilts so far backwards that it looks ready for take-off. *Noblesse oblige.* Facing me across our plates of preserves and warm bread, Grandma folds her fingers demurely and clears her throat. Hrrm, hrrm. Then she unfolds her fingers again and pats the tips on the table. Hrrrm. 'Shut your trap and don't interrupt for a spell, if you please. I got something to say.'

Hrrm. 'On Midsummer's Night in 1949, Thomas Suche – my husband, your grandfather – told me to get all gussied up because we were going out for dinner.

'"Oh really," I says to him, all fired up already. "And just how do you expect to pay for our meal?" Thomas don't answer. He just stands there before a beautiful mirror he bought to hang over his bureau, a mirror with carved mahogany leaves all round it, and he's givin' real close attention to his hair, applyin' pomade and slicking it back 'til it lies smooth and chestnut-shiny. I put on a fancy dress and plait my hair, then we're off, stoppin' first to drop off the boys – your Dad and Uncle George – with my Ma.

'"You young folks have a good time," Ma tells us, winking at me. Thomas fooled everyone. We drove to The Elway Club. I remember takin' a deep breath when I figgered out where we're headed, and my lips draw tight even now when I think how Thomas *paid* a boy to park the car. Gave him a *dollar*. That was a great wad of dough back in 1949. And us without even two beans to rub together!

There we were at the door of The Elway Club, gettin' ready to chow at the most expensive restaurant in Indiana, about to have a meal in five parts – because Thomas would never think of eatin' out on the cheap – and we'd got no way a'tall to pay for it. We were flat broke.'

Grandma sighs and butters a bite of walnut bread. 'Thomas made us broke,' she says indistinctly. 'When we got married in 1932 he had a real good job, or at least it seemed to me. My family were people of the earth and how well we ate depended a good deal on how well the rain watered the crops, and on how well the rain watered other folks' crops. Good years meant corn at twenty-five cents the bushel and five cuttings of hay. Bad years meant no corn, two cuttin's, and a loan from the bank to pay for the cows' winter feed. But Thomas ate real well all the time, 'cause he worked for Indiana Oil, surveying sites and negotiating min'ral rights.

'"Marry my daughter", my Pa told Thomas Suche, "and I'll give you a piece of land and build you a house." And Pa did. That was fine for startin' with, Thomas reckoned, but what he *really* hankered after was a fine dwellin' in Evansville proper, not a little farmhouse on the outskirts of town. So that's what all his money went towards. For sixteen years all our money went for a big brick house with oak panelled walls and cut-glass doorknobs – fancy stuff, eating up every last cent of Thomas's pay. Thomas arranged all the trappings, too. We had a nanny for the boys and a day girl for dustin' and moppin', and two years before the end, I even had a cook. Thomas'd hire those women, but I paid for them. I still ran the little bit of land my Pa gave us with our house. I raised beef cattle all day, then came back to find that the cook I paid for had made the meal I should've, and the nanny I shelled out wages for had taught bridge to my sons. It made me mad, but I never did nothing about it. I guess I see now that doin' nothing about it was actually doin' something. I'd made my first decision regarding your grandfather, even if I didn't know it at the time. I stayed with him though it was plain as day we didn't want the same things. Then, come spring of 1949, Thomas lost his job.

'"Let's sell the house and move out to The Farm," I said to Thomas, real confident I'd got the solution. But he wouldn't hear of it. "I'll find a position in town," he said. Funny thing was, no one'd hire him. Not a man in Evansville, Indiana wanted Thomas working for him. So Thomas went travelling, hoping to get lucky, hopin' to find oil work, because he really did love that. While he was away I let the maid and the nanny go, and I paid two months' worth of notes on his house with two years' worth of savings from my cow money. Then Thomas came back to Evansville still without a job and wanted to take me to dinner.

'At the Elway Club, for corn's sakes!

'"Maude," he says over a Carpetbag Steak – his favourite, stuffed with oysters – "Maude girl, we are going West. It's a whole new life out there, and though we may have a few rough times at first, it won't be long before we'll have everything we could ever want." I pick at the skin on my roast chicken and I don't look at him. When we finish Thomas pays with cash, leavin' a big tip. Huge! Equal to a pair of shoes for the boys or the vet's fee for attendin' a rough calving. I never knew how Thomas got the money for that Elway Club dinner 'til years later, when Ma told me Thomas'd asked her for money to change his tyres, just as a little loan. To be paid back when he was up on his feet again. He'd wire money from California, he told her, California where he was gonna give his family all they dreamed of.

'But everything *I* ever wanted was on a little farm just outside Evansville, Indiana,' Grandma says. 'I had no need to go West, not if I was lookin' for everthing I ever wanted.'

I become aware again of the breakfast sounds all around us, but Grandma and I sit in silence, each of us paying exquisite attention to how the other butters bread. Then without warning she jumps up with her camera and walks away from the table. She stalks to the far side of the room and aims at me, then at the decorations and the walls and the curtains. No one in the crowded room pays her any attention, a fact I would have been too embarrassed to note when I was younger.

My years of public experiences with Grandma have taught me that old people float in a bubble of immunity through existence. They can belch in public and they can wear checks, plaids, and Paisley all at once. Older people can sing loudly and off-key in church. They can grow calluses on their consciences and dish out devastating truths which in younger persons would result in social quarantine. And no one ever berates old people for their *faux pas*. I suppose that once someone passes retirement, constructive criticism seems pointless.

Pointless. What connects *old age* and *pointless*? Is anyone ever too aged to learn something constructive? What on earth does Grandma learn from opening her eighty-five year old past to me? To *me*. Would she pour out her soul, a drip at a time, to anyone who made this trip with her? Or do the drops land on me for a reason? Grandma's voice chips into my thoughts.

'Well, la-di-dah. You know, I was expecting real high-class folks at The Greenbrier, but everybody here looks like they put on their underwear the same way I do. At The Elway Club you really felt like you had to mind your 'p's and 'q's, 'cause there were some high-class folks set down to eat.' She examines the guests at nearby tables and looks deflated. 'I s'pose they took one look at us and we got hustled into the second-class dining room.' Nevertheless, remembering where she is, Grandma sits up firmly, holding her spine parallel to the chair and elongating her neck.

Our food comes in a swirl of waiters, and it looks as good as it should. Along with her crab omelette, the waiter brings a portion of Greenbrier ham for Grandma to sample. 'Boys and girls, this is *service*!' she says approvingly. Her pleasure makes me think of the tip my grandfather left on Midsummer's Night in 1949. Somehow I doubt that the service deserved all the cash Thomas Suche left behind on the night he spent borrowed riches at The Elway Club . . .

'Hey! Come back,' says Grandma. She looks at me

thoughtfully and her eyes soften. 'How about you give me a taste of your fish for a snibbee of my eggs.'

I manoeuvre a fin's length of trout, a forkful of tomato conserve, and a piece of potato pancake on to my side plate for Grandma to sample. Her crab omelette is succulently full of backfin crab lumps in a delicate sherry cream sauce, but I still prefer my own choice. So does she.

'Of course,' Grandma says, forking in a mouthful of omelette, 'I could have fish for breakfast any time I wanted when we were living on The Farm. We had two criks feedin' two ponds – one with eel and the other just filled with bluegill. If I fancied fish I'd tell the boys to get out to the manure pile and dig me some worms. Great worms we had, really juicy and the fish loved 'em. I could catch enough bluegill in an hour to keep your Dad skinning all afternoon. Naturally, the problem was findin' a spare hour. But for all the work, I loved that place. I didn't mind settling there in 1955, when we got back from six real unsuccessful years out West. Thomas never did find a steady job in California, or by rights I should say he couldn't *keep* a steady job. Wasn't much of a farmer either. Don't ever know that he gave it much of a chance.'

Aimlessly I cause wispy troout bones to travel around my plate while I search for opaque questions. 'When you talk about "The Farm", Grandma, I can hear the capital letters. The place belonged to your parents, then to you – didn't you ever give it a name?'

'Only city folk give their farms a name, and those people only got farms as a hobby. Do you remember my Farm?' Grandma looks away from me and tears the tip off a croissant. She guides it around her plate, mopping up sherry cream sauce.

'I was only five when you sold The Farm, but yes, I do.'

And do you know what, Grandma? My intuition tells me to remember to myself. In a magical haze of five-ness I remember riding a cow pony called Uppity, and hunting the skins of black snakes in the rafters of your barns. Your kitchen garden always had watermelons to thump – I would listen for the ready sound – and corn on the cob every night. I remember, Grandma, that you always talked about installing something called indoor plumbing, but it never happened. What did happen were trips to the outhouse and baths by the well with a cake of Ivory soap and a washcloth. Big and novel fun for me. I remember shrieking and running naked along the creek bed with a towel in hot pursuit. What I don't remember is my Grandfather Thomas being around to help. A succession of colourful neighbours pitched in when it was time to hay, or when a load of old cows went off to the butcher. In America, Grandma, in the latter half of the twentieth century, what sort of life was that to live as anything but a holiday?

'It's amazing how much better your manners are when Mom's not around.'

Grandma twinkles suddenly, as though I have exposed a guilty secret for which she has no remorse. Before answering me she flaps a piece of ham into her mouth; it is a large piece, and the edges wave like sting-ray wings. When she speaks, however, she does not even spew. 'There's company manners and there's family manners is what I tell those kids I babysit. And I know when to use which. Sure is peculiar how Liz gets in a snit when I eat at your house.' Examining the engraved handle of a Greenbrier fork, Grandma smiles to herself.

When our bill comes, the waiter vacillates over to whom he should present it. I nod slightly, and soon Grandma is stretched nearly flat across the table, trying to see how much our meal cost. 'Give that here. I got to see if we're gonna be washing dishes.'

'Why did we come to The Greenbrier today?'

'Weren't you listenin' to me?' Her eyes widen in disbelief. 'The Greenbrier's my Elway Club. My first trip out West began with a great meal and this trip had to start the same way! I thought you'd be able to figure it out! Sheesh!' Her final monosyllable says, 'I am goin' West with my granddaughter who is thick as a post and it's gonna be a trial to me, I can tell.'

Not as thick as you think, Grandma. 'If your intention is to replicate that grand meal you ate in 1949, just before you learned you were going West, then the least I can do is help you out. I am paying for this meal, and as an added layer of authenticity, you can ponder with what I'm going to pay. Right now, while I'm reducing my med school loans, I don't have two beans to rub together!'

Handing the bill and my credit card back to the waiter, I sign the chit quickly when he returns.

'That's real thoughtful of you,' Grandma acknowledges. 'But I'd kinda like to know what our breakfast here cost. You really ought to let me help with that bill.'

'Forty-six years ago did you know how much your dinner at The Elway Club cost?'

'No. But I can guess, 'cause Thomas and I went there regular in the good times. He liked to be seen in such places. I never been at The Greenbrier before, so I don't know what it costs. Maybe I haven't made it real clear before, but I'm making *two* trips this week.'

'What do you mean?' Back into the wallet goes my credit card.

'One trip for me, a trip that nobody'll ever know about except you – that's the trip I need *Li'l Maude* for. But I got to tell my girlfriends back in Washington something, so accordin' to my cover story I'm travelling as a tourist. The gals'll think it real queer if I don't send postcards, and take an album-ful of pictures, and tell them about this breakfast.' Grandma is leaning over the table again, attempting to examine the receipt.

I feel perverse. Like a little kid who suspects his deskmate of cheating, I cover the numbers with my hand.

Haughtily, looking vexed, Grandma pushes back from the table and walks out to the lobby. Once there she waits for me, recovering her good humour as she palms another pack of matches and a pen. When she tries to take my hand, I offer her my arm.

'Well, that was real good. And I've got plenty of proof I been here. I'm gonna put these Greenbrier matches in an ashtray for everybody to see.' The pleasant thought has Grandma almost waltzing down the path. 'Isn't it just beautiful . . . just look at these roses, and the pretty delilahs.'

'Dahlias,' I murmur.

'Now *this* is a garden. Your mother should do something

like this with *her* garden.' Grandma stoops to break off a blossom which she plants behind her ear. It matches the pink of her jewellery. 'Isn't this lovely,' Grandma demands, pointing at the flower which flops over her ear. 'This is monilia. I want Liz to get some of this.'

Thrusting my nose into a rose, I laugh until the petals fall off. Without turning to look, Grandma asks what makes me snort so loud, but I am certain she knows that monilia is a vaginal yeast infection. Suddenly I wish for Mom and Grandma and me to be sitting under Attila the oak tree, sipping tea and awaiting my mother's response to this shot across her bow.

'So how much did our breakfast at The Greenbrier set you back? I wanna know so I can tell the gals.'

I can imagine Grandma working the subject of our breakfast into the conversation around her bridge table. She and her friends will have stopped for coffee and a 'nibble' – some abominable fruit concoction of canned pears, synthetic whipped cream, diet mayonnaise, and gelatin all chilled and moulded into a ring – and Grandma will say, as if she's only just thought of it: 'Oh. You'll never believe what my granddaughter the doctor paid for our brunch at *The Greenbrier*!'

I glance at the ground, a standard preparation for any departure from the truth, and then I stare at Grandma's eyebrows. 'It cost two hundred dollars.'

Grandma's jaw drops. 'Jeezle peezle, is that how much you paid? You make your Grandfather Thomas look like a skinflint!'

'Actually it cost little more than an eighth of the sum I just mentioned.' *Are you trying to precipitate coronary failure?* The doctor in me reproaches the granddaughter, but the granddaughter is too preoccupied to care. 'Listen, Grandma, and forgive me if I'm accusing you of something unfairly. Don't cast me as the Thomas-figure to your reluctant Maude, because I, too, am a reluctant traveller to California, and I'm not up to bearing the brunt of any left-over anger you feel for Thomas Suche. Really. I'm not up to it at all.'

We have reached the car, now. Grandma arranges herself quietly on the passenger side while I settle behind the wheel, and when I look over at her I see a tear running down her cheek.

'Grandma!'

'I don't have any left-over anger for Thomas. I've got it for me! Me, me, yours truly, Maude Orpwood Suche, *me*! All Thomas ever did was all he ever could do, if you get my meaning . . . but me, I made the wrong decision, and I did it over and over again.' Her glasses have begun to fog, and Grandma removes them so that she can wipe her eyes. 'I'm a different person now, but once I was real strong, a survivor, and I've never figured why that gal made the wrong decision, time after time . . .'

Oh, Grandma, don't. I don't know if I can bear to see you cry. 'Grandma,' I begin.

'Hush! Just hush up! I decided over and over to stay with Thomas Suche, the last time bein' nearly twenty-five years ago when I wrapped up *Li'l Maude*, and I kinda wrapped up me as well. Told myself I'd never think on my decisions again. No use cryin' over opportunities you never took up, I told myself. No use thinkin' on the chances you had to leave for good. But by the time a full twenty-five years passes – and that'll be on July twentieth, 1995 – I want to have it thought over. I got to know why I stayed with Thomas Suche and why I picked him in the first place. There's got to be some other reason than just bein' darn stupid, and I'm going to work on it. Learnin' why'll be a real stone mile for me.'

'Milestone?' My smile is small, uncertain.

'You heard it, that's what I said. And I reckon you could learn something outta my mistakes.' Grandma nods, a tear that she won't acknowledge dropping on the atlas open in her lap. 'Now, keep your eyes peeled for an exit – Route 60 to Charleston, West Virginia.' She flattens the atlas by running the heel of her palm up and down the spine with tremendous, unnecessary pressure; my atlas is, after all, a paperback, and Grandma seems intent on destroying it. 'That road should be heaps faster than 64 West, and prob'ly prettier too.' She wipes her glasses before giving a final swipe to her eyes. Without those thick lenses her face looks shrunken and unprotected. She is tiny and fragile and full of so many years, but she is infinitely more powerful than I am. I would not dare reach over to hug her for fear of being repulsed.

Gauley Bridge, West Virginia

My car's trip odometer registers 300 miles. 'We . . . need to fill up the gas tank,' I tell Grandma, rushing the words so I only hiccup once.

'What'd you say?' Her gaze is fixed on my torso, which heaves with every hiccup. Even though my eyes are fastened to the road ahead, I can tell that her eyes are fixed on my torso, I can *feel* them. Maude Orpwood Suche is paranoid about hiccups.

'Would you check the . . . atlas and tell me when we pass our next town?'

Grandma looks quickly down at the map, then back at my chest. 'Gauley Bridge is about three miles away,' she says. 'Gauley. Gau-ley,' she rolls the word around in her mouth like a connoisseur. 'I once knew some Gauleys. Kind of a fat family, raised real good pigs. Mrs Gauley took a shine to the strawberry pie I made for the Indiana State Fair in 1956. I didn't get the blue ribbon, but Mrs Gauley bought my pie in the auction following the competition – she ate it right there for a snack – and she said it was the finest pile of pastry she ever wrapped her big old lips around. I always think compliments from fat people are the ones you can count on. Fat people've surely got more scope for comparison, and if they give you a compliment on your cooking, you know they're talking on a subject they care for. At every State Fair from 1956 to 1964 Mrs Gauley badgered me 'bout my recipe.'

From my mouth a noise escapes, alerting Grandma to re-examine my upper body. When she continues she sounds absent-minded, and she stares still at my torso. 'I reckon the secret – '

'Will you *please* stop staring at me!'

'I got reason to fret, you're my granddaughter.'

'Hiccups aren't deadly! A . . . hiccup is an involuntary . . . spasm of the diaphragm, sudden closure . . . of the glottis and a characteristic . . . noise!'

'I'll fret if I want to.' Her stare is now a glare. 'As I was sayin', the secret to my strawberry pie was in the crust. See, I moistened my pie dough with chilled rye whiskey 'stead of ice-water, and I only used Monday's butter. Monday's butter came of Sundy's milk, which was just that little bit richer because on Sundy mornings I'd sleep in 'til six o'clock instead of gettin' up at five. To make up for the extra hour of shut-eye, I brought the cows in from the fields on Saturday night and left 'em in the paddocks. Those paddocks were just filled with clover, dense green clover which the bees worked into a fine feedin' ground. The rest of the week the cows just ate whatever they could find in the fields. There wasn't much, and that made my poor cows so mad that six days a week their milk was bitter, and bitter milk makes sour butter. I liked Sundys too, because I waited all week for that extra hour of sleep.

'You woke up ev . . .ery morning except Sunday at five o'clock? Did you have . . . any help? Did my grandfather wake . . . up with you? What . . . about Dad and . . . Uncle George?'

No answers.

At the gas station Grandma hops out and follows me right to the hole in the side of the car. She watches me constantly, paying particular attention to my chest.

'I'm fine, Grandma. You're hanging over me like a har . . . py!'

Lowering her gaze momentarily, she positions her nose above the shimmering oily area which surrounds the nozzle. 'I just love this smell,' Grandma says, closing her eyes and inhaling deeply.

'Wuh!' I try bumping her gently out of the way. 'Petroleum fumes . . . can deviate your septum!'

Not alarmed but sated, the great nose retreats, accompanying Grandma to a stance some three feet away from me where once again she can stare at my torso. 'You got bad hiccups,' she says accusingly.

I feel the force of an unusually violent hiccup rock my body. ' . . . Yes, I do. I . . . ate too much at The Green . . . brier!' The hiccups come in earnest, now, thick and fast. Taking a deep breath, I attempt to halt the onslaught.

'Oh, laws,' Grandma says, 'I hope you're not going to be like Great Uncle Eustace. Great Uncle Eustace once hiccupped for two days solid, and when he was done the doctors had to slice him open and unhook his stomach lining from his tonsils.'

Grandma is absolutely serious. Unable to hold my breath any longer, I erupt with a huge airborne hiccup and a gasp of laughter. Seeing my mouth stretched wide, Grandma rushes at me with a packet of The Greenbrier sugar which she has wrenched from her purse. 'This'll help,' she tells me. 'It's the old-fashioned way – a teaspoonful of sugar on the tongue. Best cure I know.'

She must be nearly deranged with worry; instead of a standard sugar packet, she has used one of her carefully collected status sugars. I gesture to the green logo on the tiny white envelope. 'Why not . . . a McDonald's sugar, Grand . . . ma?'

'Sheesh. I was gonna put a load of these out on a fancy plate, to offer my girlfriends with their coffee. Sheesh!' She stares at the empty packet in her hands until my next hiccup interrupts her reverie. 'You just stay put! This ain't a laughing matter!' Grandma sets off at a trot for the little hut where the gas station attendant sits.

While I seal the gas cap, I see Grandma gesticulating. She returns with a paper cup full of Coke and the attendant in tow. Whereas when we drove up the attendant looked grumpy and certain of my intention to depart without paying, now he simply looks mystified. With his hands in his pockets, he stands watching while Grandma orders me to drink the full cup of cola.

'Drink it upside down and backwards,' she commands, and, choking, I comply. We all pass a breathless moment, waiting for the success or failure of this cure. The seconds collect into a safe, solid, minute-long chunk of eternity.

'All gone,' I say at last as Grandma smiles in toothy relief.

'That'll be ten dollars even,' the station attendant reminds us. 'And if you're paying in cash, then I'll throw in the Coke for free.'

I know, because I hear the litany often, that not only did Great Uncle Eustace suffer life-threatening hiccups, but he also had hangnails which nearly did him in. I should stress *nearly*, because that antique gentleman died in 1931 after enjoying almost a century of ill-health. I can recite names, dates, and diseases *ad infinitum*; Grandma's obsession with her forebears is ancient history to me. Because her genealogy is more a gnarly, twisted orchard than a simple tree with many branches, I have difficulty in determining who hovers where in my ancestry. But I know all about Grandma's Blood. Rife with loyalties and destiny, the word is Grandma's term for her kin. Kin as in one letter shy of skin, which is what any member of the Blood would be expected to peel, slowly and painfully, off his back for you. And vice versa.

The single aspect of her Blood which never fails to puff Grandma with pride is that her people are 'of the earth'. When I was young, that oft-repeated phrase made me wonder if we were related to trolls; it seemed a reasonable assumption, especially when I took Grandma's height and nose into consideration.

Trolls? No, but I accurately chose the working environment. My ancestors were coalminers, or at least they were on my grandmother's mother's side, the Clumpeys. On Grandma's paternal side the people of the earth were actually farmers, and they were called Orpwood. Early on I learned the characteristics Grandma ascribed to the two branches of her family, better known to me as the Blood. I learned that the Orpwoods and the Clumpeys were hard workers and plain talkers who went to the Presbyterian Church every Sunday and did not fall asleep during sermons. Notably thrifty, they never bought anything on credit. Blood always knew how to handle their weapons – guns and fists – and they never shot anything they didn't plan on having for dinner. Sometimes Grandma makes our mutual forebears sound like cowboys, but they weren't. They never went far enough West.

Blood were not frontiersmen. They alighted from German and Scandinavian sailing ships at an indeterminate time in the early nineteenth century, and they only travelled far enough from the East Coast of America so that they would be safe when God dropped Boston into the sea. The hunger of roaming did not drive the Blood. Nor were they interested in social climbing, they could conceive of no one greater than themselves. The Orpwoods settled in Evansville, Indiana, and the Clumpeys settled in Otsego, Ohio, and for generations no one budged.

My mother once referred to the Blood as 'The Boors Who Didn't Go Over the Mountains', and the name has stuck, shortened to an adulterated acronym, BOTM. Mom pronounces it 'BOTTOM', and I suspect she relishes the word. It is fecund with undertones. When I was young, playing BOTM was a favourite pastime. 'Mom, where do I get my green eyes?' I would query. From her side of the family, of course. My eyes glow the vibrant jewel-green of steamed broccoli, just like my mother and my mother's father.

'And where do I get the webs between my fingers?'

The answer was equally obvious. From the BOTM, my mother told me and laughed. Definitely from the BOTM. Along with weird knees, a tendency towards bugged-out eyes, complex Planter's warts which look like colonies of baby cauliflowers, and a hard and inconvenient stubbornness of character. 'You are as intractable', my mother told me, 'as the skin of an unripe avocado.' It meant little when I was young, but it was undoubtedly BOTM.

Though BOTM was a game for me, attributing my characteristics to the Blood presents Grandma with an important and absorbing task. Ever since the day she first saw me, lying newborn and featureless as a pink gum eraser in my crib, Grandma has been ascribing my parts to her past. My father says her congratulatory words to him consisted of, 'It's too bad you got a girl, but at least you can be sure Liz wasn't havin' a thing on with the mailman. That child is of your loins just as sure as if you'd pooped her.'

Grandma could not play 'This little piggy . . .' on my feet without reminding me that I have Great Aunt Aster's long, piano-playing toes. According to Grandma, the inherited second toe, which is a half-inch longer than the big toe, will give me a duck's gait in later life. And, just like Aster's, all ten of my toes will be inclined to arthritis.

Grandma declares that these toes made Aster's life a misery.

Aster Clumpey's son by her second husband, Thoburn, was Clarence Fenwik, and his genetic decree upon me is a pair of saggy lower eyelids. 'Everybody said of Clarence Fenwik that if he went on a round-the-world tour, he wouldn't need to buy any luggage, he could just pack the bags under his eyes!' Grandma told me this for the first time when I was twelve. At that point I stood five feet and one quarter inch tall, just the right height for Grandma to peer searchingly into my face.

Looking back through our mutual predecessors, Grandma can account for nearly every aspect of my anatomy. On bad days she backs her assertions with documentary evidence. On bad days she brings out the heavy artillery – the indisputable photographs, snapshots, and albums. Using her pinkie as a pointer, she introduces me to the previous possessors of my parts. In the stiff bodies of my forefathers and mothers I view my destiny, and denials are pointless. Grandma's pinkie rams the point home: you bear the brunt of Blood in your bones. The photographs are old, the colour of weak tea, and, as I meekly hold them, they exude the smell of dust bunnies. Spare the Blood and spoil the granddaughter is Grandma's motto.

But what does Blood really tell? I know that our ancestors are important to her and that she likes to look on me and be reminded of great aunts, uncles, and other second-class kin; they are the only part of her past she acknowledges. But ever since my childhood she has distracted me with these bit-players in her life, and I no longer care if my stomach lining is prone to looping around my tonsils, or if my lower eyelids are going to sag down to my nostrils. The doctor in me is highly sceptical, while the granddaughter is simply impatient. I want to know about Maude Orpwood Suche and her husband, Thomas. And I want to know about Nerf Fleishman. I want to know why she never talks about him, or my grandfather, or *Li'l Maude*. This woman is my grandmother, and somehow I feel that her decisions, though made long ago, affect me. I want to have her complete confidence, and ask questions she has never answered.

I believe the answers are loaded.

The West Virginia/Kentucky State Line

'I smell dung,' Grandma says, taking a long, deliberate double nostril-ful of air. 'And it's surely from horses, so we must be approachin' Kentucky.'

'Can you really tell the difference – cow, horse, sheep – by manure stench?'

'Oh sure. And even more, I can tell if it's a healthy cow, or whatever, by the smell of its dung. In fine fettle, a horse's manure should smell rich and rotting and kinda like cocoa underneath. If it smells acid or sugary, you got a sick pony on your hands. With a cow it's another matter entirely, 'cause a healthy cow's pie *should* be a little acid. It oughtta pluck at your nostrils same as a warm pickle would.'

The physician in me is fascinated, and the granddaughter is impressed that Grandma has used old-fashioned sagacity to determine where we are when she feels utterly lost. 'The last time *I* had any notion of our geographical whereabouts, we were fifteen miles south of a town called Fraziers' Bottom. Who names these places? While you were dozing we passed through West Virginia towns with extraordinary names, Hurricane, one of them was called. And there was definitely a Nitro and an Ona. Bizarre.'

'I don't know 'bout towns, but I got to name five new roads around The Farm, once. The way it works is you pick out the names – nothin' dirty or rude, mind – then you tell the county roads man, and if nobody else's used that name nearby, then you can have it. 'Bout six weeks later some fella comes out with a signpost and hammers it into the dirt.'

'What did you call your roads?'

'I called 'em *Deer Run, Fox Run, Rabbit Run, Rooster Run*, and *Rooster Run Over.* That last was to mark where Thomas ran over the best darn rooster I ever had. That bird was cock of the walk! He covered some thirteen hens and had another five fightin' for his favours.' Grandma resettles her glasses and coughs out a strange sound – partly a phlegm loosener, and partly a surprised laugh. 'Rooster's name was Walter, but I reckon as it should have been Thomas.'

Before I can comment or question, Grandma hurries on. 'The one Farm chore your grandfather used to like was running the tractor with the bush-hog stuck on the back – that was good for takin' out the poke weed and the brambles along the lane up to the barns. Thomas'd sit high and proud up on that tractor seat. Then one morning, for no reason I could ever see, the steering column snapped on the tractor. Thomas was so surprised he fell off the seat and landed on his head. Meanwhile the tractor kept goin'. Walter just stood there . . . waitin' for it. That lane was his struttin' ground, his personal place, and he was as dumb as a post. I got a theory about too much ruttin' makin' your brain go soft, and Walter was pure proof. He just stood there while the tractor wheel rolled up and over him. Made a feather pancake out of Walter! Lookee there!'

'Good Lord, that is the most enormous insect I've ever seen!' The bug resembles a twig with sails, and its tail is snagged under the windshield wiper on Grandma's side. With seventy-five mile an hour wind plastering it into the glass, the creature has little chance of exodus, but still it wriggles wildly. Grandma hunches forward in her seat, all the better to view it.

'Looks like one of them prehistoric birds,' she says, tapping the glass and trying to attract the bug's attention. 'You know, a terraduckie.'

'A pterodactyl?'

'That's just what I said.'

As the road crests into an unprotected hill, a sudden gust of wind nearly wrenches the steering wheel out of my hands. When next I look, there is nothing left of the insect but its tail, jerking electrically.

'Jeezle peezle, I can't stand lookin' at this.' Rolling down her window all the way, Grandma leans half-way out so she can hook her arm around the side of the car. She stretches until, with a lightning flash of her talons, she flicks the tail away. 'There,' she says with satisfaction. She pats at her hair, trying to arrange the disarray.

Kentucky is a pretty state, with the sun high on

remarkably green hills which turn even greener when the shadow of a small cloud scuds over. As we drive I steal sideways glances at Grandma; she has her fingertips pressed to her chin, and she seems to be deep in thought. The processes of introspection have no bearing on her surface conversation, however. She discusses a single flower she noticed a quarter of a mile back, a billboard advertisement for her preferred bouillon cube, and an obese driver in a tiny car. All the while, on a mental level one layer down, I am convinced Grandma ponders in the quiet pastures of her mind.

And I think this is how she has lived her whole life, by covering anything important with a diverting layer of surface activity. She has fooled me for years. Does she fool herself?

'What do you think,' says Grandma slowly, and then stops. 'I want to know', she begins again, slowly and weightily, 'what you think of your mother's hairdo.'

Her words follow an instruction to 'Look, look at this lovely little colt – fine height to his withers', and I am caught off guard. So much, too, for my theories on Grandma's psychology.

'Mom's hairdo?'

'Yes. Liz's hairdo. Can't say as I like it. That Muriel she always goes to did something kooky last time she cut it.'

'Muriel's been cutting Mom's hair for absolutely ages,' I say blankly.

'I know. I go to Muriel now, too. Do you think Liz's 'do would look good on me?'

Rallying my mental forces, I try to respond intelligently.

'You have to consider, Grandma, that Mom has shoulder-length hair which is wavy and thick. You have fragile, inch-long curls which cluster close to your scalp. And you've often told me that you like your style, because it stays fresh throughout a busy day. If you want my honest opinion, which is hardly *ever* what people want when they put someone else in the position where she must say, "if you want my honest opinion . . .", then, no, I don't think Mom's hairstyle would suit you.'

'Oh.' Grandma does not agree with me. The 'oh' has definite undertones of 'you may be a doctor of medicine, granddaughter, but what would you understand about hairdressing?' 'Well,' she says, 'I think it would.'

I consider the strange contradictory role which Nature allocates to mothers-in-law and the ongoing feud between my mother and Grandma. Then I decide to change the subject. 'Did you get along very well with Thomas Suche's mother?'

'Never knew her.'

'Why not?'

'I don't know if she was dead or what. Thomas couldn't tell me much about her.' Grandma flaps her hand in the air and the gesture looks strikingly similar to waving goodbye. It is Grandma dismissing the subject. 'Pretty soon,' she says, flipping open the atlas, 'I'm gonna have to decide whether we're stoppin' in Evansville to look up my old house. Not The Farm, I don't need to see that ever again. Chances are it's been swallowed by a suburb or somethin', anyhow. But that big town house Thomas poured such money into. Some swell probably bought it and did it up even more fancy. That kind of house don't ever get knocked down.'

'*I'd* like to see it, Grandma. Until a few hours ago, I didn't even know that you'd had a home besides The Farm.'

She remains silent for longer than seems natural for her personality, then shakes her head sharply. 'I've made up my mind. That house means nothin' to me now. I said goodbye to it twenty-four years ago when I left Evansville for Washington, and I don't want to be gettin' mad at Thomas for his foolishness all over again. Maybe it'd be different if any of the folks I knew still lived in Evansville, but they're all dead. No, I don't think we'll be stopping. I made the real start to goin' West back at The Greenbrier, and Evansville'd do nothing but stir up the wrong thoughts. When the time comes, let's make sure we got enough gas to ride right through.'

Obviously, my wishes have no weight in Grandma's decision. I am disappointed and don't bother to be circumspect, don't bother to consult my intuition as to whether it is an appropriate time to ask. 'How did you know you wanted to marry Thomas Suche?' And then I hold my breath.

'Well, I didn't really *know* myself, but everybody else knew for me.' Grandma is talking to her lacquered fingernails, not to me.

'What do you mean? Were your mother and father very fond of Grandfather Thomas?'

'Well, that's a real good question. Pa never said much about him, but then Pa never said much anyways, and if he *had* an opinion on Thomas, it woulda been the mirror image to my Ma's. As for Ma . . . well, I don't recollect how took she was with Thomas as a person, but it thrilled her to bits that he wanted to marry me. Oh my, yes.' Grandma falls silent and pats her budge.

'You see,' she says, and it sounds like a sigh, 'among my Blood Thomas Suche was a kind of competition. All the unmarried girls wanted him, with not a nod to fair fighting. He'd come to town on a survey trip, and it was Aunt Mastiff who spotted him first. She saw him standin' at the bank on a Monday mornin', and she went up and asked him to next Sunday dinner, 'cause she said she could tell a man who'd been eatin' too much restaurant food. Do you know,' Grandma says suddenly, seeming to ask my rearview mirror, 'I can't for the life of me remember Aunt Mastiff's Christian name. Was it Henrietta?

''Course it was, I got it now. Henrietta Orpwood Haig. But Aunt Mastiff is what everybody called her on account of she was six foot tall with loads of facial hair and droopy ears. She was my father's sister. Aunt Mastiff married Elmer Haig and bore just one gal, a year older'n me, my cousin Nettie Haig. She was not her mother's child. Where Auntie was a mastiff, Nettie was one of those bald little dogs with ears like soup bowls and a name that sounds like a banana – Chiquita, I think.'

'Chihuahua?' Out of habit I correct her, and then I grimace, fearful of having disrupted Grandma's thoughts.

'Yes, that's just what I said. My cousin Nettie Haig was certainly in the contest to catch Thomas. To start off with it was just Aunt Mastiff who wanted Thomas for Nettie –

Nettie had her heart set elsewhere, so she wasn't real keen on the idea – until Mr Thomas François Suche arrived for dinner and Nettie was smitten. 'Course by that time five days'd passed, and my mother'd set her cap on him for *me*.

'Ma had a fight on her hands. Thomas'd eaten at the tables of my kin every night that week, and everwhere he ate he made eyelashes flutter. My grandmother's sisters were castin' for him. Grandma Hilda Grimwald had two sisters – my Great Aunts Elsie and Myrtle – and they'd got some grandgirls – my second cousins Isabel, Ann, Jane, and Emma – who were all getting on in age. Nearly twenty-five Isabel was, an old maid in the making.

'When Thomas started courtin' me my relations just couldn't believe it. See, I never paid Thomas much mind, and they didn't think it fair. All those girls who washed their hair in kerosene to make it shine the nights Thomas came 'round! They sorta wilted out of the picture like the wallflowers they were. All except for my cousin Timola, who never gave up.

'Timola was two years younger'n me and real headstrong – thought she was the greatest thing since all-beef bologna, and nobody could say nothing that'd persuade her any different. Her parents were Verona Haig and Norton Orpwood, who was my father's twin brother, for all that they didn't look alike or share the same views on anythin'. And get this – Verona Haig was Elmer Haig's sister, the same Elmer who married my father's sister, Aunt Mastiff. Don't you find that a tad peculiar? My Pa's brother and sister hitchin' up with a Haig sister and brother. It was all too infestuous for my liking. The only babies that ever came from those unions were girls, and none of 'em lived very long. Why, Timola died at sixty-one, and here I am at eighty-five!' Grandma drums her fingers on the atlas while her head swings, thoughtfully monotonous, from side to side.

'You know, something set Timola Orpwood apart from the rest of my Blood, and I could never figure it out. Maybe it was her disease. She got polio when she was young, and it was the best thing that could've happened to her. Polio stunted her growth. See, Timola took after our Aunt Mastiff, so God only knows how tall she might've grown. At three years old Timola was four foot eight and three quarter inches tall. She *towered* over me. Aunt Verona and Uncle Norton got sweet-talked by a travellin' freak show which wanted to make Timola a star attraction when she turned thirteen. The freak show manager had a contract ready and everything, loads of money, 'cause he reckoned that Timola'd be over seven foot tall. He figured it out by measuring her bones. And then, of course – four years old and five and a half feet tall – Timola took polio.

'And she stopped growing. The change took place so sudden it seemed she was shrinking. I was just six then, but I still remember the whole family holding its breath, waitin' to see if Timola was gonna live. Not only did she live, she came out of it just fine *and* she stopped growing. Everybody said it was a blessing and a miracle. Timola grew up knowin' she was a miracle, and it went straight to her Aunt Mastiff-lookin' head. She thought she was beautiful, and she thought it so long and so hard that she made other people think it, too. Have you ever noticed how good-looks're often like that?

'Timola wanted Thomas from the very beginning. Even after Thomas'd made it clear he was courting me, Timola wouldn't give up – she was always flirtin' with him, taking him lemonade at his survey site. Then one night she asked him over for a real heart-to-heart. I can just picture it, her snugglin' up to Thomas on the swinging settee Aunt Verona kept on their front porch. She got him sitting near her, then, so he'd lean *real* close, she whispered to him. "Thomas François Suche," Timola whispered, "you're too good for the likes of my cousin Maude Orpwood! You mustn't throw yourself away! Why, she doesn't even appreciate you!"'

'What!' I have forgotten completely that Grandma did not want Thomas Suche for herself; the deceitful murmurs of Timola Orpwood make me furious. 'What a bitch! How on earth did you hear about those two having a tête-à-tête on the sofa?'

'That's no mystery. Timola told me. She thought all she'd got to do was tell me, then when I knew that *she* wanted to marry Thomas, I'd roll over and play dead. But her little chat with Thomas didn't have the effect she planned. It was only after talkin' with Timola that Thomas came after me for *real*.'

'When I asked him flat out who he'd rather have, Thomas laughed and said Timola was real sensuous and looked like she needed a man bad, but I'd got the attractions of honesty and no imagination. "A man like me", Thomas said, "needs a gal like you." I'll never forget him saying that. We were sittin' on a bale of hay that'd been out in the rain too long, and the smell of mould was just starting. I remember thinking that Pa'd have to burn that hay, else the young bulls'd get a fungus in their brain and be no good for market.

'Funny thing is, I feel sure Thomas wasn't paying no compliment when he said those words to me. Yet he wanted to marry me when he could've had his pick from out any of my Blood.' On her fingers Grandma ticks off her rivals, then sits still except for that gentle sideways shake of her head. Back and forth, back and forth. It makes me think of disbelief and self-disgust that never end, a perpetual motion. I want to put my hand, gently, against the side of her head and stop it.

'I won. I won the contest, but Thomas was no prize. I was a strong woman, and what I can't believe is that I got to thinking he was great because all the others did. I just can't believe that I married him because I was *flattered* that he wanted *me*. Even after all these years you don't accept being stupid too easy.'

I shake my head once, so hard that the car swerves. 'Grandma, you can't be harsh on yourself. It's human nature to enjoy the envy of other people. Particularly someone like Timola Orpwood – she sounds like a fiend. I had an ancient professor at med school who used to tell us about polio patients. His stories were like tall tales for physicians, about how polio survivors have an almost supernatural invincibility about them, a phenomenal immunity to viruses, heart disease, even physical accidents. It's a strange superiority which is mostly medical, but sometimes egomaniacal. I can imagine Timola's persistence pushing you into doing something you wouldn't normally have done.'

'Things . . . *happened* between Timola and me all our lives,' Grandma says haltingly. 'Maybe she done it on purpose. I never thought this out before, but maybe Timola deliberately pushed Thomas into marrying me that night she whispered to him on the settee. I wasn't the prettiest girl my Blood threw at Thomas, I was just the only one *not interested.* If something looked hard to get, Thomas thought it had loads of value. He was a real simple man, at the core.'

Beside me Grandma sits with balled up fists pressed into her lap. Out of sympathy, I don't look at her.

'I'd appreciate it', she says, her voice slow and bitter, 'if you don't mention this to me ever. Being dumb hurts. It hurts near as bad as being dumber than Timola Orpwood, if that's what I was. I'll never know, but I can guess. Up at the Pearly Gates she and I'll prob'ly meet again, and when we do . . . when we do, Cousin Timola, you're gonna have a lot to answer for. Because thinking about it now, I reckon you pushed me into marrying Thomas Suche – you did it for revenge. That and everything after.'

Carefree, Indiana

Grandma's slumber distresses my doctoral side. Tight-lipped and agitated, the doctor in me discourses on how mental stress takes its toll *physically*, particularly in old people. *Timola Orpwood was bad luck in life and I don't believe she's harmless even though she's dead. Avoid the subject! You see how talking about Timola for a few minutes sapped all of Grandma's strength – she has slept for two hours without moving! Physically, the woman has to be absolutely* drained; *how else could she have fallen asleep under the stimulus of such highly-charged emotions? All I ask is that you let the past lie.*

But the granddaughter in me is not so pliant. You talk, she tells the doctor, the same way Grandma must have talked to herself for sixty years. Don't you think it's sad that Grandma has only just figured out how Cousin Timola duped her into marrying someone she didn't love? *I* think it's sad.

'Very sad,' I say out loud, and the doctor hushes me. *Let Grandma sleep.*

The excellent thing about internal dissension is that it causes time to slip by unnoticed. The seventy miles between two major Kentucky towns along our route – Louisville and Lexington – disappeared in a puff of exhaust, and about ten minutes ago we crossed the border into Indiana. Shadows are lengthening, and my clock reads six-thirty p.m. On any normal day, in my usual position 640 miles east of here, I'd be at the hospital. On any normal day, the granddaughter in me informs the doctor, you'd regard the woman sleeping next to you as little more than an amusing artefact.

Right on the heels of a hauntingly quiet interlude, Grandma snores so loudly that the sound brings her to consciousness with a start. 'Ahhhhoooow.' She yawns like someone who yearns to discolate his jaw, then says, 'That was a good spell of shut-eye. You got some sandwiches for us? I'm feelin' peckish.'

'Better than sandwiches, Grandma, I have . . . damn. I have foil packets full of *raw* chicken breasts marinated in olive oil, lemon, and thyme. Two hours ago they were supposed to begin slow cooking under the hood. Chicken roasted by heat from the engine if I hadn't been so preoccupied. Can you wait two hours for dinner?'

'Not on your nellie.'

'I thought you might say that. How about sandwiches, then? I had some packed for lunch.'

We park just off the road near a pretty, wooded area, and Grandma squats to rest her hand on the front fender. 'Laws, that's hot. I guess chickens could've cooked in here after all.' Experimentally, she touches her fingertips to various points on the hood. 'No problem a'tall, we could fry a chicken underneath and an egg on top.' Suddenly Grandma begins rooting around in her pocketbook.

I wait hopefully, half expecting to see her flourish an egg, but she produces nothing more than a box of dental floss. Expertly she winds twine around her fingers, wielding the string like a saw at her tooth until something thin and white flies out to land at my feet.

'What was that?'

Grandma looks relieved and sucks at her front teeth. 'Little dabbie of crab shell. Let's eat.'

Under the trees the shadows lie very long and the quiet is startling. But this *feels* right. If I close my eyes and overlay the silence with sounds from the Chesapeake Bay, I can feel at home in Carefree, Indiana. My eyelids are pressed shut as I ask Grandma what she prefers. 'We have chicken salad, roast beef and houmous, miniature bagels with smoked salmon and chive cream cheese, or a half of pitta stuffed with tomato, black olive, and feta.'

The silence remains unbroken and my Middle Eastern soundtrack fades away. Opening my eyes, I find Grandma peering hard at me. 'Sheesh,' she says. 'I reckon you'll call me ungrateful, but don't you have just plain bologna and iceberg lettuce on bread? No? Well then, I guess I'll have the chicken salad. But you gotta keep that thing', Grandma points to the pitta bread, 'away from me. Looks like somebody sliced off a sow's ear and ralphed in it.'

'OK.' Slightly offended, I examine the pitta bread, then I start to laugh. 'Maybe I should have packed the tomato separately from the feta and black olive . . . still,

Grandma, describing this mix as vomit seems unduly harsh. Try the roast beef and houmous instead – I think you'll like it.'

'What's "humps"?' Grandma speaks through an enormous mouthful of chicken salad.

'Houmous. The marriage of mashed chick peas to lemon, sesame seed paste, and probably a whole bulb of garlic. It's a Greek speciality.'

'Ugh!' says Grandma. 'I'd never trust a Greek person. The neighbourhood around Thomas's big house in Evansville was just fulla Greek families. Every day at twelve o'clock the Greeks'd come home to have their lunch, then a half hour later you'd see their underclothes on the upstairs railings. They were rutting! Right after lunch! It happened regular, the way most folks follow their dinner with coffee. And let me tell you, the Greeks weren't quiet about what they were up to. Such yappin' and moanin' as I've never heard! You just couldn't trust people like that. I got a real low opinion of people who rut too much, 'cause it makes your brain go soft, and it brings trouble. Now take your Grandfather Thomas. He –'

Grandma stops speaking in order to fish something out of her mouth. 'What's this?'

Goddamnit! I want to hear about Grandfather Thomas. 'Grandma, don't be distracted by trivialities –'

'Why's there a big white hair in my chicken salad!' Frantically shaking her hand, she flicks a thin white tube from her fingernail on to my cheek.

'It's not a hair,' I say, peeling it off my face, 'it's a bean sprout. I put them in the chicken salad to make it crunchy.

Just so you know, there are also toasted almond slivers and the odd golden raisin.'

'Oh, for Heaven's sakes!' Grandma looks disgustedly at the last bite of her sandwich. 'It's not so bad, I guess, but I liked it better when I didn't know what's in it. Gimme a bite of that Greek stuff. Ummmm. That's not so bad. But I'm not gonna call it humidity, or whatever you said. I'm gonna call it chick pea mush, and maybe you'll be good enough to send me the recipe.'

Behind us, at a distance of fifty feet, a branch crackles and falls. The noise startles us both, and then we hear a howl and further crashing.

'Jeezle peezle! What was that?' Grandma's eyes, behind her thick glasses, are wide, and they scan the trees like a hunter. 'Awwww,' she says as a thin brown dog sidles into view. 'Lookee there. Poor 'ittle thing. Him's hungry, and that cwashing tree scared hims.'

The dog pays Grandma no attention; it is too wild for doggie talk. With bony heaving flanks it stands some two car lengths away from us, and I have the impression that nothing but hunger could persuade it to venture so near. The dog's eyes are fastened on my bagel, but they jerk away when Grandma rises to her knees. As she leans forward, the dog backs up the precise distance that Grandma advances. Then its eyes are drawn back to my bagel, frozen mid-way up in a leisurely lift to my lips. Slowly, slowly I lower the bagel to my napkin, and the dog, its eyes never leaving my hand, mimics the motion by dipping its nose to the ground.

Without turning her head to look at me, Grandma says

softly, 'Lemme give it some of that sandwich in the pitta bread, 'cause that surely ain't fit for *human* consumption.' She tosses half the sandwich back into the woods where the air is darker and the dog sits rapt. But only until it realises that Grandma throws food. Snuffling frantically through the leaves, the dog searches out chunks of feta which scattered like shrapnel. Then it sits down and resumes the stare. Because the dog's nose is pointed directly at us, I see when a delicate burp ripples the skin of its jaws.

'That is one hungry dog,' says Grandma thoughtfully. 'And I think she's a bitch and nursing. Look at those tits.' Grandma transfers her gaze to me. 'Too bad we've eaten most of our dinner. That is sure one *hungry* dog . . . wait here a minute, I got an idea.'

Mumbling something under her breath. Grandma rises briskly to her feet and trots to the car. Though the dog looks distressed by her movement it does not slink away, and I decide to toss my bagel by way of encouragement. Then Grandma reappears, clutching something shiny to her breasts.

'My tinfoil packets!'

'Hush! Gimme a hand here.' Grandma occupies herself completely with tearing two oily chicken breasts into strips; without a knife the job is a difficult rubbery exercise, but she tells me it must be done. 'That dog'd just choke on this little broiler's boobs if we threw 'em whole. It'd be killin' with kindness.' Applying her thumbnail like a scalpel, she separates a tendon from the meat.

We look up to see the dog balanced on its haunches,

excitedly sniffing the air. And then, taking aim, Grandma heaves the chicken tidbits. She throws in accurate handfuls which scatter in a two-foot radius around the dog. Occasionally, a piece hits the animal, but it doesn't care, it just turns to seek out the place where the chicken bounced off. Though I throw a few pieces myself, this is Grandma's doing, and she seems as happy to do the feeding as I am to watch the dog eat.

'There,' she says. We see the dog dart, snuffling, through the trees. It combs the area perhaps three times, intent on searching out any last morsel, then it retreats into the forest. In the quiet we can follow its movements for several minutes, and while we listen, neither of us speaks.

'Oh, sugar!' Grandma says at last. 'I forgot to feed sweet 'ittle hims the rest of this ralph-on-bread.'

'I'll take that, thanks, since you've given away all the rest of our food.' As I speak I smile, making certain that the words have no sting, and Grandma nods back at me.

'Well, I just can't stand to see an animal go hungry,' she says. 'People can fend for themselves, I reckon. I know *I* have. But when an animal starves, he only knows he's hurtin', and he can't explain to himself why.' Meticulously, Grandma folds the waxed paper which held our sandwiches. When each piece is a neat and cloudy square, she tucks it into a side pocket on her pregnant purse. 'Never know when ya might need some waxy paper.'

I give Grandma a hand up from our picnic blanket. 'You know what?' I say as we walk to the car. 'Your handbag must be the ultimate survival tool, because inside that purse you carry enough waxed paper to make a pup tent, the matches to light a thousand campfires, and the exact number of fizzy indigestion tablets to blow up a bear!'

'Ha ha very funny,' says Grandma, sounding indulgent. 'I don't need to blow up a bear when I got *Li'l Maude* here, so you just go 'head, Doctor, and have your little laugh. You don't have the faintest notion what all I got in my pocketbook.'

Seven years ago, during my first year as a medical student, I discovered a strange new smell that hangs in hospital corridors and doctors' waiting rooms. Over the subsequent years of my medical education I have become more adept at detecting this odour, and now I can smell it outside of hospitals, too. I've learned how to *smell* tension. A person in the grips of fretful anticipation breathes faster, expelling more breath into a room, and that person perspires, making an odourless humidity which the nostrils never fail to register. The smell of tension makes my neck prickle.

Fifteen miles before the turn-off to Evansville, Indiana, I smell tension in our car. If I didn't know how to smell it, I would never feel it, because Grandma sounds and behaves normally.

'Want a goodie?' she asks. It is eight-fifteen p.m., and Grandma wants to give me sugar because she fears that I won't have the energy to drive three hours further to St Louis, where she says we must stop for the night.

'Yes, please,' I say as my nostrils flare wide, trying to take in the tension.

Grandma roots in her purse for the plastic sandwich bag

which carries her aged repository of chewing gum, icy blue mints, red-and-white swirl mints, and sugarbomb mints which look like tiny pastel cushions. 'What's your fancy?' she asks. The sandwich bag is creased and yellow and fastened shut with a rubber band. Grandma calls this the 'dittie' bag, and I have asked for it by name ever since I could speak. In fact, the current plastic bag is probably the same one for which I clamoured when I was five; Grandma is a great one for washing out and re-using plastic.

The back of my neck is prickling insistently. 'I'll have an icy blue mint, thanks.' After the rustle of a candy wrapper, Grandma hands the mint over. I inspect it carefully before laying it on my tongue, because the dittie bag collects little bits of paper and pocketbook lint, and quite often Grandma's goodies come without wrappers. The mere rustle of a wrapper doesn't guarantee clean candy. Sometimes Grandma crinkles some unrelated plastic as subterfuge, because she knows I think unwrapped candies are unsanitary. When I was five I don't think I cared.

The tension asks to be tested. 'We're getting close to Evansville, Grandma. I haven't been here since I was five.'

'Last time I was here, I was sixty-two. How we doin' on gas?'

'Unless you wish to, we don't need to stop in Evansville. That's what you're really asking, isn't it?'

'You know good and well that's what I'm asking.' Grandma takes a deep breath. 'See, if it weren't so dark, I might be havin' second thoughts. If it weren't so dark I might have somethin' I got to do in this town, somethin' that's been occupyin' my mind lately. We won't do it tonight, but I have to do it soon. I got to come back to Evansville and find me someplace pretty, with a good view. For my final resting place.' She pauses. 'I'm gonna need it sooner than you think.'

Inside my head I'm shouting, 'What!?' Just as the doctor in me says *I told you so.* And then, under both voices, sounds my friend Nathan, saying quietly, just as he always does: 'I'm dying.'

As calmly as possible, I address Grandma. 'Are you ill?'

'Nothin' like that. No, I'm just interested in where I'll end up, that's all. It's not something young folks consider real seriously, but you will do when you're eighty-five. And you think about who you want to lie next to for all eternity.'

Tension is like flatulence – it's hard to smell your own. I wonder if Grandma can smell my tension, which is dissipating now, but only slightly. I am sorry I ever brought up the subject of Evansville, Indiana, because I don't want to discuss Grandma's grave site. People die all the time, and sometimes they die in front of me; it's a hazard of my profession. When Grandma dies, my family will expect me to be capable and competent, because I am the *doctor*. I will need to *feel* less and *do* more. Starting right now I'm going to practise the detachment which my position will require.

'Why do people care where they're buried?' I ask casually, while the sweat on my palms makes the steering wheel hard to grip. 'Why do *you*, Grandma, want a hole in a pretty place?'

'Well, I reckon nobody'll come visit me if my grave's not

in some scenic spot. I want my Blood to visit me regular. I don't guess I can hold you to it once I'm dead, but a solemn oath before I kick the bucket would mean the world to me.' She stares straight ahead into the dark framed by my windshield.

Can Grandma feel all the puzzlement in me? When people are alive you visit them. You have tea with them, and talk, and you travel West with them, but once a person dies that changes, obviously. You don't visit them any more. I have never visited Nathan's grave. Don't make me promise to visit you, Grandma. Once I return to my Middle East home, I won't want to go West again *ever*, and I definitely won't go West to visit a dead person.

In the dark I know Grandma can't see me dry my palms on the fabric of my shorts. 'It's illegal, but how about being burned and scattered on the waves in our own Chesapeake Bay? You've never learned to swim while alive, so what could be better than floating on the water once you don't have to worry about drowning?'

'No.'

How does she do it, these monosyllables which elaborate upon themselves in a single sound? Simultaneously, her 'no' rejects unorthodoxy for propriety while underscoring her mistrust of the water. And still I feel I've missed some nuance of this 'no'.

We pass by Evansville, Indiana – my grandmother's first home and perhaps her last – without stopping, and only when the lights of the city are a dim orange glow behind us does Grandma speak. 'It doesn't matter that we didn't tour through Evansville. I got it all up here,' she says, tapping the expanse of forehead just above her eyebrows. 'You don't ever leave the place you love. Don't be sore at me, Doctor, for wantin' to drive right through. It wouldn't have looked like home to you.'

St Louis, Missouri

'Let me do the talking!' Grandma says, her eyes clear and bright.

I can do no more than nod. It is midnight, and the combination of confidences, upheaval of my roots from the Middle Eastern Coast, and more than eighteen hours of driving has left me limp.

'Remember – not a peep outta you,' Grandma warns again as we walk through the parking lot of a twin-towered hotel on the left bank of the Mississippi River. The moment we reach the lobby, Grandma thrusts her arm through mine. Her step slows and her head hangs, and suddenly my elbow seems to be carrying the entire weight of her body.

The doctor in me ought to be concerned, except she seems to be asleep – as a senior resident she often gets to doze through the night. Still, I come out of my stupor enough to ask whether Grandma is OK.

'I'm dandy! Now move, and not another word.'

Pulling me along by our interlocked elbows, Grandma

manoeuvres towards the front desk. In the eyes of the lone receptionist I see compassion for the aged.

'Good evening. Can I help you?' she asks sympathetically, leaning over the counter to look down on my enfeebled grandmother.

'Reservation,' says Grandma whose voice suddenly sounds shivery. 'In the name of Maude Suche.' Out of her budge appears something which looks like a credit card, and she slides it under the receptionist's nose. 'American Association of Retired Persons – I'm past president of the Washington DC chapter. What kinda discount you got for me?'

'Ahhh,' says the receptionist while she examines the card.

'I'd like a room way up high, closer to Heaven,' says Grandma, who appears to be drawing nearer the grave with every word she utters. 'My room's got to be near the emergency stairs, and I'd like a real good view 'cause I'll probably be dead before I get to St Louis again. Does my granddaughter get a free newspaper in the morning? Lot of the good hotels do that now'days.'

Flustered, the receptionist fiddles with her computer. 'I believe when you called to make the reservation we quoted you a rate of – '

'That was too much,' Grandma interrupts with tremulous indignation. 'Listen, dear, I'm eighty-five years old and I'm weary to my bones . . . what're you gonna do for me?'

Room number 1008 has a 'stunning view of the mighty

Mississippi', and at fifty per cent discount it's a bargain. However, Grandma does not wish to be congratulated on her triumph; her interest lies elsewhere. Sweeping the curtains back with one hand, she stands at the window and surveys St Louis. 'Look,' she says, 'this is what we're here for.' And she sounds awed.

High as a skyscraper and wide enough for an aircraft carrier to pass underneath, a silver half-circle soars over the city. It can only be man-made, but my mind boggles as I try to imagine its construction. 'My God, what *is* that?' I come to stand by Grandma.

'That's the Gateway Arch,' she says, 'built to honour all the folks who ever decided to travel West. St Louis broke ground for this beauty in 1962, and I've been hearing about it since then. Hearin' amazing things. The outside skin got finished in 1965, on October twenty-eighth, so it's near thirty years I been waiting on this sight. Do you know how important this city is, how big it reckons in the lives of folks like you and me? St Louis has seen the backsides of people travellin' for four hundred years!

'Gateway Arch', Grandma continues, sounding more subdued, 'marks the point of no return. We've come far enough West that we lose everything if we don't keep goin'.'

I am flattened by my grandmother, who speaks like an oracle, by our long day of driving, and by the enormity of how far I have travelled from home. I won't brush my teeth, because I am so tired I'll probably miss and stuff the brush up my nose. I won't bother to take off my clothes.

But a part of me flickers to life as I see Grandma approach her bed with the glint of silver in her hand; she wears her pink nightgown and has no underclothes to hold *Li'l Maude* securely in her budge. So where does the gun sleep?

Under Grandma's pillow. The princess and the pea shooter.

The Gateway Arch
St Louis, Missouri

Feeling ridiculous, I lay a pile of clothes on my hotel bed in the order of their adornment: bra on top, underpants below bra, blouse beneath underpants, and a pair of shorts at the very bottom. Though I am twenty-nine years old, right now I feel close kinship with my fourteen year old self, who used to get dressed just this way in the ladies' locker room after a Phys-Ed class. Attiring myself for the day while in close confines with Grandma is going to take some getting used to.

Nakedness does not faze her. After my shower I drop the towel to begin dressing, and Grandma comes for a look.

'It's a cryin' shame you didn't get my breasts,' she says. 'Oh, I know your breasts seem fine now, but you're just young yet. You got boobs like Aunt Mastiff – comin' out of your chest like bullets – and hers dropped to her waist when she turned thirty. Aunt Mastiff wore a brassiere that looked like scaffoldin', but after a while even that didn't much help. In her declinin' years she had this sling which fastened round her neck and doubled her over 'til she looked like a sickle moon.' Grandma shakes her head sorrowfully. 'Poor Aunt Mastiff.'

Horrified, I look down at my chest while she resumes her morning breathing exercises. After a particularly long and deflating exhale, Grandma pulls her night gown over her head and heads for the bathroom; she is stark naked. I pick up a tourist information pamphlet called *St Louis Live*! in the effort to avoid looking at her.

Stopping to stand in front of me with her hands on her hips, she says, 'How come a doctor's so peculiar about nakedness? The birthday suit is a human bein's natural state, I reckon.'

'Maybe so, Grandma, but I have a well-developed sense of bodily humility – evidently *not* something I inherited from your side of the family.'

'But doctors got to look at naked folks all the time!'

'It's different. Patients wear disposable paper tents for examination. And though I see lots of skin in an emergency, or in surgery, it's never personal skin, if that makes any sense. I never see any of my family professionally.'

She's still standing here, entirely naked. I clap my hands over my eyes. 'Can't you put on your dressing gown? Just to humour me?'

'No.' The monosyllable is peevish.

'Why not?'

'I didn't bring it,' Grandma replies, sounding as though her hands are still upon her hips. Parting the second and third fingers on my right hand, I make a V-shaped peephole and check to see.

Yes, still standing hands on hips in front of me. I watch her and feel myself growing gradually more objective, feeling like a physician. Images of old people unclothed could never be pornographic, just interesting and curious, a matter of textures and exhausted curves. Grandma has spent her entire life outdoors, and as a result her skin is wrinkled and craggy like a cowpat in the sun. Without her clothes she resembles a petrified pear.

'Hrrmph.' Grandma goes off to have her bath, and when she does, I take my hands away from my face so that I can look down on my legs. Most of this spring I have spent indoors, making my legs the colour of heavily creamed coffee. They are long and thin and firm. But seeing Grandma naked makes me realise something: for the same period of time that my legs are at the peak of young and smooth, at the end of my life they will be at the apex of old and flappy. One day my relatively pale legs will look like desiccated blue cheeses – a strange revelation, and one which I find frankly unbelievable at twenty-nine, eleven years away from the onset of middle age.

The bath water has ceased running now, and the silence jolts me into action; Grandma's ablutions are like lightning strikes, and they leave me little time. Wildly, I rummage through my suitcase seeking my own bathrobe, which I lay on the floor in front of the bathroom door. It takes me a few moments to arrange the robe realistically, as though a person is wearing it. I put two ice buckets where the chest should be and tie the belt into a bow at a cinched-in waist, and then, just as I hear Grandma lift herself from the tub, I step back to admire my work.

'Hmmph!' Naked as the dawn she takes a giant step over my dressing gown. 'You've got another thing comin' if you think I'm wearing that. You got to leave your pits free to dry after a wash, otherwise it's no good havin' washed a'tall.' Grandma lifts both arms high in the air and walks like that over to her larger suitcase. After she snorts her way into a girdle, I turn to see her don a gauzy tee-shirt with opaque pancake-sized patches under the armpits. I can feel my forehead furrow in puzzlement.

'What're you starin' at, Dr Modesty?'

'Forgive me, Grandma, I have no idea. What is that contraption?'

'It's a dress shield. I always wear one if it's gonna be a sultry day. Nowadays you can't buy 'em anywhere, so I take real good care of this one. It stops the sweat goin' through my blouses where it dries and leaves a stain. The old-fashioned ways are best, you know.' Looking smug, Grandma straightens her perspiration armour on her shoulders. Then she arches her back to make sure that the patches are snug in her pits. 'This new generation thinks nothin' of big, dark, wet spots under their arms, but in my day no lady, not even a country gal, would show herself in town that way. You could use a dress shield yourself.'

'Yes, I probably could. The Amazon River is probably wistful that I am not a tributary. And I inherited my sweat glands from *your* side of the family. Do you know, Grandma, sometimes after a tough consultation with a patient, my labcoat is *soaked*.'

'Well, that just shows you're from good workin' people. Not like those airy fairy college types your mother hails from. Now, quit your gabbin' and let's grab a bite for breakfast so we can get out to look at Gateway Arch.'

St Louis' buildings loom over the streets like the walls of tall canyons. For three blocks we stride along in silent confusion, having lost all sense of direction as soon as we left the hotel. Then Grandma grips my arm to check my momentum.

'Stop!' Setting her nose free upon the wind, she sucks in a considerable volume of Missouri air. 'I'm sniffin' for the river. We just follow the river to get to Gateway Arch.' She fills her stately nose a second time. 'Over there!' she points.

As we walk I look all around me, comparing this city with my own familiar Washington DC, and I forget to watch Grandma as closely as I should. This is a Tuesday morning, in the midst of rush-hour, and I hear brisk footsteps everywhere. Only when I turn to speak to her do I realise that none of the brisk footfall belongs to Grandma. Automatically, I step towards the kerb and bend my knees as long experience of losing Grandma in crowds has taught me to do. Don't panic, stoop! I stoop because I stand ten inches taller than she does, and if I search through the crowd at my height, I tend to miss the five foot tall person whom I seek. So I stoop, alerting my eyes to scan any fluffy, rosy whiteness which might be Grandma's hair.

I don't see her. 'Grandma!' I shout.

No one turns to look.

Across the street from me stands a building which

resembles a church, and one of its front doors stands ajar – just slightly, only a matter of two or three inches keeps it from being flush with its twin. I start to move before I even realise it: Open doors draw Grandma like bowls of beer draw slugs! Acting not on rationale but on instinct, I dart through the traffic and discover that the open door belongs to The Maritime Cathedral. Just inside, in the vestibule, stands Grandma, and as I come panting up, I see her furtively dip her fingertips in a font attached to the wall.

'Holy water,' she whispers loudly, looking outrageously pleased with herself. 'The Catholics do this. Now I got to go and light a candle for our safe journey.' She walks briskly up the aisle to a glowing bank of wax tapers, and, after folding a dollar into the collection box, she lights a candle and sinks to her knees. I walk softly around the edges of the church, admiring the dark wooden beams and feeling the bluish cast of light from the walls and windows. The Maritime Cathedral is a beautiful church. It makes me feel small and quiet, the way a beautiful church should.

'I lit a candle for your car, so it don't break down. And I lit a candle for me, so I learn what I got to know from this trip, and one for you, so that the homesickness don't cripple you.' She reaches up to pat me on the back of the neck.

'Thanks, Grandma.' I look away so that she doesn't see how close her words bring me to tears. Struggling to get control, I recollect my forebears, the steadfast Presbyterians who never fell asleep during sermons, and I say, 'But do you think God minds? You are a thoroughbred Protestant engaging in Catholic ceremony for your own ends . . .'

As a distraction this works brilliantly. 'God is not a Catholic,' says Grandma firmly. 'So He don't mind. I do this in every new city I visit, prayin' for somethin' or other. And I reckon if I weren't a Presbyterian I'd be a Catholic – I got some Catholic friends in my bridge club. Did you see all those statues of Saints? Which one d'ya think was St Louis?'

Outside again, we walk parallel to the Mississippi River, a bubbling brown affair no more than 200 feet across. It moves at a lively pace and carries small sticks and branches, as though it attacked and ravished a flotilla of Huckleberry Finn rafts earlier in the day. Without the flotsam this river might pass for a flow of molten milk chocolate. It is neither as wide nor as assuming as I expected the Mississippi to be, and I have difficulty in associating such a demure water with the devastating spring floods of 1993.

But then, the Mississippi is a Mid-Western river. It is not a river I understand. The rivers I understand are the rivers of my Middle East – the clear, fast-running James and the sultry, sometimes smelly Potomac. I know those rivers, and, suddenly, I'm jealous for them; on the banks of my rivers stands nothing so magnificent as the Gateway Arch.

'Lookee here!' Swinging one arm airborne, Grandma traces and recreates the sinuous silvery curve for herself. I follow her arm's path until it ends with an oustretched index finger pointing to the nearest terminus of Gateway Arch.

'If I recollect right,' she says, 'this thing is 650 feet tall and made'a pure stainless steel. It's the biggest monument in the world, and it's all for folks like you and me. Folks headin' West! I been wantin' to ride up into this Arch ever since they opened it – July 24th, 1967!'

Grandma appears to be hyperventilating. The doctor in me radiates concern, but the granddaughter is highly intrigued. The only other time I have seen Grandma so visibly excited was at the Devil's Knob, the mountain she nearly died to see. What is it about this Gateway Arch?

White concrete blocks the size of a basketball court support this end of the structure, and if I shade my eyes and squint into the distance, I can see the white blocks which support the other end of Gateway Arch. In between the two enormous sets of blocks, the monument rises thin and delicate into the air. I follow the curve of the structure with my eyes and consider what Grandma has said.

'What do you mean "ride up into the Arch"? More than half-way up it doesn't look wide enough for a human!'

''Course it is. That's an optical delusion. People been ridin' to the top of Gateway Arch for years. Down at the other end there's The Museum of Western Expansion, and you go in there to ride up in the Arch. Come on!'

'Ummm. I don't think so, Grandma.' Logically, I realise that I don't see the Arch waving in the wind, but viscerally, I know something different. 'I like looking at Gateway Arch from right here.'

'Chicken!'

'No, I'm not.'

'Chicken. Bock, bock, bock, chicken.' Tucking her fists into her armpits, Grandma does a flappy little dance. Then she's off.

Damn. I hate heights. Not as badly as I hated heights when I was a kid, but almost. I'd like to look out over thirty miles, though, and if this truly is the point of no return, I'd like to have an advance view of what lies West. I walk slowly, with my head tilted back to take in the wide spread of the monument.

All the while Grandma moves away from me at an unbelievable speed. She is headed towards the far terminus and The Museum of Western Expansion, and I must run to catch up. Someone must have replaced Maude Orpwood Suche's coccyx with a motor.

To my astonished eye, the line looks as long as the Mississippi is wide. The foolish people who want to ride to the top of Gateway Arch form an orderly queue which dominates the entire museum. And this is just the visible part of the queue – I can't estimate how many people are down in the holding pen directly *beneath* Gateway Arch.

'Are you sure you wish to wait *hours*, Grandma? Is the view worth it to you?'

'You got *no idea* how important this is!' Steering me over to the end of the line, she looks up into my face with pale eyes that command obedience, and when she speaks, she punctuates her words with three-fingered prods to my breastplate. 'Stay . . . in . . . line!'

'All right!'

Looking up once into my bewildered face, Grandma draws a deep breath. 'You got to understand, this here's a kind of a penguinage for me.'

'What?'

'One of them trips to a holy place. I'm here on a – '

'Pilgrimage. The word you want is pilgrimage.'

'Don't matter!' Grandma bounces on her toes, giving the impression of a rocket anxious for lift-off. 'Round the walls of this museum are all kinda exhibits tellin' how the Arch was built. I'm gonna have a look, then I'll come back and hold our place so as you can get a look. OK?' Taking my compliance for granted, she merges with the crowd.

If I squint I can just barely make out photos on the walls, and if I lean forward I can read captions. Eero Saarinen designed this monument, and it is 630 feet tall. The main structural component is – I lean so far forward that I step momentarily out of the queue – stainless steel. Well! Now that I stand out of view of the Arch, I can consider it without feeling under a spell. What soars into the air over my head is the misuse of enough stainless steel to provide cutlery for the entire country! Certainly a dessert fork for every man, woman, and child . . .

Someone is poking a finger at my *butt cheek*.

When doctors are surprised they forget to use terms of anatomical exactitude. Whipping around, I see the culprit – a tiny male person of about six years with hair the colour of french fries cooked in old oil. A creature who must certainly be his older brother stands, slightly taller, next to him, and they both smirk at me.

'Momma, tell that lady to move up,' says the smaller one.

Quickly I step forward, then turn back and look at the boys as if to say, 'There!'

'Momma' shoos her brood into the space created by my advance. She is a massive smiling woman, with hair bleached white by seaside sun; just like her child, she speaks in an Alabama coastal drawl. 'Hold yowah hossis, l'il sugahs.'

'You done this befowah, lady?' asks the older of the towheads. 'Do you know how it wuhks?'

'No,' I say as serenely as possible.

Like dogs, the two boys scent my trepidation. So while Momma smiles above us all, the older boy does the explaining, and the younger brother provides sound effects.

'See, thayuh'sa tube in its guts, and an elevatuh rides up the tube. It's reyul loud and it sounds lak it huhts the Ahch.'

The boy with the french fry head groans wretchedly and makes noises like an automatic weapon. On cue, his older brother pauses, all the while eyeing me covertly to gauge my response.

'Fahnly,' he continues, 'when ya get to the top, y'look out these little windahs and ya can see forevah. And when the wind blows, ya can feel the floa *shivah*.' The older brother quakes theatrically. 'We already done it two tahms.'

Materialising at my elbow, Grandma nods pleasantly at our neighbours in line. She looks her normal self and outwardly does not *appear* driven by the pilgrim's strange fervour. 'Now,' she turns to me, 'you go learn something from this museum.'

* * *

Number two prod into my *gluteus maximus* comes while I examine a set of architectural plans. Not so surprised this time, I pivot to see the larger version of the two boys who stood behind me in line. The creature seems perturbed that I don't require the administration of a second poke.

'Mah Momma sent me ovah 'cause yowah Mamaw's been callin' you and you ain't heard. Y'all gonna go up in the Ahch with us, and it's neahly owah tuhn. Yowah Mamaw's all excited!' He grabs my arm, pulling me towards the head of the queue, and he doesn't pause as he says over his shoulder, 'This's just mah thuud tahm up in the Ahch. Ah'm gonna do it all day!'

Down in the tunnel beneath the Gateway Arch, Grandma stands with sucked-in cheeks and watches the drama of loading massive Southern Momma into the elevator.

Whoever designed this ride to the top of the Arch did not consider the girth of all possible riders. The opening into the elevator is roughly four feet high by two feet wide, and so Momma, who stands nearly six feet tall and three and a half feet wide, has a problem. Good naturedly, she puzzles her way into the elevator. First she attempts a head-on approach, then a hopeful sideways squeeze, then at last she straddles the doorway, inserting first one thigh then the other.

'Suck in yowah gut, Momma, just lak last tahm,' says the younger boy dispassionately. He and his brother are not embarrassed by Momma's trembling Mount Everest of flesh and the problem it creates.

'Poor, poor woman,' Grandma says behind her hand. 'I just bet it's her glands . . .'

Momma squeezes in. All by herself she takes up most of the tiny elevator, yet, somehow, Grandma and the two boys and I ooze in too. When the door shuts, the air is close and fetid with the odours of previous inhabitants. Momma needs a bath. As the car begins to rise, slowly, with a faint but growing list to the left, I think fiercely of fresh breezes off the Chesapeake Bay. Next to me, Grandma chats happily with Momma from Mobile, Alabama and her sons, the Butt-cheek Pokers.

'Ah hope the brakes don' fail,' chuckles Momma comfortably. 'We'd be a grease spot.'

Her sons' eyes light up. 'Really, Momma? Y'think it maht fall?'

'Nothin's shua but death and taxes, l'il sugahs.' Momma shifts round to look at Grandma and when she does, I feel the elevator shudder to a stop. Maybe it's a coincidence. Oh God.

'This's the boaz' thuud tahm today,' Momma says, completely comfortable with a stationary elevator. 'We're heya visitin' mah sistah who married a Yankee. Ah thought the boaz maht lak to ride a rivahboat, but they just want ta keep ridin' up in this Ahch. Ah even tempted 'em with the National Video Games Museum, but nothin' doin'.' She gazes fondly upon the 'boaz'.

I have my face turned close to Grandma's head and am hoping to placate my nose with the scent of Chanel No 5 talcum powder, which Grandma dusts all over her neck and shoulders. I see when her cheeks go inexplicably pink.

And then she draws in her breath sharply.

'It ain't an amusement park ride,' she says harshly. The silence in the elevator inflates, balloon-like with her sudden fury. 'I got something to tell you young fellows,' she says, leaning forward to stare into their eyes. And she begins by repeating herself.

'This ain't no amusement park ride! Remember that! Every time you ride up into Gateway Arch you're travelling back 400 years. For 400 years now folks been meeting here before going out West. It's a natural spot, near where the Mississippi and Missouri River waters mix together. Me and my granddaughter, we're heading West to the Pacific Coast. We're from Norway, my family, but the first folks here was Spanish and French, in fact a Frenchie named this city in the first place. Named it St Louis, for a dead king, Louis the ninth, who rose up a saint. But by rights this city oughtta be called St Jefferson, after Thomas Jefferson who bought it in the Louisiana Purchase! It matters, boys, listen up! In 1860 a courthouse stood on the land where this Arch is today. Real famous cases got tried here, and people just naturally met here and organised to go West in wagon trains. A gateway to justice and freedom! Can't you feel it?!'

Momma holds her boys to her protectively, one on either side, nestled under her arms like baby birds. All three of them stare at Grandma while she speaks. Do the boys understand the meaning of this history lesson? I don't think so, but Grandma's passion glues their eyes on her. She is more than frightening: bewitching, and her hopes for this place pervade every word. She takes my breath away.

Gateway Arch matters to Grandma. She believes it

could change her life in the same way that mountains, with their awesome magnitude and grace, once prepared her for personal apocalypse. Forty-six years ago a mountain made Grandma hope her future life would change. Now at eighty-five years old, my grandmother has come to this Mid-West monument so that she can look back to the past, in the hope she might change something there.

Can locations be catalysts for mental metamorphoses? I don't know, I just don't. My only shrine is almost a thousand miles away, my home on Herring Bay. For me it's a place of comfort, of haven and ease. Not a place of epiphany. I worry for Grandma, who expects so much from a ride to the top of a stainless steel tube.

'Why,' says Momma, 'that granbaby of yoahs is white as a sheet! They bettah get this elevatuh movin' right quick!' Momma shifts her weight, like she's going to reach over and pat my forehead, and a creak sounds, maybe from her seat, maybe from the elevator.

'Don't move!' I shriek.

'Are you gonna be sick?' asks Grandma, her anger instantly deflating. 'Oh, laws, let me just get a baggie.' Extracting a folded plastic bag from her purse, Grandma says to the elevator at large, 'You know, I always keep one of these handy so's I'm prepared if I can't finish all my dinner rolls when I'm eatin' out. It turns my stomach to think of all the food restaurants throw away.' Grandma sounds sorrowful as she aims the bag at my face.

'Oh, yes,' says Momma. 'Ah keep a bag for that ahdentical puhpose. Waitahs just throw all that bread away and its a cryin' shame. Such waste. Think of all the starvin' chilluns.' Momma sounds dismal, though her cheerful expression never wavers. Her gratitude at having been born in the first world looks to consist of three-fifths fatback pork and two-fifths cheese grits.

I really do feel queasy. And equally uneasy.

The ominous quiet of the machinery changes into a grinding whine, and finally our cage tilts upright to indicate a completed ascent. For agonising, gullet-constricting moments, the tiny door remains shut . . . jammed . . . In our little box the silence is thick and my green cheeks draw all eyes. When at last the door opens, Momma holds her sons back so that I can squeeze out first. Greatefully I stagger to one of the tiny airplane-like windows here at the top of Gateway Arch, 630 feet above the earth. I don't even stop to think that I hate heights and that maybe I shouldn't let my body realise where it is.

Because that doesn't matter.

Grandma struggles to absorb the view. It looks to me like she can see more than thirty miles in every direction. She sees back to Evansville, Indiana, and ahead to the farmlands of middle America. And I realise for the first time that Grandma suffers from *mylocusphilia.* Because she has lived for almost a quarter of a century on the shores of the Chesapeake Bay, I assumed that the waterside community of Deale, Maryland was *her place.* It isn't. Maryland never was her place and it never will be. Grandma belongs to the Mid-West. This immense land-locked flatness is where she fits.

Maybe the whole world divides into water people and land people, and on top of the two categories people layer their regional preferences. I am a Middle East water person, and Grandma is a Mid-West land lover. It's that simple. But it becomes complex when I think of Thomas Suche. As long as Thomas Suche lived, Grandma stayed with him in Evansville, Indiana, and she begrudged him every moment. As soon as he died, she left Evansville and went *East*, not West. I don't think she came East just to be near my father. Somehow, it was a penance. The way Grandma stares out the window, forgetting even to raise her camera for a picture, the way she drinks in the view, going East to Maryland must have been a penance. I don't know for what. Does it change anything for you, Grandma? Will you tell me?

'My brothah', says a voice from below hip-level, 'has just been sick as a dawg.' It is the smaller of the Southern boys, and he points to his sibling, who is doubled up and choking. As Momma swoops down upon her elder son, a dreadful odour powers its way around the viewing room. Unlike the hospital, where vomit stench is quickly civilised by antiseptic solutions, the smell here is highly, repellently, assertive.

Stains on the carpet attest to others who have felt the virulence of vertigo, but I barely have time to notice. Grandma grabs my hand and pulls me across to the far end of the twenty by ten foot viewing area, where a down elevator is just opening. Though some dozen people already plan on boarding the car, somehow Grandma and I enter first, and our ride back to earth is short and sweet.

'You go on outside if you want to,' Grandma says, 'but I'm gonna wait here by the elevator.' She is dying to offer Momma a fizzy lemon indigestion tablet for her son's solace.

Five minutes later, Grandma exits the museum. Blinking against the sun, she trots over to the bench where I sit, looking out over the Mississippi. 'What a lily-livered woman,' she says and shakes her head in disgust. 'That fat gal's back in line with those boys, waitin' to ride up into Gateway Arch a fourth time. She thanked me for the 'digestion tablet and ate it herself! They didn't understand a thing I said – the Arch is a once in a lifetime thing, not a carnival ride. No good comes of spoilin' children.'

Grandma snorts. 'What that gal really needs is a pill to stiffen her backbone. You know any medicine like that, Doctor?'

Odessa, Missouri

If anyone ever asks me what Missouri looks like, I will say it doesn't look like the Middle East.

Grandma directed me to Route 70 on leaving St. Louis, and now we have travelled two hundred and thirty miles to the western side of the state. Missouri rolls out *flat*, the flattest place I've ever been, and *sweltering*. The temperature hovers near ninety-five degrees, making air hang over the black highway in shimmering waves. As for the way this land feels, well, it feels like hot homesickness. Missouri *feels* like a land-locked state, without even the memory of an inland sea.

'Laws,' says Grandma, patting under her eyes with a hankie. 'Let's find a nice hotel where I can get a bath – can't you just picture loadsa ice cubes floatin' in 'bout an inch of cool water? Then I want a pizza. After that long drive yesterday, we oughtta have us an early rest.'

'All right, but better still, we'll find a hotel with a pool. Even if you won't swim, just swinging your legs in the water will make you cool.'

Out of the corner of my eye I see that Grandma looks apprehensive. I've always known that water makes her nervous, but I don't know why.

We register at the counter.

Maude Orpwood Suche's 'I'm old and tired' routine deserves a lifetime achievement award from The Society of Travelling Shysters. I'm on the inside of her con game, and my conscience gives me a twinge, albeit not too large a twinge; I pay half our hotel bill, so I'm pleased to share in Grandma's fifty per cent discounts. It's just that I feel a bit sorry for the bamboozled hotel clerks.

'So,' Grandma asks, her voice a quavering shadow of its usual self, 'what're you gonna do for me, Miss?'

Her mark is an enthusiastic mass of dark hair attached to a girl whose name-tag reads Arabella Noire.

'Oh, *puhleeze*, Mrs Suche, don't call me *Miss*, just call me Belle. My Mom and Pop call me Belle of the Night, on account of my dark hair. No one can figure out what side of the family I favour, because the majority of my kin is blond and German. I don't look like either of my folks, but they swear I'm not adopted!' Arabella Noire beams widely at Grandma.

Grandma, charmed and disarmed, beams widely back. This is Blood talk, and, therefore, music to her ears. Leaning into the front desk she peers searchingly at Ms Noire's face. 'Not German. You haven't got much from your German kin at all. Somebody from your past came outta Eastern Europe – you got Hungarian eyes. I recognise 'em because Great Uncle Eustace married a Hungarian gal with eyes,' Grandma taps one perfectly manicured fingernail on the countertop in between each word, 'just . . . like . . . yours. Hungarian, no doubt about it.'

Reaching for a plastic room key, Arabella Noire asks, 'Do you think they're pretty eyes? My brother Jeff says they look like cows' eyes!'

'Take that as a compliment, dear. Cows got beautiful eyes. I know because I used to keep cows.'

With a big wide smile, Arabella Noire proffers a kite-shaped orange plastic room key. 'You get free buffet breakfast tomorrow morning, and I've given you a great room on the ground floor right next to the pool. You'll have barely five steps from your doorstep to the diving board! Isn't that a fine thing on a hot day like today. You enjoy yourself, now.'

No discount, but Grandma is not perturbed. She had a brief but vitalising encounter with genealogy, and she'll get our money's worth from the free buffet breakfast. Inside her pocketbook are little plastic bags to pack in enough eggs, bacon, and toast to last out a famine.

In this heat, even Grandma slows her usual quick step to a stroll. We ooze along the hotel's outdoor corridors, looking for our room, until Grandma commands me to 'Stop!' Pointing to a dusky alcove which looks like it smells of cat urine, she says, 'Bet there are some vending machines back there. Why don't you see if they got a machine sellin' those little cans of orange juice. Get two. I got a flask of gin in my purse, and I reckon we should have cocktails by the pool.'

* * *

Incredulity makes me choke on my drink.

Here in our solitary neon-blue swimming hole, under a broad Missouri sky gone deep purple with sunset, Grandma acts in an unprecedented way. She wades out into the pool up to the level of her belly button! This is Maude Orpwood Suche, who grows nervous if bathwater closes over her thighs, who agreed tonight, in concession to the heat, to sit on the top step leading down into the pool, but agreed only after sucking courage from her potent gin and orange juice. Grandma is *in* the pool!

'This is real nice,' she says, pleased with her daring. She positions her hands as if to hold herself afloat – palms down and flat upon the water's surface – and plants her feet firmly on the poured concrete of the pool floor.

Grandma's cocktail controls my tongue, and I speak before I realise that there might be other, more opportune times for my question. 'Why are you afraid of the water, Grandma? As far back as I can remember, you've never entered even a puddle above your ankles!'

'I'm *not* afraid of the water,' she tells me, sounding surprised. She walks small slow circles in the pool, and a tiny wake follows her like a bustle. 'I'm a Pisces. I *love* water.'

Looking down into my glass, I swirl the ice cubes and assume that I have all the answers. 'You may love water, but you're also terrified of being in it. Then again, I don't imagine there were too many places for you to learn to swim when you were growing up. Many people who can't swim fear water. Fear of water usually masks a phobia about drowning.'

'Yes, I worry 'bout drowning.'

'I know, Grandma. That's what I mean. You used to say, "Watch out! You can drown in a ditch havin' only an inch of water!" It made a big impression on me. In medical school I learned how right you are. People drown from glasses of water – the amount of liquid is immaterial – but most lay-people never grasp the concept. Your phobia is exceptional in that it encompasses waters as big as the Chesapeake, and as small as an almost empty drainage ditch.' Setting my glass down, I lean back on my elbows and stretch my legs into shallow water; in the hot Odessa twilight, these are the only movements I can countenance.

Once again I speak without thinking. 'Where's *Li'l Maude*?' The question occurs to me because Grandma's bathing suit is low-cut in front, and it hides little of her ancient bosom. If, somehow, *Li'l Maude* were secreted on Grandma's person, the pretty pearly pistol would be sodden by now; Grandma has been slowly sinking up to her neck, and trapped air puffs the top of her bathing suit.

'The rule is, we don't discuss *Li'l Maude* in public!' Grandma glares at me like a surly buoy, but I am full of gin and orange juice and I don't care.

'No one else is around. The hotel is nearly deserted, and who would know what we're talking about anyway? Where's *Li'l Maude*?'

'Wrapped up safe in my towel,' hisses Grandma. 'Now shut your trap!'

'All right.' I nod sagely, my curiosity satisfied. 'Would you like another drink, Grandma? I thought I might get one for myself.'

She nods and circles over to sit on the highest pool step in my absence. When I return, she moves back out to the centre of the water.

'What makes you think I don't know how to swim?' Grandma asks, sounding more aggressive than the question deserves. 'Just 'cause I won't, don't mean I can't.'

'But you never swim at home, and you never canoe or sail out on the Chesapeake because you worry about capsizing. I make my assumption based on twenty-nine years of evidence, Grandma.'

She snorts. 'I learned to swim when I was fifteen years old. Learned the hard way: I got dunked in a flooded quarry pit by my friend Nerf Fleishman who threw me in, then turned himself 'round and walked away. It must have been real hard for him to do, you know. Because he loved me. But what he said when I was fifteen was, "If you're the girl I think you are, Maude Orpwood, you'll find a way to get to the side." I was strong and a fighter, but I nearly drowned. See, I was so surprised when gentle Nerf Fleishman said those words to me – "If you're the girl I think you are, you'll find a way to get to the side." I just couldn't believe it.'

'But you made it to the side?'

'Now Doctor,' Grandma points at me, 'that's a dumb question, ain't it? I'm standing here plain as day. My friend Nerf threw me in 'cause he'd got tired of me sayin' I'd learn to swim soon, and he wanted me to take a dip with him every night before supper. He figgered I'd never get wet 'less I was made to, so Nerf threw me in, and I learned to swim, after a fashion. Kinda like a dog swims, but it worked. In the end, you can see, it wasn't *me* that drowned.'

I feel my eyes go wide, and I make room for Grandma when she circles slowly back to the step where I sit.

'We were two sides of the same penny, Nerf and me. Ever since we were just little sprouts we played together. I liked him better'n any of the gals, and he wanted to play only with me. Our mothers were best of friends, so it just seemed kinda natural – what I mean is it seemed *natural* to me and Nerf. But the other kids noticed that Nerf didn't play with boys. And they all picked up on Timola's name for him. Timola hated Nerf. He was always makin' these great toys – yoyos and slingshots and guns that shot walnuts – but he wouldn't give 'em to Timola, who batted her eyes for nothing. She called Nerf a sissy.'

Pursing her lips, Grandma embarks upon a falsetto to indicate the mental arrival of Cousin Timola: '"Sissy, sissy, sissy. Sissy!" Nerf never minded folks callin' him that, but it bothered me. I don't know if it bothered me for Nerf, or if it bothered me for me, if you get my meanin'. I liked to jump rope with Nerf, but that was a girls' game, so I always said we had to jump rope in Pa's hay barn, where nobody could see us. Problem was, it was always May by the time the barn cleared out enough for jumpin' rope. September through April, there was no jumpin' rope for me and Nerf.'

Grandma can't quite reach across me for her drink, so I hand it to her.

'What did Nerf look like?' I ask. I want to see him in my head. And all the while, I'm puzzling over the strange emphasis of 'It wasn't *me* that drowned.'

'Well, he *looked* like a sissy – all fine boned and light skinned. And he wore these real thick glasses, thicker'n mine are now. If you tried to look him in the face, his eyes looked all wavy. He never took his specs off, not even for swimmin'. But underneath he had the most beautiful eyes, big brown eyes with long, long lashes. I saw his eyes just once, much later on.' Grandma sits silent, staring across the pool at a copse created by the hotel's landscaping service. There is a waving wilderness of pampas grass and a palm tree.

'Timola never called Nerf anything but Sissy. "Hey, Sissy," she'd call. "You got a pretty dress I can borrow?" Timola was one of those gals everybody clusters round, like flies on shit. She'd call those things to Nerf Fleishman, and he'd just ignore her while everybody'd laugh.' Grandma assumes the falsetto again. '"Why are *you* laughing, Maude? *You* play with Sissy every day, or doesn't everybody know that? You and Sissy play dolls, Maude?"

'To reply I always laughed as if Timola's words were no 'count. Not once did I take up for Nerf.' Grandma drains her second drink, taking all the ice cubes into her mouth. Moments later the ice cubes shoot from her lips with the force of pickled breath behind them – a salvo of ice cubes arcing out over the water.

'He sounds like he was a better friend to you than you were to him, Grandma. I don't get it. You don't lack the courage for your convictions – it's not your style. Why didn't you stick up for Nerf?' Currently my head holds more voices than just the doctor and the granddaughter. A gin and orange juice voice tells me to go ahead and ask questions. A quieter voice, muted almost to inaudible, tells me to shut up, because Grandma is talking about someone she truly loved, in a way that she never loved anyone else, and certainly not the man she married.

'I don't know why I never stuck up for Nerf. But I remember how it felt, Timola cuttin' him up. My cheeks got real warm and I'd stare at Timola while she did her yapping. I couldn't ever walk away 'til she was done. *Nobody* liked Nerf but me, which I could never figger. Sometimes I hated him for bein' so unpopular.

'Nerf didn't care what anybody thought. He didn't need to play with anybody other'n me. What he loved was makin' mechanical toys, and they were so interesting I never wanted to stray far, 'cause I might miss what he made next. He was sixteen when he took the worn out motor from Pa's John Deere and made an elevator – this rope chair which rode me up to a platform Nerf built in his big maple tree. I could see for miles. And Nerf's uncle went to China and brought him back an abbatoir – you know, one of those Chinky countin' machines.'

'An abacus.'

'That's just what I said. Don't interrupt.' Grandma sits in the deepening darkness and allows for a moment's silence.

I worry she has lost her train of thought. 'About the abacus, Grandma – '

'Oh, it wasn't so exciting as the elevator, but it spoke well for his career as an inventor. Nerf made a mechanical abacus that looked like a calculator, long before anybody'd thought of a calculator. Can you get me some more gin and juice, please?'

First I run to the vending machine, because we are out of orange juice, then to the glass I add the last dribbles of gin. Though the refill seems to take me for ever, I know my return is quick because Grandma continues as though uninterrupted. Next to her in the pool, I sit quietly licking gin and orange juice from my fingers.

'I was just thinkin' that I've never spoken about Nerf to anybody, not since he died. But he's in my head lots. Every time I have a poached egg it's like a trigger, bringin' it all back, because the last time I saw Nerf, his breath smelled real strong of poached egg yolks. It was what he'd had for breakfast. Are you,' Grandma turns to me suddenly, 'snozzled? I'm real snozzled. I can recollect only one other time I've been so snozzled, and I'll prob'ly tell you about it soon, seein' as I've opened my trap so wide already.'

'Oh, yes, Grandma, I'm snozzled . . . weird word. Doctors usually say *intoxicated*, or *inebriated*, but perhaps I could introduce a hybrid. How about "snoxicated"? Or maybe "snebriated"?'

'Shut up,' she tells me. 'I was talkin' about the last time I saw Nerf Fleishman. I was thirty-one years old, with two children, and your Grandfather Thomas was out surveying in Ohio, somewhere. That was the last time I saw Nerf. He came over to the big brick showplace Thomas had built for himself, and he came 'cause his Ma sent him. Mrs Fleishman asked Nerf to come breathe on me.' Grandma nods her head vigorously; even in the darkness she can see my questioning look.

'That's right. To *breathe* on me. I told you how Ma and Mrs Fleishman were bosom pals. As a personal favour to

Ma, Mrs Fleishman always sent Nerf over as soon as he picked up the latest germ. I got mumps that way, and measles, but somehow Nerf and me escaped chicken pox 'till we was older. I recollect how Ma used to supervise the breathing and when we were only young sprigs. It embarrassed me dreadful. Ma'd ask Nerf to stand close to my face, then I'd shut my eyes while he just about blew his brains up my nose. Ma made him breathe on my eyes, too.

'So it was only natural that Mrs Fleishman send Nerf to give me chicken pox, even though I didn't want 'em. I didn't want to see Nerf. Ma didn't figure that, though, she just thought I didn't fancy spots all over my face. "Vanity could kill you," Ma tells me, real angry. "You'll get chicken pox sometime for sure, and it can be dangerous. The older you are when you get it, the more likely you are to pass away. Think of Thomas and the boys!" So I thought of Thomas and the boys, and Nerf Fleishman came to pay me a chicken pox call.

'This was in 1941. I hadn't spoken to Nerf in nine years, not since the day I married Thomas. He'd been away for a long spell, gettin' a higher education, learning engineering. But his mother called him home to be nursed through the pox, and so he came to spread the germ. "Hello, Maude," says Nerf at the front door. He looks all solemn and speckled.

'Don't come in. Just breathe on me, can't you? I wanna get this over with quick,' I say, not best pleased to meet Nerf's eyes. After I say my first words to him in nine years, there's one of those silences you get sometimes, in conversation, that seems to last for ever.

'"All right," he says finally. His voice is so gentle, quiet, that in my head I hear Timola shouting *Sissy*! "But I think, Maude, that we better do this where you can collapse right after, because as soon as I pass the germ the pox'll come on you like lightning." So we go to a settee in the morning room, and I tell Nerf he don't have to breathe on me in the old way. I can smell poached eggs from where I stand, so surely I got the germ, too.

'"Oh, no. We better be certain," he says. "Sit down." So, not really wanting to, I sit down and shut my eyes.

'"Open them, Maude. Chicken pox is a virus, and a good way to get infected is through the membrane round your eyes." So I sit there, eyes wide open while Nerf blows a chicken pox cyclone in my face – and the smell of poached eggs is so strong it makes my eyes water 'til the drops run down my cheeks.

'When he's done, he just shuts his mouth and keeps his face close to mine, and I realise then that Nerf took off his glasses when I shut my eyes. For the first and only time I see that his eyes are deep brown, like fall leaves in a cold stream. They're beautiful, they'd make a cow's eyes look plastic.

'"Don't cry, Maude," says Nerf quietly. He doesn't figure that I'm cryin' from his breath, so he puts his arms around my neck and holds me with him. And then the tears really start. I'm bawling like a baby, because it feels so nice havin' Nerf next to me again, better even than when we'd been friends. I missed him. And I knew I loved him. He held me for hours, the finest hours I can remember. My friend Nerf stayed the whole afternoon, but when he left, we weren't speaking. I never spoke to him again.'

I can see tears running down Grandma's face, and they land in her drink when she takes a swallow. 'You see, I told Nerf I could never leave my husband and marry him. For nine years he'd held on to the hope I would. Nerf'd reckoned someday I'd come to my senses and leave Thomas Suche, but I said it wouldn't happen 'less I was a widow. Nerf walked out of that fancy house a broken man. And I took sick right after, just as he said I would.

'My chicken pox went everywhere. I'd learned from Nerf that they could – he had them in some peculiar places for sure. But I got a fever, too, and it went higher and higher. I started talkin' nonsense. My Ma called Thomas Suche back from his job, and then, because she was almighty fearful, they got a doctor in who said my brain was burnin' up, and that I might go mad. But I didn't. The fever broke, and it left me fragile as milkweed floss.

'For all the months it took my pox to scab and dry up, and my strength to recover, I kept askin' for Nerf to come see me. I told my Ma I wanted to see if his pox were healing, to give me hope. But what I really wanted to do was patch up our quarrel. For one afternoon we'd been friends again, after nine years, and I couldn't lose that. I wanted Nerf to understand why I couldn't leave Thomas. I just had to see him.

'The doctor who'd come for my fever had left instructions about my health bein' shaky and my mind being soft, so nobody told me Nerf Fleishman was dead. About the same time the pox raced along my spine and popped out on my elbows, they found Nerf Fleishman floating face down. He was in the quarry pit where I learned to swim.'

'Oh, Grandma, no. No, no, no.' I am shivering. The heat has left the air and the water feels not buoyant but clammy. 'He killed himself for you? Because he loved you and you loved him but you wouldn't leave Thomas Suche?'

Grandma hears the hostility in my voice. When she turns to look at me, I can make out her pale eyes but little else. 'I had a child by Nerf Fleishman,' she says.

I am stunned, and my silence is an answer enveloping everything I could ever say.

'My third son was not Thomas's, though he never knew. The baby was born dead while Thomas was surveyin' in Pennsylvania, so Thomas could never look at it to see it wasn't his; he would have *known for certain*,' Grandma sighs.

'Babies growing during a bout of chicken pox don't do so well, and Nerf gave me his child the day he gave me his germ. We lay together on the settee, and Nerf couldn't believe I wouldn't leave Thomas after that. He couldn't believe I'd sleep with him once not to sleep with him for ever.' Grandma's voice sounds exhausted. Setting her third drink down, empty, she speaks so quietly that I must concentrate entirely on hearing her.

'Nerf Fleishman isn't the reason I got to go on this trip out West. I wouldn't have to *take* this trip if I'd married him. My whole life could've been different. All I had to do was say once that I cared for him. I wouldn't even've had to say it directly, Nerf would have taken it as proof if I'd just stood up for him once against Timola. Just *once* in the thirty one years we were friends. She got nastier an' nastier as she got older. "Hey Sissy, why don't you go on and marry old Maude, so I can stop calling you Sissy and just call you Sister." She had all my Blood laughing fit to kill, and I never said nothing. It was 'cause of Timola I never stood up for Nerf. She didn't just make me marry a fella I didn't love, she made me lose the only person I did love.

'Yes, I reckon I can say it now, after three shots of gin and all these years: I loved Nerf Fleishman, and he loved me. Timola just couldn't stand it.' Grandma shakes her head and rises, dripping, from the pool. I rise with her, because if I don't, I can't hear what she says.

'Timola had fellas around her all the time . . . she had the pick of Evansville, Indiana. But she knew nobody'd ever love her the way Nerf loved me, and she just couldn't stand it. Jealousy ate Timola alive.'

On a plastic *chaise longue*, Grandma sits down as though her knees give out. I shake out her towel without thinking, to cover her shoulders against the chill, and, as I do, the clang of silver on concrete makes us both jump.

'*Li'l Maude!*'

'She'll be all right,' says Grandma listlessly, pulling the towel close around her. I pat the fabric into her shoulders, but my eyes are steady on silver.

The handle. I pick up the gun by its handle; *Li'l Maude* is not a 'she' to me. I'm careful to point the barrel away because I don't know whether it's loaded. Slowly, gently, irrationally worried that my steps might induce a misfire, I move to a spotlight buried in the pampas grass copse, and there I examine Grandma's personal pistol.

It is not a simple piece of work. Though I know nothing of guns, I gain instant tactile understanding that anything complex which looks this fluid is a masterwork. The engraving on the barrel is deep; running my index finger over the gun's name, I know I could read *Li'l Maude* even if blind. Gingerly, I turn the gun up to examine the grip. Between the two halves on the pearl inlaid wooden handle, connecting them, runs a metal strip, and on the metal strip is stamped *FLEISHMAN 1932*.

Grandma shivers violently on her *chaise longue. Get her inside and into a warm bath*, says the doctor in me urgently while the granddaughter holds a gun on the mutual palm. *Think of radiation cooling. This flat land loses all its heat the moment the sun goes down! Get her inside now!*

Putting my arm around her towelled shoulders, I help Grandma to her feet. '1932 is the year you got married, isn't it.' I pose not a question but an observation; I know very well what year Grandma married Thomas Suche, but I want an explanation.

'I told you. Nerf made her as my wedding present.'

'Yes.' I realise that I am supporting her for real. Around our feet dewy cold grass closes like shrink wrap. 'It's just that a deadly handgun seems like a strange wedding gift.'

'I can't explain that now,' Grandma says wearily. 'You got to wait 'til we get to Colorado.'

Unignorable.

Old, alcohol-relaxed muscles and officous adenoids make the vibrations of Grandma's uvula and soft palate unignorable.

I sit with my chin on my knee, mindlessly picking my toes and watching Grandma snore at seven am on Wednesday morning. My attention catches on my little toe, where a blister floats.

'We din ea las nigh, di'we?' asks Grandma, sitting bolt upright in bed after her own ferocious snore wakens her. The sudden movement startles me.

'I'm sorry, Grandma, could you repeat that?' She does, and still I'm befuddled. 'Can you put your teeth in, please?'

She fishes in the bubble-lined glass standing on her bedside table, then settles the dentures in among the remnants of her natural teeth. 'Ohhhhhh. All that gin and juice on an empty belly. No wonder I feel like somethin' the dog coughs up after chewing a little grass. I feel like dookie. Maybe a little more shut eye's the ticket.' Sinking back into the pillow, Grandma settles the sheet under her chin and closes her eyes.

Her colour isn't very good says the doctor in me, to which the granddaughter replies, Ha! If you were as hung-over as she is, you wouldn't be the soul of fresh colour, either!

Looking like a wizened white currant against the pillow, Grandma's head asks, 'Are you hungry?'

'Yes. But I'm surprised that you are.'

'Well, why don't you go to that breakfast buffet and bring us back two real heaping plates of hashbrowns and eggs. No bacon, 'cause I can feel the ralph waitin' just back of my throat. Ohhhhhh. Bring loadsa toast.'

Blue Springs, Missouri

'Still stinks in here!'

Thirteen miles west of Odessa, Grandma continues to wrinkle her nose at the strange smell we found after the car was shut up all night. The smell is insinuating and unsettling, the scent of a place where humans nest. It is one part banana skin, one part foot odour, one part unidentifiable, and all parts comfortably ensconced in the upholstery, the carpet, and the evaporation beads clinging to the inside windows. Whipping an atomized bottle of Chanel No. 5 out of her purse, Grandma works her finger on the pump until a frenzy of spray fills the car.

'Ummmmmm,' she says appreciatively. 'Fresh air.'

Grandma's notions on the subtle application of perfume make me think of monsoons. I cough, flapping my hands in the air. 'That bottle won't last very long if you use it as room spray.'

'Listen,' she says, chuckling at me through the mist, 'I got enough of this stuff to drink a shotglass with dinner for a year. Your Uncle George gives me a bottle each birthday, Christmas, Mother's Day, and Valentine's Day. I got twenty bottles, every size, along with three things of talcum powder, two body lotions, four soaps on a rope, and some kinda body cream with ground up pearls in it, for Pete's sake. I oughtta set up a store!'

'Oh!' It is a monosyllable full of amusement, and it's the last word I say for some time. My whole body is taken over by a violent fit of sneezing. Because no one in Grandma's family has a history of virulent sneezing, my sneezes don't concern her the way my hiccups did on Monday. She continues to speak, fitting the essential words into cavities of calm between my terrible nose explosions.

'You know how your Uncle George knew to buy me Chunnel No. 5? Liz. It's her fault. 'Bout five years back your mother took me shoppin' at a real la-di-dah place in Georgetown Mall', here Grandma waves the fingers of both hands in the air, as though she's tickling the ivories on some ethereal piano. 'You know, that real fancy place where everything costs double and they got a girl who's standing in the bathrooms, waiting for you to pee so you can wash your hands and she can give you a towel. Liz tipped her fifty cents!

'Anyways, at the perfume department Liz sprayed me with scents 'til I had no plain-smelling scrap of skin left. I was so powerful I made my head swim. But out of all those bottles I liked Chunnel No.5 best, and I told Liz so. Boy, was that a mistake! She told George, and I've never gotten any other present since.'

My eyes water, soothing the blood vessels which bulged

when I sneezed. 'How do you thank Uncle George year after year for the same present?'

But Grandma doesn't answer me; she looks pensive.

I am mystified. Resigned acceptance accords ill with the Grandma I know. Last year I gave her a pair of slippers for Christmas only to find that she preferred an electronic gizmo to shut her curtains automatically.

'What is it 'bout this car, Doctor? I say things I try real hard not to say, never, even to *myself*.'

Puzzled, I look over to see Grandma shaking her head.

'Every time George gives me more perfume, I kinda clap my hands and act real excited, when, a'course, I'm not. I've started giving out bottles as prizes at Senior Citizens' Bingo. Last Mother's Day I started to tell George maybe I'd like a nice cactus or somethin' next time had had to give me a present. Then I stopped myself and acted real delighted again. It seems disloyal to tell my son I'm tired of his gift. George has a lot of his father in him.

'Thomas gave me jewellery. Each anniversary, my birthday, and Christmas. Always jewellery. He wanted me all dressed the way he dressed up his big brick house. But unlike the house, he forgot what he'd bought me after the first year, and I started gettin' repeats. In my safety deposit box at the bank I got ten thin bracelets made of hearts linked up, and I got sixteen pairs'a pearl earrings in filigree settings. All the same. The best jeweller in Evansville used these blue velvet boxes. They were real pretty, sized like small, medium, and large mushroom caps, and I always knew what was comin' according to the size.

'I couldn't tell Thomas my tenth gold bracelet wasn't

just perfect, and I don't tell George not to buy me my twenty-first bottle'a Chunnel No. 5.'

'Chanel No. 5,' I murmur under my breath. 'But you can tell *me* these things.'

'Yes, things I don't admit to myself. Never have, really. I s'pose if I'd talked to myself about it, I'd've had to do something about it.'

Inside I feel a great glow which has nothing to do with the smugness of secrets. The glow spreads and delights me though I don't understand it, any more than Grandma understands breaking her silence to someone who just listens, though she can't do anything to help. Me.

Junction City, Kansas

I expected to follow Highway 70 straight across Kansas today. I expected wrong.

'Here,' says Grandma, 'turn right here.' Staring into our atlas and communing intensely with the page, she is oblivious to physical realities; a right turn in the foreseeable future will dent a parade of parked cars. When the car fails to do her bidding, Grandma looks up from the map.

'Oh. According to my book here, we should've come upon Route 18 by now. Should've been a right-hand turn. For corn's sake! A town oughtta look like it does on paper!'

'What's special about Route 18?'

'Don't ask questions. I told you I might have to change our trip now and again, so as to follow my purpose. You agreed not to ask why; those were the rules. Lookee there!'

Route 18. A practical, two-laned provincial highway which looks to me like the kind of road where we could get stuck behind a gargantuan farm vehicle travelling fifteen miles an hour. It does not look like a shortcut. 'Did something happen here on your first trip out West?'

Grandma shakes her head. 'I never been here in my life. It's likely looking, that's all.'

Paradise, Kansas

Every so often, Grandma looks away from the window down to her fingernails. She works on each one until it is a fine and shapely point, then she moves on. The motions are mechanical, and the sound is soothing, a sort of slow-motion anatomical sanding.

Gently, with the tip of a freshly sharpened talon, Grandma pokes me in the shoulder. 'Hey. How's your head?'

'I'm fine. I only had *two* gin and orange juices. You had three. How's *your* head?'

She chuckles ruefully. 'I've not been that snozzled . . . snozzled. Is that the word you kids are using nowadays? I'm not asking you as a doctor. What does a normal twenty-nine year old kid call it?'

'Different things for different occasions. "Drunk" has hundreds of synonyms. I like "fuzzy". The more vulgar versions – the ones you learn at college – are "rocked", "crocked", "wasted". Back at home, Grandma, when we drink a margarita on the dock before dinner, you sometimes say you feel a little "high". Nowadays, "high" has connotations of illegal substance abuse. As a general rule, one becomes "snozzled" on port, "tipsy" on sherry, "toasted" on cocktails, and "fucked up" on beer. It's a class thing.'

'Oh.' The monosyllable reflects puzzlement and a *soupçon* of scorn. 'I'll just stick to snozzled. Didn't reckon on it being so complicated.' She goes back to filing and looking out the window. Then I hear her inhale sharply.

'Last time I was snozzled like I was in the pool', she says eventually, 'was October 20th, 1965. I was in Miami.'

'Miami, Grandma?'

Miami, a far point south on the East Coast of America. It is not my place, but I feel a twinge of *mylocusphilia*. Miami, 1,000 miles east and 1,000 miles south, is more my place than Kansas, more home-like than my ultimate destination. 'What was a Mid-Western gal like you doing in Miami?'

'Running away as far as I could go,' says Grandma steadily. 'I was fifty-five years old, in Miami, with a man who wasn't Thomas, and I was snozzled. Bet it's hard for you to picture.

'In 1955 when Thomas and the boys and me got back from California, everything felt strange. I noticed that the moment we came ridin' into Evansville. I'd been lookin' forward to that moment for six years, and I looked all around me, so eager my tongue was nearly hangin' out, but I didn't recognise my hometown.' Grandma's voice cracks, full of a bewilderment which has aged with her. 'I don't mean the buildings were changed, I saw those just the same, but my heart didn't holler out, if you can understand that. Nothing *inside me* recognised Evansville. I expected to feel just as happy to see the place as I'd been sad to go away, but I didn't. Which was funny, 'cause all the circumstances was the same. We were still ridin' in that old butcher's van, and Thomas still didn't have a job. I looked around me and things looked the same, but they *felt* outta kilter.

'While we were gone, Evansville society changed. A new oil company bigwig lived in Thomas's brick palace. My cousin Timola headed the Garden Club I used to run, *and* the church social committee back at First Presbyterian. She didn't want my help on either. I went to a few meetings of the Garden Club, but Timola was so big with her sympathy – in front of all the gals who used to be more my friends than hers! – that I couldn't take it. "Oh, Maude," Timola'd say, her voice fulla cousin-love, "how terrible that you should have to come back here empty-handed. Thomas has just had the *worst* luck in his career, hasn't he!"'

Grandma inhales until her shoulders press back into her seat.

'I want to punch her – even now – her saying that to me in public! I could *shoot* her. I almost did. But of course, Timola had lots to lose with me comin' back, lots more to lose than just a few friends. It meant I took over The Farm.' Again, Grandma inhales hard. 'My coming home hit Timola where she lived, right in her pocketbook!'

'What do you mean?' I ask gently. The physician in me notes Grandma's quick breathing and her too-bright eyes, while the granddaughter worries that Grandma has lost herself in the sandtrap of remembered enmity.

'What do you mean,' I ask again.

'What do I mean? My Pa's Farm was never meant for Timola, but takin' things that didn't belong to her was pretty much her way of life! She married Horace Allbright, whose farm was next to ours, and while I'd been away Horace had been running his own operations on Pa's land. Taking three hayings a year for his cows – free! – and selling off Pa's dairy for a walloping great commission! Pa'd got too old to do anything about it. Ma might've stopped Horace; she was stronger and still together up here,' Grandma taps her forehead, 'but Timola sweet-talked my Ma. So much that Ma thought I was doin' an unkindness when I came back to take over The Farm and booted Horace and Timola off! Timola came bawling to Ma and said she didn't know as how she could feed her cows without free hay from The Farm. As I live and breathe! The nerve!

'In 1955 Evansville was *her* town. Timola's. I lasted ten years under her thumb. She played around with Thomas, *under my nose,* on the same settee where once she told him that he was too good for me. This while I was out in the fields, worming cows and covering bales of hay. Milking every mornin' at five o'clock. Making loads of money. Putting four dollars out of every five I earned into the bank, while Thomas travelled round lookin' for work. He didn't need to travel to find work, it was right there, on The Farm. If he'd worked with me, I wouldn't've had to hire help. Farming wasn't the work Thomas fancied, but he coulda done it. Instead he had schemes; sellin' a load of old jewellery here, trading used cars, then vacuum cleaners. You name it. Every time *he* made a bit of money he'd take us to The Elway Club, or buy a new suit, or another bracelet for me. Then there'd be nothing left. We went like that for ten years.

'On October eighteenth, 1965, the bigwig in Thomas's old brick showplace died. And on October nineteenth, Thomas went to the bank and took out fifteen thousand dollars cash to buy back his old house. And he never told me he was gonna do it. Accordin' to the bank, Thomas was just as entitled to that money as me, 'cause I'd put the money into an account with both our names on it. It never occurred to me I'd got to do different. So I left.'

Grandma looks down into her lap. 'I just *left.*'

'October twentieth, 1965 was a beautiful day for going away, the finest Indian Summer day Evansville'd ever seen – you couldn't believe it was October. I just went down to the Greyhound Bus Station and bought a ticket to Miami. Seat 22A all the two-day trip south. Up 'til that ride I'd got a bladder the size of a corn kernel – all the Orpwoods're made like that – but things change. They got to. I couldn't make myself flicker on a moving bus, and sweet Jesus, how long it took between stops! By the end I mastered bladder control. Pity now I've lost it again . . .'

Cultivated wheat fields begin ten feet from Highway 18, and in between pavement and field grows grass. The green of the grass and the gold of the wheat look fabulous together, the leaves and shafts swaying to the same wind which buffets the car. In my forearms a dull ache tells me how hard I've gripped the steering wheel to keep the car steady on the road. Kansas blows gale force, which seems appropriate, a tribute to the strength of the woman next to me. Maude Orpwood Suche up and left Thomas Suche!

'You better pull over,' Grandma tells me, accompanying her words with another firm prod to my shoulder. 'I got to go. Since we're in the middle of nowhere, I reckon I'll do my duty in that wheatfield. The wheat's tall enough so if I hunker down, anybody passing'll just think I'm tyin' my shoe.'

'You can't stop there!'

She looks at me, astonished.

'Sorry, that's not what I mean. I'm not talking about peeing, Grandma, you can stop anywhere you please, for God's sake. But the story!'

'I been keepin' this story for thirty years, so it'll keep a mite longer. And you can just hold your horses.'

Here in the middle of the state, on a provincial highway, there are no official exit ramps, just tiny tracks which lead off Route 18 like tender shoots. Turning down the very next tiny track, we see the silos of distant farms rising out of the wheat, and we drive into the grass to clear the single-lane road. I massage my arms and wait impatiently for Nature to take her course.

'Let's walk a spell,' calls Grandma, rising out of the wheatfield like some cereal Venus. I wade in behind her, following the path of a tractor's wheel to avoid damaging any of the wheat. Underfoot the dirt lies dry and crumbly, with large clods which look like rocks but disintegrate under Grandma's pristine sneakers. Around us the shafts of wheat, our future flour, spread in every direction. The heartland of America, one great big bread loaf waiting to happen. In silence we walk while wind fills our ears. The tautness of gale-stretched skin keeps Grandma's face devoid of expression, but I watch her anyway, because I want to know what happened in Miami, with a man who wasn't my grandfather, when Maude Suche got snozzled.

'You know,' says Grandma, and I step closer to her so that I can hear over the wind, 'I planned on staying put in Miami. I brought a big valise with me, and if I liked the place, I planned on staying. But it took me two days to get there. *Two days* after leavin' Indiana the bus pulled into Miami, and I just thanked the Lord for havin' lived through the trip, bowels intact. Then I looked around. Even down by the bus station Miami was beautiful – painted all light pretty colours like candy floss at the State Fair. I found me a cheap pink hotel, then I caught a bus to the beach so's I could look at the ocean. I'd never seen the Atlantic before. I sat on sand so hot, even in October, that it burned. Then I walked up and down the beach, tryin' to decide what to do.

'Nobody just sits in their room in Miami, not at night, when the place is jumping. So I went out dancin' with a fella who picked me up on the boardwalk that afternoon. Would you believe it? I can't recollect his name for the life of me, but he was a fine figure of a man, looked like Will Rogers. And he was such a smooth dancer. He said he was fifty-five, like me, and I called him a liar! Even as a young gal I was never much of a flirt, more of a friend to fellas, and I got rustier with time. But he didn't mind me calling him a liar. He just laughed. We laughed a lot.

'At first we drank ginger ale, but then we went to a supper club and somebody had this pink punch which I tasted. Then I wanted one too. He paid, and I liked that. We drank loadsa these pink drinks which kicked like a mule, and he held me in his arms, and then we drank some more. Soon I was floating – snozzled! I could've been a balloon for all I knew.

'After a spell I said I was hungry, so he took me to Wolfie's Deli. I'll never forget the money in that place! All the swell folk in Miami must have been there, wearing flashy diamonds and sweatin' like pigs in their mink coats. I ordered one of those sandwiches with corned beef – a Ruby they call it – and it was so crammed full it wouldn't fit in my mouth. We laughed fit to kill when sauerkraut and thousand island dressing dripped all over the front of my dress. "That's the only drawback to having big tits," he said. "You always wear a little of what you eat!" Because I had a shelf to catch it on, you see. Anyway, some part of my brain that hadn't gone dumb with drink told me to go straight to the ladies' and wash that gunk off. My dress was my best flowered polyester, with hat and gloves dyed to match, and I didn't want it ruined.

'Do you know, when I got back to the table that man was gone and four people sat in our booth. They were whoopin' and hollering like we'd never been there at all, so I left. Laws, the state I was in! I couldn't find my hotel, but I passed the bus station. It was four-thirty in the morning, and there was a bus that stopped in Evansville leaving at four-fifty-five. All I took back with me was my pocketbook, and I was lucky I still got that.

'I got back into Evansville on October twenty-third, and my pride made me pretend to Thomas that I never left. I could do that, you see, 'cause he hadn't noticed I was gone. But the gals in Evansville all wondered where I'd been, and when I told 'em, they believed my story on how I'd gone visiting my Clumpey kin in Ohio. Until Timola told them otherwise.

'"What were you doing in Miami, Maude?" Timola asked me after church when she had a guaranteed good audience. I pretended I didn't know what she was on about. "Oh, yes, Maude. That nice young man at the Greyhound Station told me you bought a ticket to Miami. You keep a secret beau down south, Maude?"

'Thomas was standing right there, listenin' hard, and that night he came out to The Farm with me, to sleep in the same bed for the first time in years. All because the thought of another fella wanting me got him randy. I hadn't missed rutting – I never really minded when Thomas tended his needs elsewhere. Timola did me no favour.'

'What in God's name brought you back to Evansville after you'd found the courage to leave?' My voice is loaded with disappointment in her. I was born in 1966 and I know Grandma lived at The Farm then; she never spent sunny sandy years in Miami. The way she told her story, however, made me hope that the ending would differ from the reality I know.

Grandma stops and puts out a hand. 'Sit,' she says,

pressing on my forearm. She sinks into the dirt until wheat waves behind her head. If I sit next to her I can't see her, so I sit opposite, crushing plants. The force of the air gives me goosebumps and thrashes me with the smell of warm wheat, a tangy gold odour like pine needles in the sun. When Grandma finally speaks, she won't meet my eyes.

'I felt so dumb when I came out of the ladies' at Wolfie's Deli and I found that man gone. I just felt so *dumb.* Kinda ashamed at what I'd set out to do.'

'Ashamed? Of what? I think you tried to instil some happiness in what sounds like a very bleak life! Do you mean you're ashamed for having an affair? Did you sleep with him?'

Grandma stares at me as if I have asked the most ridiculous impertinent questions on earth. 'What for corn's sakes do you think? No! Where I came from, men who had affairs made for gossip and *women* who had affairs made straight for Hell.' She glares at me glaring back at her. 'But I could've. I reckon he wanted to.'

Would that have been a bad thing? The doctor in me opposes casual sex violently, on hygienic grounds. The granddaughter in me says Oh, yes, Grandma why didn't you? 'Did it ever occur to you that your Miami fellow could have looked for you after you came out from washing your dress? Just because he wasn't at the table doesn't mean he was gone. You could have been *ages* in the bathroom, and if Wolfie's Deli was busy, they might have wanted your table for people who hadn't eaten yet. I know how you feel about stains, Grandma, and being drunk accentuates a person's natural compulsions. For example – and you may not remember this but I do, it impressed me clearly: I was eight; you took me to meet Mom at the Zoo, and somewhere on the trip into Washington I sat on a wad of gum. It obsessed you! We had to go to McDonald's and ask for ice cubes so you could freeze the gum and scrape it off with your fingernail. It was two hours before you were satisfied that I was gum-free. And you were *sober* that day. If you were an hour in the bathroom at Wolfie's Deli, Miami Man might have thought *you* ditched *him*!'

'Are you finished?'

'Yes.'

'Well, I thought of what you say. I thought about it on the bus back to Evansville after I'd slept a coupla hours and wasn't so snozzled.'

'And still you went back to Evansville. What was it you set out to do in Miami, Grandma? Do you even know? Or were you just running away? Would you have stayed if you'd slept with that man?'

Her gaze dips down to the earth and she reaches for a clod. 'This is good dirt,' she says, crushing the clod with her fingers. 'Look at me gettin' dirt under my nails after all these years. We could've had three, four hayings from soil like this.'

'I'll ask again: why did you go to Miami? Would you have stayed after a one night stand? Please answer, Grandma!'

'I don't know,' she says, working dusty disintegration on another clod. 'I reckon not. I can't tell you what I was settin' out to do. I wasn't thinking clear. Something just *snapped* in me after Thomas took all my money and bought his house a second time. Maybe I left so's I could figure out *why I stayed with Thomas all those years.* I'm tryin' to figure out the same thing now, thirty years on. But I learned one real important thing when I ran away in 1965. Laws, Miami made me realise how strong it was.

'You understand what *it* I'm talking 'bout? I mean whatever kept me in Evansville with Thomas. Over and over I thought about leavin' him, then I'd decide to stay. So many times I made that decision. The day I left, I acted real quick, without even thinking. I never made no decision, I just left. By the time I'd thought about it, I was in Miami, and pretty soon I was headed straight back to Thomas. Pretty dumb, eh? But powerful. I was a smart woman, fulla courage 'cept about this one thing.'

'Not dumb. Stubborn. Part of me admires you, Grandma. I believe in marriages, good and bad, and I believe in bearing responsibility once you decide to marry.'

She nods at me firmly. These are home-truths to her, the kind of beliefs her Blood has revered for generations.

'But the promise you made, Grandma, was only *'til death do us part.* Thomas Suche is dead, and he still worries you. Maybe the problem is that you want to punish yourself for the first time you made the wrong decision.'

'I should have left him right away, you mean. Soon as we married.'

'No. I'm talking about Nerf Fleishman. You decided wrong about him. It sounds like you first decided wrong when you were children, and then you repeated that decision again and again, right up to the day he died. It's not the decision you made about Thomas Suche that disturbs you. It's how you rejected Nerf Fleishman, who loved you and whom you loved.'

So long, that the wheat seems to grow a little higher, we sit still and quiet. I am utterly unprepared when Grandma looks at me with hatred.

'This . . . trip . . . *is not about Nerf Fleishman*! It's about me! And how I was my own best enemy!' She glares at me and I look back, blinking against the warm wetness of sudden tears. 'Don't you *ever* say that again! You got no idea what went on with Nerf and me! *He's got nothing to do with this*!'

She takes her eyes off mine and the relief is physical.

When I was five and my feelings were hurt, the lump in my throat felt like this. Does she expect me to listen only, never offering another angle on thoughts and actions which are mothballed and over-familiar to her? What did I say wrong? I've never seen Grandma this angry, like someone has thrust a pin into her sorest spot. And somehow that someone is me.

Was I ungentle in my judgement on her past? I am a physician because I have an overriding wish to help, an instinct which is ever present. The instinct brought me here today, on my way out to California in a move to frighten a *mylocusphiliac* rigid. I can't turn the instinct off. But it's dangerous in combination with comaraderie such as this trip fosters. Until five minutes ago I felt close enough to offer a different slant on her history, one I thought would help. She doesn't want it, and though I've said nothing else, Grandma shouts at me.

'Just shut your trap! Shut it! I haven't told you true! I

didn't go to the bathroom in Wolfie's Deli to wash my dress! I excused myself and went to the bus station. And *there I washed my dress*! I left that fella sittin' there, wondering where I'd got to. Because I was ashamed at what I was thinking of doing! I ran out on my husband. I was drinkin' with a man I wasn't married to and I liked how I felt in his arms. A voice in me said "For shame, Maude Suche! A virtuous woman don't act this way!" I made my bed. It was mine to lay in! No forgettin' that, because that's what I told myself every time I wanted to leave!

'Want to know how your grandfather died?' Grandma is calm enough, now, not to shout, and she stares at me until I raise my eyes to her. Though the gaze is no longer vicious, it is uncompromising and demands fullest attention.

'Thomas took sick in 1970, and I had to decide one last time to stay with him. Decidin' was easier, somehow, when Thomas was weak and sorry-looking. You don't need love to feel pity. Prostitates cancer, he had, you know that man's thing doctors check for with the glove and jelly, only Thomas never let anybody check for it 'til too late. Those germs spread all over him, and in the end I was feedin' him nothing but clear chicken soup and cream cheese sandwiches on white bread. I broke the sandwiches into little bites and we'd sit in front of the TV and talk about the shows.

'Watching TV, Thomas'd fall asleep, because the drugs made him real tired. Then a part-smoked cigar'd fall out of his fingers to burn a little hole in the carpet. Thomas loved that rug, an Arab carpet made of silk. He bought it with my money once he bought his big house back again, and he got real upset 'bout the burn holes. I thought to put a cookie tray full of sand right underneath where Thomas's hand rested, not because I worried over the carpet, mind. But I feared a house fire'd get him before the cancer did.

'He always, always, *always* sat in the same chair. It was like a leather throne, and he bought it special for reclining. He marked that chair – it was the oil in his skin and the pressure of his body that did it. The leather took the print of his legs and his backside and the lie of his arms. Even after Thomas died it looked like he was still there, stuck in that chair.

'I kept it. When I sold the big house the only thing I brought with me out to The Farm was that chair with Thomas pressed in it. I kept it 'til the end, when I left Evansville two months later, and then I burned it.'

Into this clean wild field of wheat which strains at its stalks, comes an uncomfortable image of Grandma in the jeans – she called them overalls – and green corduroy shirt she always wore at The Farm. I envision her out by the creek, standing by the wire basket in which she burned rubbish. And out there next to the little fire which consumes toilet paper rolls, newspapers, and cereal boxes, burns a bigger fire which is Thomas Suche's chair. That chair would have hunkered down there by the creek, too big a thing to set on top of the fire, so Grandma probably laid a fire on its seat. Even in a wide open wheatfield I can imagine the smell of leather smoking.

'My God, Grandma!'

Leather is skin. When it burns it remembers that it once had hair and was alive. At the hospital I became nauseated only one time, when I assisted two surgeons trying to save a woman with seventy per cent third-degree burns. Her charred skin surface bore the stench of holocaust and Armageddon, and I vomited. 'My God! How did that chair *smell*?'

'Bad.' Grandma raises her eyebrows. 'And once I'd got the flames lickin' hot, which was no mean feat, I can tell you, I ran back up to the farmhouse and brought down one last thing I'd got from your grandfather's bureau drawer at the big house. One last thing to fire up, something I found when I cleared out Thomas's stuff.

'That old whore had a big box of condoms. In my day we called them prophetlactaries, but that's old-fashioned. I don't guess you'd know what I was talkin' about if I called 'em that.' Grandma uncrosses her legs and stretches them in front of her. 'Mind you, not just a few condoms, a whole big box. Cheaper by the dozen's what Thomas thought. The box was only *half* empty. Unfinished business, that's what my husband left behind. Unfinished business.'

I must say something. 'It makes sense why I seldom saw him out at The Farm. Is that how you both lived all the time? You at The Farm and my grandfather in his town mansion?'

'How people would've talked! No, I lived with Thomas in his palace. Except for calving season and when you kids came. See, I wanted you to know The Farm. Thomas's town palace had nothing to do with a child. When Thomas died I felt nothing about selling up.'

Expecting her to tell me about how they lived together in Evansville proper, leading separate lives, I wait for Grandma to speak, to tell me more about Maude and Thomas Suche. But she doesn't.

'Timola,' Grandma says finally, 'wore a bright red suit to my husband's funeral. Everybody talked about it. And she had hat and gloves dyed to match.'

Campus, Kansas

After Paradise, Kansas, we hit Natoma, Codell, and Plainville – tiny towns along tiny Kansas roads looking like they were laid just so people could travel from one side of their expansive farms to the other. These fields cover an area so vast, so completely uninterrupted that I feel lost. Lost and negligible and *seasick*, because wind moves in waves across the wheat, making the land look so fluid that I, riding windswept but stable through the middle, experience a disorientation like seasickness. *If it becomes a problem* says the doctor in me, *remember that the first aid bag contains fifteen milligram capsules of cinnarizine, for travel sickness. It might make you drowsy, but nothing that caffeine won't counteract.* Ask *Grandma if* she *needs some. And ask her why she's got her head poked out the window, her tongue waving in the air like a dog. It's not normal.*

'Slow down!' hollers Grandma, pulling her head back in the car. 'Slow . . . it . . . down! There's unpaved road ahead. We can't be drivin' at the speeda sound when we hit it!'

'Highway 18 is unpaved ahead? You mean there's construction?'

'Of course not. I bet there's been no construction on these roads for fifty years. The roads're just unpaved, that's all. It's no good to pave 'em. Roads out here get baked in the summer and frozen in the winter and ruttier all the time. I wanted to find some roads like this. To remind me how we all travelled in 1949. You reckon we travelled on big state to state highways just five years after World War Two quit? Is that what you think?'

'I don't know.' Honestly it never occurred to me, a world without the smooth motorways which slide across America like thick snakes, going everywhere I want to go. Highway 95 connects all the dots for me in my beloved Middle East. If I wanted to travel it, Highway 95 could take me all the way from Bangor, Maine down to Miami in one uninterrupted trail. The sum total of my highway knowledge is contained in this: the numbers for east-west roads are even, for north-south roads, odd. Highway 70, our current westward path, has taken us through one state and most of another, and will carry us deep into Utah.

Grandma is trying to tell me that she first travelled cross country following a patchwork thread of pavement. No super-highways.

I can't imagine it.

'It was only the late Forties when the government started buildin' big roads. Our butcher's van rattled along on little dirt roads 'longside men laying down highways, with Thomas swallowing his pride and asking all the time if there were some little dabbie of work he could do for cash. We were purely broke.

'"What can you do," some foreman in the work crew would want to know. Thomas knew how to answer. We'd been watchin' how they laid those roads. First it was just the boys and me who were interested. We'd ride along with the van's back doors wide open, partly to air out the stink of hot blood, but mostly to see the men layin' the highways. It was an art, how they did it. Almost as exciting, I reckon, as when the railtracks were first laid cross country. But no gold spike got driven in when the highways got round to joining America east to west. Somebody just painted a yellow line from end to end.

'But it was real exciting. Your Dad and Uncle George sat either side of me, my arms pressing each one tight to keep my boys safe in the van. We sat on the wooden floorboards and dangled our legs out the back. And all the while we watched the crews buildin' roads. We followed the little roads 'longside future Highway 80 for nearly a year. And it was the best year of being married to Thomas Suche.'

Grandma smiles.

After all that she has told me about her relationship with Thomas Suche, to see a happy face in conjunction with my grandfather's name surprises me into a grin. I don't enjoy thinking of her long marriage as joyless. 'What makes you so happy,' I ask, watching her as she laughs to herself.

'Well, it wasn't such a bad year. Not bad at all. I only asked myself one time why I stayed with Thomas. We lived outside and slept outside, we were like pioneers . . . Hey! I said no rocket speeds, but you don't have to drive like a snail to please me! We got to get to Denver tonight.'

Arvada, Colorado

Grandma yawns, and while she has her mouth open and tilted back, she flashes her fingers in and out of her mouth. Plop goes the lower plate of dentures into a water glass on the hotel bedside table. Plop goes the upper plate. Another yawn. It is eleven o'clock in the evening, and we have stopped for the night in a suburb of Denver, the mile-high city where Grandma and my father and uncle danced their glee at finding an entire state filled with mountains.

'Gef what,' says Grandma, now nearly toothless. She waits for me to say 'what', and when I do she nods in satisfaction.

'Fer tha firs time, tomorrow, I'm gon fire *Li'l Maude*.'

When I come out of the shower, puddling on the carpet as I never dare at home, Grandma is on the telephone talking to someone she doesn't like – I can tell by her tone. She has the atlas spread before her, a finger tracing the line of some road.

'As the crows fly, it ain't so bad, but I reckon it'll take an hour . . . We're in some two-bit l'il part of Denver, Aardvark I guess they call it – '

'Arvada.' I say it loudly, while examining my towel turban in the mirror. Turbans are a convenient way for some of my chemo patients to deal with the hair loss: for women I recommend turbans over wigs because they look better, and because wearing one with panache builds confidence. Many faces gain shape under a turban, and some gain ascetic beauty. I just look like I have a towel on my head.

To whom is she talking?

'Arvada,' Grandma repeats irritably. 'Well, I said ten o'clock when I wrote back to you, didn't I now . . . Sure, sure . . . Fine . . . Fire away.' In our quiet hotel room the sound of her writing scratches loudly.

'OK,' says Grandma into the receiver and she hangs up without saying goodbye. Reading her writing as though to herself she says, 'Interstate 70 West to Highway 6 on to Rural Route 119 North.'

'Where are we going, Grandma?'

She shakes her head, looking irked. 'You ever try and bend the quill on a buzzard's feather? One of those real sturdy feathers on the underbelly of the wing? Bet you haven't. Let me tell you, it's rough to do, and that man I just talked to has a buzzard quill pushed way way up his rear quarter, I could tell even by his letter. There's backbone – that's a fine thing – and then there's havin' a ramrod up your rump, and that's different.'

'Oh.' My monosyllable says 'I know better than to ask,

Grandma. I'm sure you'll tell me if I keep my mouth closed.' But she doesn't. Instead she picks through her suitcase, fastidiously collecting an entire ensemble of lavender, including a lilac mohair cardigan which I gauge as knee length on Grandma, though it hung just to the hips of my mother, who owned it first.

'I don't know if you got any fancy duds in that suitcase of yours, but if you do, put 'em on. Today's no day for looking cheap.' Grandma knots a purple silk scarf around her neck, fastening one flailing end upon her shoulder with a pin that looks like a dove and is made from wooden popsicle sticks. Then she pulls *Li'l Maude* from under her pillow.

'To your way of thinking,' she says, holding her pistol by the barrel and shaking the butt end at me, 'what do guns and fishes have in common?'

I look at her with my face reflecting that I don't have a clue. Without thinking I turn slightly away, loosening the towel wrapped around my torso, then pulling and tucking it tighter. Modesty.

'It's a riddle, for corn's sake! *Li'l Maude* and a fresh bluegill got one thing they share . . .' Shaking her head disgustedly, Grandma continues, 'Guns and fishes – a gal oughtta know *how to clean her own.* A woman's got no place catching a fish or holding a weapon less she can clean one up pretty.'

I smile at her, feeling quite smug in the half knowledge gained from my Middle Eastern upbringing; knowing how to deal with live seafood is a by-product of my childhood. 'I can gut and skin a fish, Grandma, *and* fillet it. I can pick a crab clean before you've cracked your first claw.'

'That's just the half of it – you got no i-*dea* how to clean a gun. Hand me my toilet case.'

I do so without mentioning that I don't own a weapon, so, naturally, I have no notion how to clean one, and that because I never will own a weapon, the knowledge is interesting but superfluous. Sitting down next to Grandma, with *Li'l Maude* between us, I realise my attitude to this particular weapon has changed completely; from horror to appreciation and curiosity. I'm not sure why, but I don't connect this Fleishman firearm with the wounds I treated in the emergency room in Washington DC. Maybe it's because *Li'l Maude* looks more like a piece of art. And she's never been loaded. But she will be today, loaded and fired. I wish I knew the target.

From an ancient leather box Grandma removes one brown prescription bottle with a white stopper, one glass vial of cotton swabs, a plastic bag with scraps of handkerchief silk, and a bottle of fingernail polish with the label scratched off. 'Gun oil,' Grandma says, pointing to the last item. 'Now watch.'

'Why are you cleaning her? You said she's never been fired.'

'So what? Pretend you got a real fine dining table, mahogany, carved pretty, and too nice to eat off *ever*. Thomas's brick showplace was fulla stuff like that, so nice the occasion never came up fitting to use it for. Even so you got to dust and polish your table, just like *Li'l Maude*. Now pay attention.'

I obey. *Li'l Maude* lies between us, looking dainty and beautiful on top of the white sheets. I can't imagine that she needs grooming.

'First we break her open and scrub the barrel,' says Grandma. 'Dip the swab in alcohol, never water – she'd rust with water, but ethyl alcohol dries quick – and stuff it down. Use a *fresh* swab only, 'cause we don't want no cotton threads down there. Now, suck the spit off your teeth and swallow. You got to clear your mouth so as you can blow a dry breeze. All dry now?' Grandma rubs a finger on her incisors then checks to see if it glistens. 'All dry, so I'm gonna blow.' She puffs into the slender barrel, making a sound like wind in chimney tops.

'Then you take a snibbee of silk and brush it with oil, always havin' care you don't apply oil straight to the gun – that makes a puddle, and oil puddles collect dust. Dust makes gunk and gunk gummin' up your pistol lays waste to a weapon! Rub your oiled cloth into the barrel joint – '

'Grandma, this makes no sense. If you intend to fire it today and make it dirty, then why are you cleaning it now? Why not clean it later?'

She continues pushing the oiled cloth into crevices on the gun as though she didn't hear. When Grandma finishes the pistol looks exactly as it did before, and she slips it into her budge. 'Well,' says Grandma at last, and there she stops. She pulls *Li'l Maude* out for another look and a second shine, balling the cloth into a tiny wad and squeezing it against the wooden handle, rubbing hard until a higher gloss rises on the wood. When she puts *Li'l Maude* away again, her pale eyes are watery, and I see that her spirits have sunken like her cheeks.

'Well,' she says solemnly, 'that's a good question.' Grandma's breast puffs and falls with a sigh, while her hand covers her budge protectively. 'For days I've known this hour was coming, don't know why it should make me so sad now. Why's *Li'l Maude* all fancy in her Sundy best when it ain't even Sundy?'

The question is rhetorical, and not meant for a further query. When Grandma does not answer herself immediately, I pat her shoulder and rise to dress myself in a long corduroy skirt, stockings, loafers, and a cabled fisherman's sweater. I know it's late May and two days ago my blood boiled, but today, in the foothills of the Rocky Mountains, there are snowflakes blowing past our hotel window. I can stand and peer out the glass, pretending to watch the snow, while I gaze at Grandma's reflection in the window. She flutters abstractedly around our room, folding underwear, checking under the bed for left-behind shoes, collecting glass ashtrays, a Gideon Bible, and single-serving packets of freeze-dried coffee provided by the hotel. Then I see Grandma's image sit down suddenly on the bed, and concerned, I turn back to her.

'What's the one possession you care 'bout most, in the whole world?' Grandma asks, plucking threads from the bedspread's hem.

'Right now? Here in the middle of Colorado?' I don't even have to think. 'My car. It is the means of returning home.'

'It's also how you got here,' Grandma looks at me sternly. 'You love it for that too? Seems to me you love a gun that smokes from both ends.'

'I think any possession is a double-edged sword. One day my car may cripple me. Remember, Grandma, that it, and *you*, nearly killed me in West Virginia on Monday. And if my most cherished possession was an exquisite piece of heirloom jewellery, a mugger might knife my abdomen to take it. I truly do believe that a person loves solid, molecular constructions at her peril. What material thing do you love best?'

But I already know, though I don't know why her most cherished possession makes her eyes water today. Big Maude loves *Li'l Maude*. Grandma cherished her gun even while it lay for a quarter of a century in a safe deposit box. I pat my chest and nod at hers, hoping Grandma will smile at me and perhaps remove her pistol so it can preen in her palm.

Instead, looking at her richly lavender sneakers she says, 'Did you know Nerf made his first gun when he was just fifteen? He worked on it for weeks, checkin' the picture in *Encyclopaedia Brittanica* and fiddling with bits. Later on folks'd say they thought it peculiar how he fell in love with guns and ammo, because Nerf seemed such a gentle fella. But it wasn't, peculiar I mean. Nerf liked the mechanics of a weapon. That first gun was more like a cannon, just jury-rigged, out of wood, and it used black powder – that's charcoal, saltpetre, a little sulphur – which is powerful stuff, I can tell you. Nerf and me loaded that gun with black walnuts for shootin' at Timola, and we waited days, carting that thing all over town, before we got off the perfect shot – a direct hit to her bosom, just at the teats. Timola's bosom had one quality makin' it a fine target – she always covered herself in a pure white shirtwaist that stood out a mile. On the downside, her breasts were just bitty small things – we were amazed we could hit 'em.

'Do you know how bad black walnuts stain? They stain like a handful of runny cowpie, and that stain don't ever wash out . . . We got her just as she set down on her porch's swingin' settee to read *The Saturday Night Post* with a glass of cold lemonade. We were about twenty feet away. Nerf touched a match to the black powder, then there was a fizzing noise and we held our breath . . . BOOM! BOOM again! Timola dropped the magazine and clapped her hands to her tits! Nerf and me threw arms around each other's necks and danced behind the bushes while Timola screamed 'til her lungs gave out! I never saw her so mad. Tattling was one of her talents: she told Ma and Mrs Fleishman and then she wrote the sheriff to say Nerf Fleishman and Maude Orpwood tried to murder her!'

Grandma and I grin at each other. She knows and I can imagine how thrilled she and Nerf felt to fire on Timola. I can picture them gathering black walnuts, discarding nuts too big to fit the barrel of Nerf's cannon, prodding the walnut husk to ensure suitable resilience for maximum sting and stain, chortling as they do so. This revenge of the underdogs satisfies deeply: Cousin Timola's very name tastes like rancid air to me, and I hate her.

'All through upper school Nerf kept his guns a secret, showin' only me the designs and the finished pieces. And then when we finished school he started work for his dad. Mr Fleishman was a seed merchant half the year and the other half he fixed tractors, or cars, or anythin' with a broke motor. Nerf was real good at that part of the business, he kept it goin' year round. But in his spare time he kept on making guns, and they got finer and finer. He figgered out how to wax-cast metal for parts – triggers, hammers and barrels – and he made bullets and cartridges. Sometimes after milking I'd sneak out and we'd drive in Nerf's repair truck to a strip 'a land where nobody could hear us shoot and we'd test the guns, shooting at targets Nerf pinned on trees. We had a drawing of Timola for fun – Nerf loved to shoot her between the eyes and pierce her earlobes. I asked him one day why he never stood up to her, because that bothered me. And he said, "It doesn't matter, Maude. I never notice her; she and I just aren't on the same planet. Sometimes, when I pass her on the street, I can blink my eyes, look straight at the spot where she stands and see blank space. That's how much I think of her. Nothing Timola Orpwood says can hurt *me*, but I notice it surely does get you into a funk."

'Yes it did. Nerf spoke the truth. The older we got, the more energy Timola put into tauntin' me, and she loved it public. Funny thing was she let up on Nerf in person, kinda like she feared him – I don't reckon she spoke a word to Nerf after he and me left school. But she had no fear for teasin' *me* about him. Most often it'd come at church, when folks gathered in the fellowship hall for coffee and doughnuts after a service.

'"Maude!" Timola would call, all tinkly-voiced and joky. "I nearly got run over, yesterday a.m., by you and Nerfy Nerf heading out of town like you do. You two were in such a hurry you blew my hair! Where'd you go? Here, Maude, don't have a doughnut, you sit down and rest, and let me get you one of these *hot biscuits*. I'm sure that for *you* there's *something in the oven*!"

'She'd snicker behind her hand and everybody'd laugh with her, wondering if Nerf and me were rutting. It was a shame for my parents, who reckoned me a good girl. And a different shame for me – you could tell by how folks laughed that Timola's words surprised them. Not because they thought I'd never go out ruttin' – it was often the way gals in Evansville got married – just sorta shameful if more than one fella figured and the baby came less'n six months after the hitchin'. No siree, my fellow Christians laughed 'cause it was too peculiar that somebody like me, fulla piss and vinegar, would be so desperate as to go down on somebody like Nerf Fleishman. Can you reckon it, after Thomas Suche came to town and set his sights my way, the ladies whispered I got him on account of all the rutting practice I'd had! And all the men reckoned they were jealous of Thomas if it were true!'

Beside her, in a fold of the long lilac cardigan, Grandma deposits a tiny ball of thread and plucks another from the bedspread. 'Do you know, I guess I thought I could marry Thomas and me and Nerf would go on being friends like always. I never considered makin' a triangle – it would still be me and Nerf, but off on the side in the place I slept, there'd be Thomas. It never occurred to me Nerf might have something to say about that. It never occured to me he'd go *crazy*. I'll never forget what he sounded like when he first shouted at me!

'"YOU WHAT? YOU ARE DOING WHAT?" And I . . . well, I feared him . . . he came at me with his arms stretched out and he squeezed his fingers around my neck and shook it 'til I thought my head would fall off!

"YOU WHAT? WHO ARE YOU MARRYING?" he said over and over. He didn't say he loved me, he never had. He never said he loved me. Finally Nerf stopped shaking me, and then he stared at me, and I stared back. I don't know what he was looking for, and I guess I was waiting for him to kiss me or maybe say he cared for me. But he didn't.

'We was out at our target range that day, testing a design for Nerf's first rifle which he wouldn't let me shoot, and I was fired up about that. "It might explode in your face, Maude," he said. Nerf was always cautious. See, he'd designed a chamber new for that rifle and he didn't wholly trust the bullet to exit smooth. But *he* fired it, over and over, testin' the spin of the bullet down the barrel at different angles. He'd finished, and we were breakin' down the guns for cleaning, before I told him. Someplace, in some part of my brain that weren't so dumb, I knew he might not take kindly to me marrying Thomas Suche, and I didn't want to talk while he held a hammer-cocked rifle.

'When he was through with shakin' me and through with sayin' nothing, he turned back to his truck and loaded all the guns inside.

'"Drive back to town, Maude," he said. "Go now." The way he said it, all flat like my friend Nerf wasn't behind his mouth any more, I'd got no choice but to do just that.'

Sighing, Grandma pulls a tissue from her sweater sleeve. She blows her extravagant nose without enthusiasm, then balls the tissue up and shoots, concentrating on the throw, for a wastebasket by the window. 'I left Nerf's truck off at his house, then walked a mile out to The Farm. It was lucky Mrs Fleishman didn't see me, to ask where Nerf'd got to. Don't know what I could've said, I really don't.

'Not until one week before the wedding did Nerf speak to me again. He walked out to The Farm and brought me a ball of paraffin wax. "What's this for?" I asked, all smiles at seein' him. He smiled back kinda funny, but all he said was "Squeeze, Maude." And I did, I left the print of my right hand in the wax, and Nerf took it away with him. The next time I saw him was two o'clock, the morning of my hitch to Thomas Suche. He knocked on my window at The Farm.

'"Come for a ride," he said through the glass. I couldn't sleep, he was my best friend, and I figured I might as well. Nobody had to know. I just threw on my overalls and a sweater and followed him to his truck. I was pretty sure we were goin' to the target range.

'We did. And on the way out we talked just like normal, just like we'd been speakin' every day since the last time we had target practice. Nerf laughed loads, but he kept lookin' at me funny, like he was disappointed. I'd leapt outta bed, excited, and I never thought to put a brush to my head, so my hair was all a-kilter. Whenever he wasn't looking, I reached up to smooth it.

'I expected him to go round and get the newest model of his rifle from out the back of the truck, but he didn't. He just stuck out his hand to me, dropped four shiny balls in my palm. "Put these in your pocket," Nerf said, "and don't lose them. There won't ever be any more." Then with kind of a flourish he opened the lid on a beautiful, dark brown wooden box and inside was *Li'l Maude*.

'She was the prettiest thing I ever saw. I told him so. I held her up to the truck's headlights and examined every inch, overjoyed with that finest piece of Nerf's work yet. And he was proud, I could feel it. But all he said was, "She's for protection against Thomas Suche. You're going to need it." I asked what he meant, and I was still smiling a little, but he wasn't, he looked as solemn as could be.

'"You're marrying a bad man, Maude, and you're far too good for the likes of him. Don't go throwing yourself away! Thomas Suche doesn't even appreciate you. He and Timola fit, not you and he!"

'I'd heard those words before, but they'd come out of Timola's mouth when she was talking to Thomas about *me*. All of a sudden, I was furious so cat-mad I spit when I said, "Are you questioning my decision, Nerf Fleishman!" And he said "Yes Maude. I think I have that right!"

'And then we fought there, so bitter I knew I'd be walking home. I said things Timola would've been proud of, I remember every word and I'm ashamed. All the mad I had from twenty-two years of wishin' he had the backbone to stand up to folks, wishing I could be proud to be seen with him. It all came out. He got so pale and then he just looked at me like Thomas looked at my second cousin Isabel, widely reckoned ugly enough to make a dog howl. I could tell Nerf suddenly saw me as below his notice, just the way he saw most everybody in Evansville.

'"Keep the gun," Nerf said. "Use it to shoot Thomas Suche one day, after he comes home from laying with someone else. Use it on yourself when you realise what you've done." He turned for his truck.

'Something in me just . . . went *wild.* I wouldn't have Nerf Fleishman look at me like that, like I wasn't there! I wouldn't stand for it! Quick as a wink I pulled a bullet from my pocket, cracked *Li'l Maude* and filled one chamber. She fit perfect in my hand 'cause of the wax cast Nerf made, and that good grip helped hold her steady as I aimed at him. I said, "Don't think you're leavin' me here to walk fifteen miles home *on my wedding day*! I won't shoot me or Thomas, but I might shoot you, Nerf. You step back from that truck! I mean it! I'll shoot! When I'm in the truck you can come to the wheel. I'm gonna hold this gun on you while you drive me home!" I sighted on him and he stared at me. It was so quiet, I remember hearin' when a big boar beetle crawled up tree bark. I heard owls hooting and I heard Nerf break wind. He had beans for supper, he'd told me, and any other time I would've waved my hand by my nose, laughing fit to kill.

'Without a single word he drove me home while I kept the gun on his neck. I pushed so hard I left a print of the barrel on the side of his throat. The last thing he said to me when I climbed outta the cab was, "I didn't drive you because I had to, Maude. If I hadn't wished to drive you, nothing in the world would've made me, certainly not you with a gun *I* created. You're going to look rotten later on, having no sleep, but I couldn't care *less.* Maybe for Thomas Suche you'll find time to run a comb through your head."

'For nine years after that, we didn't speak, Nerf and me. Not until he came to give me chicken pox.'

• • •

'So that's how you come to possess a gun,' I say slowly, in a daze from Grandma's words. How could she possibly be so *dense*, so incredibly *stupid*. Does Grandma know even now what a mistake she made? She can't. She wouldn't tell me, otherwise. I wouldn't! If I made a life mistake such as hers I would never tell *anyone*, not ever. More than a minute passes before I realise that I shake my head in constant denial. How can someone, my grandmother, for God's sake –

'I know what you're thinking,' Grandma tells me furiously. 'Shut your yap and take my suitcase outside! We got a ten o'clock appointment in Central City, and I got to get some food in me before I *die*.' She glares at me, her final word pressing into my brain, activating a motor neuron motion command.

'And just you remember, Miss Granddaughter Know-It-All! Who-Reckons-She'd've-Made-The-Right-Decision! You wouldn't be breathin' today but for my mistake!'

Raging, speechless I meet her eyes with enough force to prove that my glare descends from hers. *What mistake, Grandma?* I'll bet you still think that the biggest mistake you ever made was marrying Thomas Suche.

The air this morning carries the cold wet smell of frost, and the skies over Arvada show the mottled grey colour I associate with phlegmy expectorations – those of city dwellers in places like South Central Los Angeles. Grandma said last night that Colorado's skies average six days of sun for every one day of rain. That's more than three hundred sunny days a year, but today is not one of them.

'Breakfast,' Grandma says. 'Pull over.' By speaking to me like a minimalist she conveys her ongoing irritation. I presumed to criticise her, albeit mutely, for how she handled Nerf Fleishman. It is a very sore subject. But I know she turned her anger on me because it's easier than turning it on herself. I understand that she's angry about Nerf; I'm angry at her for Nerf's sake, and also frustrated. Frustrated with Maude Orpwood Suche for a marriage missed. Enjoy your taciturn interlude, Grandma, if it makes you feel better. I think you're an ass.

In the restaurant we concentrate our energies on burrowing into the back corners of our booth – me because I don't wish to talk, and she to keep warm. Grandma's theory seems to be that the intersection between the orange Naugahyde seat and the pine-veneered wall offers a spot more conducive to heat than any other.

'Brrrrr.' It is a vibration more than a sound, and it escapes her without intention. 'Brrrrr.'

I note and dismiss the thick blue veins on her hands – age not cold – but the waxy hue of her fingertips is hard to deny. As is the fact that she has sneezed her resident handkerchief soggy, and is now working her way through our table's dispenser of flimsy napkins. *Give Grandma your sweater and order her a large cup of hot chocolate* says the doctor in me. *Chills weaken old flesh. Being generous and humane may not be the inclination of your character, but it is the requirement of your profession.*

Sometimes I wish my profession was not the sum of my life.

'The one thing which may make California bearable, at

least for two years,' I say, peeling off my sweater and leaning across the table to drape it over her shoulders, 'is that it won't be as cold as Maryland in the winter.' I wonder how civil I sound.

'Maryland's cold ain't nothing to the cold in Evansville. And we'd no heat at The Farm, so you just had to move quick. I couldn't take it now, I don't reckon. My blood's too thin. But I tell you, only fools who've got easy ways to get hotted up talk about crisp mornings when you see your breath. What're you having?'

'French toast and a large hot chocolate. You should have some too.'

'Laws, no. All this sitting in the car and I'm getting fat. Couldn't fasten the button on my skirt this morning. If I come home lardy from this trip, all the gals in my bridge club'll laugh themselves sick, 'specially that Milicent Funly. Big as a moose, Milicent. Every summer she's got to tuck tea towels under her arms, so as her pits don't chafe. I'll have a grapefruit, I reckon. Young man! Hey, you! Young fella . . . come here!' Grandma's eye falls on the shy and comely busboy who brought us clean coffee cups. She likes young boys; they make her think of her sons in their youth, before they married women like my mother.

The busboy is barely sixteen, and at Grandma's shout he looks away and begins to turn colour, a slow red burn working up from his chin to his eyebrows.

'Young fel-la,' Grandma yodels. 'Yes, you. I want a word.'

He moves towards us, in the lolloping way of boys unaccustomed to their own height. His reluctance makes me think of a young giraffe who understands simultaneously that his existence requires trips to the watering hole and that lions lie in wait there. He hovers at the end of the table.

'You know anything', asks Grandma, 'about a place called Central City?'

Central City? I look at her, hoping for clues, until the discomfort of the busboy distracts me. He won't meet our eyes, and inside I cringe for him. He probably never has to say anything except the occasional 'you're welcome' to a customer's murmured 'thank you'.

'Cat got your tongue?' wonders Grandma, speaking at the exact moment the busboy opens his mouth. She chuckles in the poisonous kindly fashion of a person who does not remember being sixteen. But I do, and I feel indignant that a compassionate God doesn't thrust adolescents into suspended animation until they reach twenty-one.

'Central City?' prompts my grandmother, losing her patience. 'What's it like?'

'Never – ' He starts again. 'I've never been there.' Feverishly, his eyes alight on every inanimate object within a ten-foot radius.

Grandma thinks he's a nice boy, I can tell, and she's feeling charitable. 'Guess you haven't lived in these parts long.'

Great sucking in of air. 'I was born here,' the busboy says, then appears to rally slightly. 'Uh, sometimes when my aunt comes to visit my Ma, Ma, uh, takes her to Central City.' His gaze fixes to the floor, on a toast crust, and he maintains eye contact.

'How 'bout that!' As though the movement will encourage him to look up, Grandma bobs her head while speaking. No, I tell the physician inside me before she can even raise the query. No, Maude Suche's enthusiastic head movements are not titubation, the symptomatic head bobbing of a person who suffers from Parkinson's disease. So there. Then I go back to the exchange between my grandmother and her prey.

'Well then, young fella,' she says, still bob, bob, bobbing along. 'So your Ma goes to Central City. Can you tell me is it far away?'

'Unh-uh,' the boy shakes his head and turns to leave. But contact with Grandma has diminished him, and he must rise to the occasion or surrender possession of his sixteen year old soul. 'I don't know much about Central City, but I know you shouldn't go up there today. Not up in those mountains with this weather. Not unless you have to.' The words sound cracked and broken, and he flings his final salvo over his shoulder as he flees. 'You're just a tourist!'

Grandma watches his retreat, then turns on me. 'It don't matter what the weather is. We got to be in Central City by ten a.m. We'll just allow some extra time for drivin'.'

Central City, Colorado

Globs of wet snow hit our windshield regularly. Each glob resembles an infant jellyfish as it clings to frozen integrity then dissolves into a fat raindrop, and I find it dangerously easy to become mesmerised while watching this assault upon the glass. I am stunned that this is late June in the same country as my sultry Maryland home. Stunned, mesmerised, hypnotised. I feel menaced by these mountains. The weather seems like a tactical weapon.

'You're driving this car like a skittish calf,' Grandma tells me. 'Are the Rockies gettin' to you?'

'Ummmmm,' I offer, not wanting to say aloud and give it credence. The Rocky Mountains give me the creeps. Maybe it's just the weather, but I've never *felt* geography like this in my Middle East.

Under the grey sky these mountains loom dark and sharp where they jut from heavy swathings of cedar trees. A sense of foreboding fills the chilled air, as though the mountains resent the incursions of man. Signs on Route 119 alert me to watch for falling rock, and, to underscore the message, enormous boulders hulk by the side of the road. All the better to crush you, my dear. My head imagines stony avalanches while my hands twitch on the steering wheel, second-guessing them.

'Hey,' Grandma says, peering anxiously out her window, then down at the atlas, 'are we going the right way? My atlas don't show these twists in the road.'

'I don't like this, Grandma.'

'Well, I don't care. We're not turnin' back. We got to make my ten o'clock appointment.'

'I don't think I missed a turn-off, though I can't be sure. However dangerous our course seems, I think we're probably right on it.'

'Oh.' It is a doubtful syllable, radiating suspicion. Henry the Navigator might have made a similar sound if his chief pastry chef had claimed to know the way to Atlantis. Suddenly distracted, Grandma holds out her left thumb so that it wavers directly under my nose. 'Lookee there! Do you see that? That red spot?'

The red spot she exhibits is actually a small pink bump on her thumb, a bump accentuated by a minute spot of blood in the middle. 'Have you impaled yourself on one of your talons, Grandma?'

'Doctor, they oughtta take your certificate away. Haven't you treated one of these back in Washington? This is a chillblain. I'm freezin' to death.'

'I can give you an ointment for your chillblain, Grandma, but I don't think that's what makes you so fretful and twitchy today. Is it this appointment you have? What is the problem?'

'I got no problem with my appointment.'

That is all she'll say.

We arrive in Central City, Colorado. It is a tiny town which looks self-consciously historic, as though it boomed during America's Gold Rush but holds merely token attractions for the twentieth century. The mountains seem to be encroaching on the city limits, sliding in over the town, lapping it up. I see advertisements for tours in old mine shafts and a queue for hot coffee which snakes beyond the door of a touristy café.

'I'm cold and we're late,' Grandma says. 'Listen up so I only got to say this once: at the end of this road we'll find a big gravel parkin' lot; you cut the motor and we'll walk from there – I got a little foot map. We're hunting *Ye Olde Antique Shoppe*.' She shows me the business card she holds.

'What a corny name.' I examine the card carefully, nearly driving into a fire hydrant. 'Who is Herbert Prune?'

'Fella I was talkin' to this morning. The one who put me in mind of a buzzard quill.'

Ye Old Antique Shoppe.

It sits in the midst of a dozen other antique–junk shops, but unlike the others it displays no sample wares, no patchwork quilts, rusted lanterns or battered tin cookware presumably used by gold miners. Outside *Ye Olde Antique Shoppe* stand two pink plastic flamingos. The shop windows are curtained and the door locked. 'Entry by appointment only' says a neat placard by the door.

'I got an appointment,' says Grandma, pressing one

polished talon on the buzzer while I eye the flamingos.

The man who comes to the door could only be Herbert Prune. He is in his fifties, and stands tall and spare with magnificent eyebrows. Though he bears himself like a soldier, his posture is less remarkable than his dress sense; he wears a plush cashmere sweater the colour of algae and knee britches of purple tartan with green stripes. His socks would better be termed stockings and they are creamy wool which disappear beneath the bottoms of his britches.

'Nice pants,' Grandma says, sneering slightly. 'That what you call camouflage in this part of the world?' She steps past Herbert Prune only to be halted by a thick glass interior wall with a keypad embedded in the handle of the transparent door.

'You're Maude Suche, I presume, and this is . . .'

'My granddaughter,' Grandma says firmly.

'Ahhh. You're not as prompt as I had hoped. You are five minutes early.'

'By my watch we're five minutes late. You got a problem with that, Mr Prune?'

'I don't know, Mrs Suche. I'm not used to people talking to me as you do. We have never met. And your rather circuitous letter gave me no indication of what mutual service we might render each other. You simply wrote that you had something I might like to see. Would you care to elaborate, Mrs Suche?'

'No, Herb, I wouldn't. I got a chillblain and I'd like you to open the door so as we can step inside. Use your head. Would me and my granddaughter drive up here in this weather just to waste your time?' Grandma glares up at him, locking on eyes that sit in a face eighteen inches above her own.

Maude Orpwood Suche's supreme confidence convinces Herbert Prune that he should open his door to us, and we step into the luxurious dark warmth of his shop. 'The rugs and furniture represent a sideline for me,' says Herbert Prune, waving at rich colours and shining wood as he leads us quickly through, 'a way of furnishing my home with an ever changing array of history. I'm currently involved with George III. But of course, I am primarily a dealer in arms.'

'Guns,' says Grandma to his back. 'I wouldn't be here for anything else, that's for sure.'

The shop looks smaller inside than it did from the outside, and in just a few steps we come to the back wall where a rug hangs. With her hands on her hips, Grandma steps back to appraise it. 'My husband Thomas would've gone for this, he had a thing for nice carpets. 'Course he would've burned a hole in it before he was through with it.' She steps forward to take an edge of the hanging rug between her thumb and forefinger. 'Real pretty,' Grandma says, 'if you like this type 'a thing.'

'Aubusson,' says Herbert Prune.

'Bless you,' says Grandma, offering him a tissue from the sleeve of her sweater.

He looks doubtfully at us, then reaches behind the rug and reveals another glass door, armed with another keypad, and suddenly we are in a room with enough weaponry to gladden the hearts of an antique army. Glass cases line the room, and in them, rifles stand butt to butt, long barrels climbing the walls. There are swords with ivory handles, daggers with diamonds on their hafts, and, on red velvet which lines a wooden display table, a collection of derringers, only one of them as small as *Li'l Maude*.

'Your letter mentioned a connection with Fleishman, Limited. I am the country's premier dealer in rare Fleishmans, particularly the early models. Last year I acquired the prototype of the Fleishman Finesse rifle. I don't know if you are at all familiar with the company's history, most people don't know that Nester Fleishman's son Nerf actually designed all the guns which made the company so renowned. He died under mysterious circumstances in 1941, but not before he'd made the prototypes of every gun Fleishman sells today. I bought the first Fleishman Finesse from the estate of Nerf's elder sister, Clara Fleishman Bulmer, and it sold at auction last year for $450,000.' Herbert Prune's eyes are shining.

'Poor Clara,' says Grandma softly. 'She sure would've liked some of that money while she was alive. She married Thurman Bulmer, and a meaner skinflint never lived. You made a nice profit outta that deal, Herb. It's a real shame Clara never got to enjoy her end of the stick.'

'I would have been as happy to buy the gun from Clara Fleishman Bulmer herself,' says Herbert Prune. 'She need only have contacted me whilst still alive.'

'I believe you on that one, Herb. Now. How much cash you keep here,' Grandma demands with sudden menace.

Instantly wary, Herbert Prune stares at Grandma. I can see him assessing her and me anew, wondering if he has made a mistake by letting us into his treasure cave.

'I keep no cash here,' says Hubert Prune surely but too quickly. 'It would be unwise.'

'More unwise not to,' says Grandma. 'Us Orpwoods only deal in cash, have done for generations. But don't worry. You and me can still talk, because I think you're lying. I bet you keep plenty of cash here.' Grandma reaches into her budge and I see Herbert Prune step sideways, closer to a small red button on the wall. His fingers reach out long and sinewy, and he turns his body slightly, so that we won't know what he's doing. He doesn't push the button, but he is wary and ready, his eyes darting back and forth between us. As Grandma slowly withdraws something from her blouse, I see Herbert Prune's eyes grow wide and his body stiffen.

My own eyes are wide, as wide as my nostrils are flared, one part of my body looking at tension, the other smelling it. *I know what Grandma keeps in her budge.* Grandma's hand moves away from the top of her blouse, her fingers extended to cover whatever she holds. She takes a deep breath and flips the underside of her hand over to reveal a . . .

. . . lace-edged hankie. Herbert Prune's shoulders slump in relief because Maude Suche has no evil intent, she simply needs to blow her nose – I can see him thinking it, and his fingers fall relaxed to his sides. My eyes go back to Grandma, who is not blowing her nose but wiping the corner of her mouth. Suddenly, in one single motion which looks oiled, she reaches back into her shirt and draws *Li'l Maude*. Herbert Prune's mouth drops open and his eyes unfocus. When he speaks his voice shakes.

'Hands in the air,' says Grandma.

'Do not . . . do anything you might regret. Really. I mean, really . . . unwise. There will be someone else here in mere moments. I have, er, I have an eleven o'clock appointment with a representative of the Imperial War Museum in London – '

'Quick thinkin', Herb, but I don't see anybody less'n God getting through the security you got here,' says Grandma very seriously. 'I could shoot you and nobody'd know for weeks. Revenge for poor Clara Fleishman Bulmer!' Her mouth shapes a cruel sneer and then she can hold back no longer. My grandmother laughs, she absolutely dissolves in perfect, extraordinarily happy chuckles which catch me out of my astonishment and coax an incredulous smile. Then I laugh too, at first uncertainly and out of relief, but soon carried along in the infectious waves of her humour. This is the funniest thing I have ever heard and I begin to cry from laughter. *Li'l Maude* drops with Grandma's arm, parallel to her thigh. Herbert Prune stares at us, shocked and disbelieving until Grandma lifts her glasses and wipes under her eyes with the handkerchief.

'Oh for corn's sakes,' she gasps still chortling, 'my *gut* hurts.'

At last Herbert Prune clears his throat and finds words. 'I don't find this the slightest bit amusing and I'd like you to leave instantly, before I call the police – '

'Shut your trap, Herb,' says Grandma, radiating an utter lack of concern. She wags her finger and carries on scolding him. 'I'll only get one moment like this in my entire life, 'less of course I decide not to sell to you, which

I might decide anyway, on account of you being such a horse's ass. If I sell to someone else I get the fun of pullin' this stunt once more. Look at my gun.' Grandma tugs Herbert Prune's slack right arm away from his side, and lovingly places *Li'l Maude* on his palm. 'Nerf Fleishman gave this to me in 1932.' Grandma crosses her arms over her chest, and regards Herbert Prune. 'She's been mine for sixty-three years.'

As he raises *Li'l Maude* for a look, his expression empties of the fact that he thought Grandma was about to commit armed robbery. I see reverence like a rapture on Herbert Prune's face. He forgets entirely that Grandma has offered to sell him this gun – there is no guile or cunning on his countenance, no awareness of traders' tactics such as downplaying the importance of a find so that it may be purchased more cheaply. The only expression on Herbert Prune's face is amazement that such a thing exists and that he is holding it. Like a coquette, *Li'l Maude* looks even prettier in the light of his admiration.

'This is . . .' he blinks, stumbling for words, 'extraordinary in the *extreme*. How do you come to have such a gun? For what purpose was she made? There's no doubt about the maker, I don't even need to see the mark, but she's not a prototype . . .'

We are here to sell Li'l Maude. The realisation astonishes me. Despite my disbelief and a strange, sudden wash of sorrow, I watch Grandma carefully. I am intent on her answers, wondering what they'll be.

'Prototype? Huh.' She flutters her fingers – her characteristic horizontal goodbye – in the direction of *Li'l Maude*.

'What you got there's the model of my *marriage*. Nerf moulded the handle specially for me. I got the four bullets, too.' She fishes in her pocket, then four tiny silver balls make metal noises on the glass of a display case.

'You would sell it?' Herbert Prune's eyes are wide. Unconsciously his fingers flow over the gun, tracing the engraved name on the barrel, smoothing the mother of pearl waves laid into the handle so carefully that the join of wood and shell is indistinguishable.

'I would. I might. *Li'l Maude*'s a burden I'd like to leave behind. Make me an offer I can't refuse.'

And he does, barely stopping to think about it. I won't make this much money in the first three years I practise as a fully qualified oncologist.

'There's a condition,' Grandma cautions. 'She's never been fired, but I'm gonna shoot her now. Let's load her up and walk outside through your glass gates, Herb.' She looks over at him and sees his brow furrow.

'Ah, Mrs – '

'Herb,' she says, instantly ferocious. 'I'm warning you. Don't tell me the price is different with three bullets. If I want to, I'll shoot every one of these bullets, and the price'll stay just the same or I'll walk right out your door. There'll be no haggling over *Li'l Maude*. Got it?'

Meekly, desire for Grandma's gun driving him, Herbert Prune nods.

'Right, let's go outside. You come, too, Herb. It might do you good to see what I'm gonna do.' Grandma sweeps all four bullets into her palm and heads for the room's entrance. The proprietor of *Ye Olde Antique Shoppe*, who has no intention of letting my grandmother out of his sight, rushes to unlock the doors.

Grandma marching in front, me close behind, and Herbert Prune trailing at a respectful distance, we walk through Central City back to the car. At a distance of fifteen feet from the left front tyre, my grandmother stops. 'Did you know that these are just balls of silver, Herb? Not bullets. Nerf had loads of imagination, and he wanted this gun fired only four times – so it's like you're burnin' a bridge behind you every time a silver ball comes from her barrel. Burning bridges, that's what Nerf thought of my marriage. Guess I don't have to tell you that a bullet's normally inside a full metal jacket, with a snibbee of powder packed at the butt end so when the hammer hits it, it fires the bullet, which is most often lead. But not here. Not for Nerf. See how he built the explosive caps into the back of this revolvin' chamber – and the chamber actually carries the housing for the bullets. Four silver bullets. Four shots. I lied when I said there'd never be any more bullets for *Li'l Maude*. Some clever johnny might make little silver balls, but even if he did, there's no way to add more explosive to this gun. Four shots, that's all Nerf Fleishman ever wanted for her.

'I'm gonna fire just one.' Grandma turns to me, ignoring Herbert Prune entirely but not maliciously. He is no longer important, only me.

'Doctor? Your eyes good enough to see the GOODYEAR on your tyre? I'm gonna put a bullet through the little triangle at the top of the A.'

'Why?' I am open-mouthed and disbelieving. It is the last thing on earth I expected her to say.

'Because that car's your most precious possession, and I wanna make it useless to you. It ain't much of a test for me, 'cept I got to figure in how the bullet's gonna go off course at this distance. With a rifle and my naked eye – and my specs of course – I could blow a beetle off a tree at a hundred yards. The A on your tyre ain't a problem.'

'I have a spare tyre, Grandma. Why are you doing this?'

'I got to teach you that nothing's too important to give up, not a person, not a thing, not if your reason for keeping it ain't a good one. I only just learned myself. I'd've loved if somebody told me so sixty years ago.'

For a very long time I look down at her as she sights over *Li'l Maude* at the A on my Goodyear tyre. Seldom does someone astonish me. The only area of my life where I wait for revelation is in the hospital, where one day I plan to snatch someone's life back from the grip of a malignant growth of cells. Maude Orpwood Suche fills me with awe and respect such as no person earns simply by being a relative. I'll bear her Blood gratefully and know that it helps me do whatever I want to do. As long as I *know* what I want.

'You don't have to blow my tyre apart, Grandma – I get the message.'

She smiles at me. And beaming, fires off a single shot which goes into the dirt one inch beyond Herbert Prune's shoe.

'Goodbye *Li'l Maude*,' she says. 'Now, Herb, let's talk turkey. Oh for corn's sake, stop whimpering. If I'd wanted to hit you I would've.'

The Rocky Mountains, Colorado

Back on Route 70 West, we drive through the Rocky Mountains, through the lofty towns of Idaho Springs and Silver Plume at twelve thousand feet, then into the Eisenhower Memorial Tunnel and gradually down again, through places like Vail, Eagle, and Rifle. Once out of the tunnel, Grandma insists that we take the scenic route which runs parallel to Route 70. Her insistence meets no opposition from me – the weather is clearing, the menace has disappeared, and I'm intrigued by our surroundings.

These mountains differ from any I've ever experienced. Back closer to my Middle East, the mountains command respect by towering over attendant valleys, the contrast between peak and trough giving a full measure of meaning to altitude. But here in the Rockies the mountains stand shoulder to shoulder without interruption; there is nothing to look down on, no way to gain perspective. I'm enlightened by road signs – *Grays Peak 14,270 feet* – otherwise the only clues I'd have to our exalted position would be snow on nearby mountain sides, and the wheeze of Grandma's breathing in this oxygen-thin air.

Under white skies this is a place of stark magic splendour, and when I have a moment to consider where I am, it makes the hairs rise on the nape of my neck. Someday I'll have to drive back through Colorado to appreciate such ancient highlands fully. But at this very moment I'm distracted – I have been ever since we left Central City – by a wad of money and a cashier's cheque replacing the familiar metallic bulge in Grandma's budge. I have no idea why she did it.

All I can imagine is that by selling *Li'l Maude*, Grandma proved she was strong enough to give up the thing she loved best. She showed the strength of her former life, before she got 'soft' and came to Washington DC. And she wanted to shoot my tyre and teach me a lesson. But what I've learned is that the force of will Grandma associates with strength attaches just as easily to cowardice. Long ago Grandma proved she had the strength to give up the person she loved best, and it was the action of a coward.

'Why – '

'Shhh,' says Grandma, giving a last arranging shove to the money mounded between her breasts. 'Shh, now. Hush. We're in the mountains. Whatever you got to say'll keep.'

Fruita, Colorado

Things are heating up: the weather and Grandma.

'"Why, why, *why*",' she mimics me. 'Like a darn why-bird. I can't stand it.'

'All right, Grandma, let's work on *how*. *How* did you know about Herbert Prune, how'd you know to bring *Li'l Maude* to him?'

She is the most irritating person on earth. Grandma's eyes glitter as though she has landed a prize-winning catfish and wants to let it thrash on the line for a while before netting it and bashing its head with a broom handle. 'I'll tell you how,' she says. 'You know that girl who always helps me with my safe deposit box at the bank? I guess you don't – it's Liz takes me to the bank. Anyways, there's this young gal called Phoebe that unlocks the door of my box while I unlock it too, and I showed her *Li'l Maude*. Her eyes got all big – kinda froggy, come to think of it – and I had to tell her real quick it weren't loaded. That's where I got the idea to pretend stick up with Herbert Prune.' Grandma stops and chortles, vastly pleased with herself. 'After Phoebe sat down and caught her breath, she suggested if I want to sell my pistol I should call The Smithsonian Institution. "Why don't you do that for me, Phoebe dear," I said. And she did. And the Smithsonian gave her Herbert Prune's number. Easy.'

'Don't you feel naked without *Li'l Maude*? That gun isn't hiding in a safe deposit box any more, waiting for you. *Li'l Maude* is gone. I don't understand . . . how could you sell her?'

'Well it weren't the easiest thing I ever done nor the hardest. Why do you care, Doctor? Thought you hated guns. Five days ago you near as ordered me out of your car 'cause I wanted to tote *Li'l Maude* along out West!'

In frustration I decide to change the angle of inquiry. 'The bundle between your breasts makes me more nervous, Grandma. What are you going to do with such a huge amount of cash?'

'Now you're a what-bird. I'll try speakin' your language – I used to be real good at bird calls out at The Farm. *What* would you say if I told you that selling my gun helped make this trip true to life, more like my first trip out here with Thomas, huh?'

My eyebrows rise so high that my ears stretch forward. 'You sold *Li'l Maude* in 1949? Pawned her? You're not serious.' Then I look sideways at Grandma and see her eyes glitter again. Doctor Catfish flaps helplessly on the line as Fisher Maude raises her sawed-off broomstick. 'You didn't pawn your gun . . .'

'Nope, but *Li'l Maude* almost got sold out from under me on account of ten bucks. That's how much some cowpoke offered Thomas for my gun, only Thomas and the cowpoke didn't figger on it bein' *my* gun. Those sorry, sorry fools – I came just shy of blasting a hole through the two of 'em. We needed that ten bucks bad, the boys, me, and Thomas, but I'd made all the sacrifices I was gonna make, even if it meant we wouldn't have food come sun-up. I almost lost my most treasured possession that day, and I lost it for sure this morning. But today was my choice, I sold *Li'l Maude* because *I* wanted to. I didn't let nobody else make that decision for me. You think on that a minute, Doctor.'

We drive in silence until Grandma says solemnly, 'It ain't this car that's your treasure. It's your cartouche.'

'What?'

'Your cartouche, that old Greek symbol doctors got engraved on their doctor crest. Your cartouche.'

'The *caduceus*, you mean.'

'Yes, that's right, don't repeat. You say you value your car most, to take you back home. I know how much your Mom and Dad and the Chesapeake Bay mean to you, but you left 'em for the caduceus. Your most treasured possession ain't a *thing*, it's a knowing: knowin' how to be a doctor. You're coming West, leaving what you love best, all to be a better doctor. But you know, I always thought you'd be a good *lawyer*. I watch *Perry Mason* re-runs on TV and I think how good you'd be at that. You were gonna go to law school, I know you were, not right out of college, but a year on. You'd'a been the first lawyer in our Blood.'

'Instead I am the first doctor. I love what I do, Grandma.'

'But I don't know why you changed. Never got to ask you. You spent that year at the beach, then all of a sudden you was at medical school. How was I to get to Charlottesville and ask what you were doin'? I recollect you used to scream at the sighta blood. And do you remember when you were in high school, and your Dad and Liz gone to Hawaii? That cat you had, Delilah, dropped kittens in a closet and you woke me in a panic, didn't know what to do? We had to tie off the cords on those kitties, and one came out and Delilah couldn't get it to breathe, so I shook it 'til it mewed and you passed out? Remember? Did you want to be a doctor *then*? You didn't even make a good vet!'

'Even if you had come to Charlottesville, Grandma, you couldn't have made a difference in my decision. Remember my friend Nathan died the year we all lived at the beach –'

'Was he your boyfriend? Were you rutting?'

'That's a bit blunt.' You *antique fiend*. 'No, and we never did or would have. He liked a friend of mine. I *had* a boyfriend.'

'But that fella gave up when you decided on goin' to medical school.' She drives a sharp talon into my shoulder to emphasise her words.

'What are you saying, Grandma?'

'Just tryin' to figger what you gave up for your cartouche. Seems like a lot. Can you tell me why?'

Why not tell her? 'Because I hear Nathan's damned voice in my head – not all the time, but often enough so I've got to do something about it. Never again will I stand by and watch helplessly while someone I love dies.'

'So you figger you can make it up to Nathan by savin' somebody else.'

I think for a moment, feeling inexplicably reluctant to confirm her words. 'I suppose so . . . yes.'

'Hmmph,' says Grandma, completely unimpressed. 'Dead people are the most ungrateful folks I know.'

Moab, Utah

This land is a baked hot terracotta hell.

'Why are we here?' I ask my grandmother, who without explanation ordered me to turn off Interstate 70 West on to Highway 191. I didn't want to. I'm beginning to have my own agenda, and it doesn't include extraneous side-trips. 'Is this a stopover from your past?'

'Not really, but 'lot of the gals in my bridge club came out here last summer, and they talked up Arches National Park to be some kinda prehistrionic Disneyland. Me, I can't believe the state didn't round up a bunch of fellas in secret and set them to work makin' a tourist attraction.' She shakes her head at the fraudulence of men.

I have never heard of Arches National Park, but at the entrance gate I snare a pamphlet, and this is what I learn: three hundred million years ago an inland sea covered eastern Utah and western Colorado. As this sea evaporated, layer upon layer of debris built up, and in between the layers, billions of tons of salt settled down to wait out eternity. Eventually the debris compacted into tremendously dense and heavy rock which shifted the salt, making bizarre transformations. The results, after several million years of buckling and caving below, and erosion above, are sandstone layers in the shapes of spires, steeples, bridges, and most importantly, arches. So many arches that the park is enormous. Some of the arches are famous and have names, like Tower Arch and Delicate Arch, and the notoriety and beauty of each individually named arch is directly proportional to the difficulty of reaching it.

'We're gonna see it all,' says Grandma. Despite the combination of intense heat, winding park road, and the prospect of hiking, she is determined.

Balanced Rock, Arches National Park, Utah

Standing with one hand on her hip and the other shading her eyes, Grandma peers up at a miraculous sandstone formation called Balanced Rock; it is just what it says, a thinnish spire of stone some fifty feet high topped by a round rock bigger than a bull elephant. 'I just don't believe some man didn't stick that thing up there with a l'il dab of cement,' she says.

'This is a further example of the power of geological forces. You accept mountains as natural wonders, why not arches and balanced rocks?'

'Huh.' Grandma's single syllable hangs eloquently between us. 'There's a sucker born every minute, and you're about an hour's worth. Some park official hoisted that pebble up there with a crane and now the park makes big bucks on every car fulla dummies that comes through the gate. In fact . . .' still speaking, Grandma stalks off to circle Balanced Rock, examining it from every possible angle. Back at my side, she pronounces her conclusion.

'No. No way the earth did this on its own. I reckon the whole place is one of them elaborate hogs.'

'I guess you mean hoax, an elaborate *hoax*.'

'Just what I said. Come on. We're gonna find out.'

Windows, Arches National Park, Utah

My watch reads six-fifty p.m. From the shadows cast on this weird and barren terrain I gain an inkling of what night might look like, all settled in: thick darkness melting over the rocks like deep chocolate ganache while overhead an explosion of stars summons thoughts of freshly hatched cosmos. It would be beautiful, but cold and other-worldly and utterly, mind-blowingly, alien. Full blown night in Arches National Park is incredible to contemplate, but not about to happen, at least not to us. It's time to go.

'We have to be out by seven o'clock, Grandma, so we need to *move*. Now.'

'Hold your horses. It's nowhere near dark yet, and I think this is real interestin'.' Crouched on a red rock outcrop, Grandma searches the underside of an arch for chisel marks. Already the skin of her fingertips, below the immaculate pearly pink talons, is dusted red from patting stone, checking for signs of modern tools. Twice a park official has driven by and stopped. Both times he asked her not to touch the monuments, and the second time he also asked us to make our way to the exit.

'The park will be closing in fifteen minutes,' he said. 'Unless you people want to be caught behind the gates you need to make your way to the exit,' and he waved his hand at a slow line of cars snaking in one direction.

'We can always come back tomorrow, Grandma.'

'We can't come back tomorrow. I shelled out the bucks so as we'd be here today.'

'*I* will pay for us tomorrow. We'll come back if you feel you need to.' The last car left our area ten minutes ago, and I can't keep the agitation out of my voice any longer. 'Let's leave, find a hotel in Moab, and be back here when the park opens at eight a.m. tomorrow! I will pay, let me just repeat that.'

'I got another idea,' she says, calmly running her fingers over sandstone. She steps behind a boulder to continue her investigations and upon emerging again, she tells me about spending the night in Arches National Park. By the time Grandma finishes speaking, we have no other option – the gates are locked, and darkness is descending in poured shadows.

Delicate Arch, Arches National Park, Utah

'The boys and Thomas and me stayed in a hotel only one night while driving West in 1949. A hotel in Reno, Nevada after Thomas won fifty bucks at the casino's stud poker table. It was a straight flush, king at the top, and it made Thomas so high he asked for the hotel's Hollywood Suite at forty-five bucks the night – money we needed bad. I couldn't talk any sense into him, and he was bound determined to spend even that last five bucks on room service champagne. So I tried to look on that suite as an opportunity. I milked it for all it was worth, and by the time I was done, the butcher's van was burstin' at the seams with my booty. Fine sheets and towels, a champagne bucket, six cheese knives, three pillows, a bedspread, a fancy mirror, and a fruit basket so big it took both boys to carry it to the van.

'But every other night we slept outside. I thought you oughtta see what it's like, Miss Civilised Doctor, under Western skies.'

What it's like.

I shift on my rock couch and ponder fitfully, exhausted but feeling too strange to sleep. The car is one and one half miles away, the nearest human is probably double that, and all we have by way of company is the largest free-standing arch in the park; Delicate Arch rises eerily massive beside us. It is barely a quarter of the size of Gateway Arch in St Louis, and not so precisely shaped, but it is awesome in its accidental splendour. Very little vegetation grows here, and the landscape, which serves also as the building material for Delicate Arch, is red rock, nothing more. This is a Martian place where the slightest noise makes me leap to my feet and cast my flashlight in wide arcs. Being cold doesn't help. When the sun went down the temperature dropped twenty degrees and it felt good, as Grandma suggested, to lie on the rock and cover myself with sweaters. The rock baked in the sun all day and it released heat into me like a brick oven baking dough. Every last bit of heat has left the rock, however, and now I'm feeling raw.

'I can hear your teeth rattling,' Grandma says charitably, 'so why not come hunker next to me – anything so long as you don't grouse about the cold. You know, it was my being bitter chilled that saved *Li'l Maude* back in 1949 when Thomas tried to steal her from me.'

'Tell me a bedtime story, Grandma.'

'I got no *stories*,' she says a little sharply. 'This is history.' But my interest whets her tongue. 'It was August 1949, in Utah, though not so far south as we are here, to my recollection. Closer to Salt Lake City. The boys and me were sleeping beside the butcher's van while Thomas talked big with a couple of cowpokes. There're loads of huge ranches in Utah and Nevada, a million head of cattle left to roam free 'til market time, when the rancher calls in riders to help him round up the steer. That's when the cowpokes show up. A cowpoke is a strange lonely fella, an American gypsy with no real home outside his saddle. He drinks his earnin's, wants no woman longer than one night, and doesn't even seem to feel much affection for his horse. But every cowpoke has a powerful obsession. You never know what it's gonna be. I met loads of cowpokes while we camped. A fire always draws cowpokes, and Thomas sometimes found a week's work talking to those fellas over the meals I cooked –'

'What did you cook?'

'Things we bought from farms. In sauces made from canned peaches, which Thomas picked up cheap in Lincoln, Nebraska. Canned peaches, mushed up, sweeten any barbecued meat, but sweet or not, it was hard work cookin' animal flesh after a day's drive in the van. I told you how that stunk – hot meat and sawdust. In all the six years we travelled never once did I clear the smell of blood outta my hooter. That's why we slept outside, the boys and me, for the fresh air. You had to want the fresh air *bad*, because at night in the open air the temperature'd drop right down. I'd give the boys my blankets, couldn't bear to see them shiver. Don't pity me! I can't see your face but I feel it, and like I said, it was my shivers saved *Li'l Maude*.

'Every cowpoke collects something – it's a footish with them. A way of makin' up for not havin' a home, I guess. I met a cowpoke who talked my ear hot showing me his stamp collection. For safety he stored it in the false soles of boots made specially for him. Another poke collected gold fillings, though I never asked how he came by them. Lotta those kinda fellas collect arrowheads or silver spurs. Always small things, for easy carrying. But the most dangerous cowpoke I ever met collected ladies' pistols: percussion caps, six shooters, the more unusual the better. He showed them to us one night around our fire after a meal of pork chops and peach chutney. He had a fine collection. He said to call him Abner.

'"Always on the lookout for a fine acquisition," said Abner. I kicked Thomas before he could say a word about *Li'l Maude*. Thomas looked hurt, like he would have never thought to tell this man about my gun. Abner had a strange glint in his eye, and a pocket flask he kept pulling on. I didn't like how he looked at me. I knew I'd like it even less if he got a look at *Li'l Maude*. But I trusted Thomas, or maybe I was too tired not to. Trusting my husband was another mistake I made over and over.

'"Move over Maude, let a man get warm," Thomas said to me while I lay there on the ground with my eyes closed, trying to wish away the cold. He smelled of bourbon. I figgered the fire was out and the cowpoke gone. Thomas seemed kinda randy, like he wanted rutting, and I remember thinking "Oh sweet Jesus, do You ask this of me as well?" Then he started after my bosom with his icy hands, and right quick I understood Thomas had no interest in my tits. No interest at all – he only wanted what was between them. He tried to draw *Li'l Maude* out from my nightgown.

'It was being cold that saved me. If the weather'd been warm, I'd've been snoring and I'd've woke to find my gun gone, because Thomas had a light touch, and I'd've slept through the robbery. Thank the Lord for goosebumps. I pretended sleep, but I acted like he'd disturbed me. Giving out a big groan I rolled to my belly, pressing *Li'l Maude* to the ground. As I rolled I saw through slit eyes that the cowpoke was standin' not five feet away, watching us with glittering eyes, and that scared me so bad I sat bolt upright. I made like I'd come awake with a start. Quick as a shadow the cowpoke stepped behind the van. Think, Maude, think. What're you gonna do? "I got to flicker," I told Thomas, "real bad." He was surely startled, but I pretended not to notice how guilty he looked. Giving his leg a little, wifely kind of squeeze, I started for the bushes. Careful, Maude, careful I said to myself. It was a quiet night, and my hands shook so much that I feared I'd drop *Li'l Maude*'s silver balls before I got 'em loaded. I loaded two. I'm an excellent shot, knew I'd need no more. Then I walked soft and barefooted back to the camp, stepping behind Thomas, who, though nervous and waiting, didn't hear me, and I looked under the chassis of that butcher's van, seeking the cowpoke's feet and seein' which way they pointed. I wanted to come up on him from behind, very, very quiet.

'"Don't move, Abner, or you're deader than the meat you ate by my fire tonight. Nod once if you hear and understand." He nodded. "Now let's you and me walk over to your horse. Don't look round for Thomas, he'll be no help to you. Go quiet, and nothing stupid, or me and my boys be eatin' you with peaches. How dare you ask Thomas for my gun, huh? How dare you! Ride away and don't come back. I'll shoot you if you do, *and then I'll take your pistols.*"

'I knew that'd send him off for good. Oh, not the threat I'd shoot him – that kind of man don't value his life like he should. But Abner valued his guns, they were what he cared for most, and the idea of me havin' them once he died was more than he could take. Bet he rode miles without stopping. I'll bet he rode *miles*. Lucky I knew that cowpoke's mind.'

'Not luck, Grandma. Native Middle Western cunning.' I huddle closer to her, wondering in this thick darkness what facial expression she wears. I hope she feels proud. Maude Suche belongs here, under this wide sky in this primitive place. I admire my grandmother's courage none the less because it is instinctive rather than social. I wish the dividends of such a gift paid off more in her everyday life, both long ago in Evansville, Indiana, and currently in Washington DC.

It's unnatural lying out here, under cover of nothing but sky. When Grandma's snores begin, like heavy stage whispers, they make me curiously content. But I can't sleep. I may as well stay awake and watch where the sun rises when it's not in my Middle East.

By eight o'clock in the morning Grandma and I are at the park entrance, ready for the opening moment. Only we're on the wrong side of the gates. I had wanted to be discreet, maybe wait until nine a.m., so we could pretend we hadn't been overnight guests.

'What are they gonna do?' asks Grandma. 'Fine me? Lock us up in jail? I don't reckon they will. We'll just sail on through like this is regular for us. Once upon a time it was regular for *me*. And good morning to you,' Grandma calls to a disapproving park ranger at the gate. 'Where do you reckon we could get a good breakfast round here?'

He sends us to Moab, a town just a few miles to the south. Grandma wants food, and I want a bank; it makes me apprehensive that she carries so much cash rolled up in her chest, but Grandma is unconcerned. And at a vegetarian café we nearly quarrel about it after a thunder-faced hippie tells her she can't have bacon and eggs at his café.

'Pinko,' Grandma mutters under her breath. 'Commie pinko! What does he mean, he doesn't serve bacon and eggs. That's what *Americans* eat for breakfast!' She sips at her second cup of coffee – a chicory blend which initially made her gag – and holds the mug up close to her head so she can glower out over the rim. 'Huh! Let's go. There's nothin' here for me to eat, so we may as well hit the road, 'cause we got 750 miles to drive today.'

'Is that how far it is to the Pacific Coast?' I try keeping my voice unconcerned, but it matters to me very much. I need to see a West Coast beach, to gauge its similarities and differences, to judge whether I can transplant myself successfully. And I want to do it quickly; my rootball cries out for sand and salt air.

'No, that's how far it is to Reno, Nevada, the biggest gambling city in the West! Outside of Las Vegas, a'course. You wanna know what I'm gonna do with all my cash? I'm gonna gamble it. We can find a bank later, if it'll make you happy, and I'll open an account and deposit my cashier's cheque. But the cash stays with me. And I don't care if you don't like it!'

I don't.

Sevier Desert, Utah

As we drive through the dry cracked countryside of Utah, Grandma shaves her legs and there seems to be a connection. Her leg hairs stand up pointy and grey from skin that looks like salt flats. Using a straight blade, she shaves without lotion and makes noises which I can hear even over the roar of the engine. Rasp. Rasp. Short rasp over her knees. Long rasp from ankle along the calf. The noise tortures me.

Reaching far back into my repertoire of unladylike noises, I bring up a sound which is half a belch and half an anguished howl. Grandma slides her eyes sideways at me and purses her lips; she knows what I am commenting on even though we haven't been discussing it. Though I haven't said a word since the rasping began, Grandma knows exactly how I feel about her scraping her legs with a straight razor. She can read it in my face that dry shaving violates the soul in a peculiarly itchy, eczema kind of way. I will have quarter inch long leg hairs all over my car forever, because the windows are open and the fur flies.

Grandma interrupts her shaving to lick her finger and plant it smack below her knee on a tiny bloody nick. She thumbs the razor's blade to gauge its sharpness, and then, without looking up, answers my disapproving silence.

'I've always done it this way. It don't hurt.'

'My God that's gross.' When I speak I keep my lips as close together as possible.

'Picky picky,' says Grandma, beginning on the other leg. Rasp. Rasp. 'I got to do this. I'm gettin' beautiful for Reno.'

'Couldn't you have shaved before now, perhaps in the bathtub? Doesn't it bother you when your leg hairs grow so long you can braid them? Many elderly individuals with hirsute habits have been deposited at animal shelters by relatives who mistook them for lost pets. I suppose, in its own way, that's better than being dropped off at the hospital for an indeterminate stay. "Granny dumping" we in the medical profession call it. Don't let this happen to you.'

'Oh, look.' Grandma pays me no attention. 'Oh, look,' she cries waving her razor out the window. 'There's a dead cow.' Grandma continues to gaze out the window, her razor poised to attack an enclave of curly hairs on her big toe. 'Sometimes a dead cow takes in the heat 'til it bloats like a balloon. It gets bigger and bigger, and then it explodes.' Grandma puffs out her cheeks and prunes her little mouth into a knot before expelling the air in a puff of spearmint denture fixative breath. 'I used to see that every so often on The Farm, when one of my old bessies'd kick the bucket on a warm afternoon, and the knacker truck was too busy to get out to her straight away. Just awful. And if you had a little breeze it'd swish that stink all over the fields. Upset the cows no end.'

Rasp. Rasp.

'We need to find you a bank, Grandma, so you can set up an account and deposit that cheque at the very least. And it still makes me nervous to have so much cash in the car –'

'Don't think on it then. Where', she waves her straight razor at our surroundings, 'do you see a bank? Nothin' here but us and cows. We'll have to go to Reno, Nevada for a bank, and that's 700 miles away. Put your pedal to the floor! I wanna be gambling by midnight!'

Moving along with her mobile toilette, Grandma removes her pearly pink fingernail polish with passes of a cotton puff dipped in acetone. The fumes are sickly sweet and my nostrils twitch.

I have been thinking about The Pocket, and I am now so comfortable with my passenger that I ask questions without taking advice from my intuition as to whether the timing is opportune. 'I know that what *you* need to discover is why you stayed with Thomas Suche after you married him. But what *I* find bewildering is why you married him in the first place. It wasn't just Timola's meddling – there had to be some connection between you both, some degree of mutual attraction. There had to be. If you think there wasn't, then you're distorting your own history, and if I were you, I'd wonder why.'

'Huh.' She tosses a pink-stained cotton ball on the

floor. 'Well. I guess Thomas was real handsome when I first met him – that helped. And he smelled of Ivory soap. My mother always made me wash my hands with Ivory soap before dinner – Ivory appealed to me. The most interestin' thing about him, though, was he was a founding.'

'A founding? What do you mean?'

'One of them with no parents. An orphan. Kind of fascinating, don't you reckon? Pick up your speed or we'll never get to Reno!'

I press my foot down on the accelerator hard, because while considering Grandma's news I have let the pedal float up. It is a measure of my surprise that our m.p.h. dipped from seventy-five to forty-two miles an hour. '*You* married an orphan? Of all people . . . you care so much about Blood and genealogy, didn't you care that he had none?'

'Well, I guess I couldn't believe it! The idea of an orphan interested me somethin' powerful. There I was, related to half of Evansville. And he had no one. That's what we talked about, most of the time – him growin' up in the orphanage – it interested us both. Once he finished tellin' me all about bein' a founding, of course, we had nothing left to say to one another, but those were good stories, more like fairytales. Want to know how he got his surname?

'He was a real pet of the matrons when he lived at the orphanage, so Thomas told me. Doesn't surprise me at all. Thomas could charm a night-crawler, so long as it was female. Every day the matrons told Thomas he was such a little devil, such a little dear, such a little charmer. So, kinda joke-like, Thomas called himself Sucha. Later on he hired a lawyer, changing his name in the courts to Suche. He corrected everybody we'd meet, smoothing 'em into saying his name the way he liked it – "Suuuu-shay. It's French," he'd say and wink. He picked out a Frenchie middle name to match: François. Thought it sounded distinguished.

'Soon as he'd grown enough peach fuzz to make up a little moustache, Thomas ran away from the orphanage. He was twelve then, by his own account, and while I know that's young for fur on the lip, Thomas always had more growth than other fellas. All you can do is guess when you set to figgerin' an orphan's age, Thomas coulda been anywhere between fifty-five and sixty-five when he passed on. I'll never know. Thomas never even had a birthday party 'til he ran with my Blood, and then he got loads of 'em all at once. It was part of the Catch-Thomas contest.

'First of all Aunt Mastiff gave him May Second for his birthday. May Second, a new suit, and she baked this big cake decorated like an oil well. Then Great Aunt Elsie said no, Thomas's birthday should be the fourteenth of May, with a five-course dinner to celebrate. It was a busy week for Thomas – Aunt Myrtle gave a big barn dance on May fifteenth to celebrate his *real* birthday, which *she* said was a day later than Great Aunt Elsie'd said it was. To prove her point Aunt Myrtle even gave Thomas a pocketwatch with "*Thomas François Suche, May Fifteenth 1908*" engraved on it. Notice Aunt Myrtle wasn't happy deciding him just a birthday, she had to give him a birthyear, too. And then my mother said his birthday would be the sixth day of the sixth month. She didn't give him a party nor a present, just wrote his name and the date in our family Bible, and he stuck with that. How my kin talked! That was the first time folks figured Thomas Suche would marry Maude Orpwood. Want me to leave my blade out? You need to shave before we get to Reno?'

'It's going to be hard for me to stop in Reno, Grandma. I know you want to in order to retrace the steps of your first journey West, but remember this trip is for me, too. I *need* to see the coast, and Reno is only 250 miles away from the Pacific.'

'Listen to you! Easy to tell you been travellin' too long, when 250 miles's just a drop in the bucket. We wouldn't get to the beach before five o'clock in the mornin', at the earliest!'

'That would be ideal. It's very important, Grandma, that I see how the sun rises at the farthest point west that I can imagine. Do you understand?'

'Sure I do. But if we don't stop to spend the night in Reno, you'll be so bone tired that all you'll do is cry if the beach don't look exactly like it looks at home. And I'll be cryin' too, because Herbert Prune booked the best suite at the MGM Grand Hotel in Reno and he booked it in the name of Mrs Maude Suche – it was parta the deal for *L'il Maude*. We got a dinner reservation for one o'clock in the morning and I got plans to spend thirty thousand dollars at the roulette table. How's those apples, Doctor? I can tell you, we're not passing Reno by! Your beach can wait, and you'll be all the better for it.'

• • •

The road to Reno bisects central Nevada, which comprises the biggest darkest expanse of *nothing* imaginable. We are out here alone in it – just me, Grandma, and at least one million jackrabbits. Every two or three minutes I brake hard, and at slightly longer intervals I leave skid marks on the road in my efforts to avoid making rabbit pancakes. My speed has dropped to fifty miles an hour.

'Sheesh! I'd get to Reno faster if I was walkin'!'

'You are welcome to try. Damn!' I swerve as a pair of long ears attached to a running body flies across the road. 'Did I hit that one, do you think?'

'Naw. When you do you'll feel a bump.' Grandma pats me on the arm, then squeezes the flesh below my elbow. 'Laws but you're tense. You muscles're all bunched up.'

'I'm very concerned about hitting a jackrabbit!'

'Easy to tell a city kid. I'm a animal lover, too, but havin' a farm you feel different. It comes down to them or you. Out here, if you hit a jackrabbit, as long as you hit it good, that creature'll never know, 'cause it's all over in a second. That is if the car's driving *fast* enough. Back on The Farm I once hit a doe, nothing I could do to avoid her, she just ran right out in front of me. Sad, sad day. You like venison? I got kinda tired of it.'

Grandma isn't helping. I am exhausted, and the desolation out here unsettles me. I care, care out of all proportion to the creature's importance on the planet, about running over a jackrabbit. The glint of a rabbity eye reflects my headlights back to me and I slow to a creep.

'Want a goodie? I got the dittie bag right here for you.'

'No thanks, Grandma. What I'd really like is a wire

mesh screen with holes no bigger than a sugar sieve. Ideally, said mesh would run the entire length of this road on both sides, permitting not a single rabbit to stray on to the road.' Then I hear the bump, though I did not see the animal.

'That', says Grandma definitively, 'was a jackrabbit. Deader'n a doornail, and not a thing on earth you could've done about it. You want to run back and take one of the paws? A rabbit's foot brings good luck if you string it on a keychain.'

I can feel my face blanch in the dark. What keeps me going is that every mile is one mile closer to the water, and now that I am so far away from home that it seems too far to go back, I'm anxious to see a West Coast beach. I want to see how much kinship I feel with Western waves. I wish Grandma would forgo her trip to the casino.

She switches on the interior light so she can count her money. It is a measure of my preoccupation that I don't notice how large the withdrawal from Grandma's budge into her purse grows until I see that she has just a tiny roll to fit back between her breasts. I thought she was joking about spending thirty thousand dollars. In her purse sits enough to pay off a sizeable portion of my medical school loans! The money is crisp and thin and new, five-hundred dollar bills which Grandma has folded so that the sheaves are in ten-thousand dollar groupings. Such amounts seem unreal to me. When it finally breaks into my brain that Grandma carries *thirty thousand dollars* in her handbag, I have to stop the car and look at it. Little details register – Ben Franklin's portentous face stares back from the one-hundred notes, and the paper actually has tiny red threads running through it . . .

'Now, *what* did you say you are going to do with this, Grandma?'

'Start this jalopy moving again and maybe I'll tell you.' She grins broadly as we accelerate, back on to the road, heading to Reno faster than before. 'I'm gonna spend it, of course. All my life I've watched my money like a mother hen. I made loads and saved loads, then other folks spent it for me. I've planned and scrimped so I don't got to worry any more, not 'bout anything – I won't be a burden on your dad if I got to go in a retirement home – I've bought bonds and I got savings. But I've never had enough to even *think* of going on a toot. I wanna get a *millionaire* feeling from this money. I wanna spend a wad and not miss it, all thanks to *Li'l Maude*. This here', Grandma pats her pocketbook resolutely, 'is wild money!'

Reno, Nevada

So late on Friday night that it feels like Saturday morning, lights begin to glitter in the far distance. I have no idea what they are but I'm delighted to see them; for the past three hours I have greeted any small sign of humanity like a Christmas present. Pressing the accelerator to the floor, I speed for civilisation and am rewarded, because less than five miles from the California border, Reno, Nevada appears out of the night like a phosphorescent fungus farm. Grandma is ready. Her nails are painted raspberry, her hair is combed, her legs are shaven, and her pocketbook is fleshy with money. I'm ready, too. I'm ready for bed in the suite Herbert Prune booked as part of the deal he made to acquire *Li'l Maude*. I thought I needed to see the West Coast more than I needed anything on earth, but I cannot drive another two hundred and fifty miles without some sleep. The last twenty-four hours has tired me more than the longest, busiest shift I ever worked in a hospital.

After driving hundreds of dark and lonely miles,

happening on this city is like chancing upon the opulent indolence of a fallen star. Millions of electric lights melt together and outline the civic topography, which is not like any Middle Eastern city I've seen. The cities with which I'm familiar, cities like Washington DC and Richmond, Virginia, have typical city layouts: a heart of tall buildings surrounded by a gradual thinning skirt of suburbs. The bigger the city, the bigger the skirt, the greater the circumference of the hemline. But Reno is concentrated, a single blob of brilliant light in a Nevada valley.

'Oh, it's so beautiful,' says Grandma, her palms rising to press flat against her chest. 'Say somethin', why don't you. You aren't saying a word!'

She looks so crestfallen that I try to muster enthusiasm. All I really want to do is sleep, but I find myself making an attempt at cheerful comment. 'Mmmmm,' I say appreciatively, 'it's very bright.'

'You bet. Land of the midnight dawn, folks call it. Let's hope Lady Luck's gonna be good to us here in Reno.'

'Why do you care if your luck is good or bad, Grandma? I thought the justification behind gambling so much money was to feel what it's like to lose money and know it isn't taking bread out of your family's mouth. Wild money isn't lucky or unlucky, it's just gone when you're finished. Do you actually expect to leave the casino having made a profit? The real millionaire feeling means leaving with nothing and not worrying about having lost all you brought.'

'Well, I reckon millionaires get used to feelin' a little

foolish. But I sure don't wanna come away from my one millionaire experience feeling like a fool. I want some luck! Hey look, these are real famous casinos!' We travel down one of Reno's main streets while Grandma reads the glitzy signs aloud. 'We got Circus Circus – I hear that's got acrobats swingin' from ropes overhead the whole time you're gambling – and The Flamingo, Fitzgeralds . . . hey! We're lookin' for the MGM Grand and I don't see it. It's s'posed to be the grandest of 'em all.'

'Look at that tall building, Grandma, there on the other side of the highway. Undoubtedly the grandest building in sight.'

'What're you waitin' for? Let's drive on over there and ask.'

Winding our way through a maze of streets and then a maze of parking areas, we find ourselves at the door of the grandest building in Reno, a hotel and casino called Bally's. It is twelve-forty-five a.m. and an entire battalion of car parking attendants bustles under a car porch lit to diamond brightness.

'Ma'am, may I park your car for you?' asks a uniformed valet as I approach the kerb.

Grandma leans over me to shout out the window. 'Can't stop young fella, we're just lookin' for the MGM Grand Hotel and Casino. Wonder if you can direct us.'

'What you're looking for is Bally's, Ma'am. Until just a few years ago we were called the MGM Grand. Even now some of our long time clients refuse to call us anything but. Of course when we changed the name we changed the ownership. Bally's', says the valet, slapping his hand lightly on the rolled down window, 'is owned by one of the biggest names in the entertainment business!' He beams.

Grandma realigns herself in her seat. 'This's it,' she says excitedly. 'I told Herb Prune to book me a suite at the MGM Grand. Hope he figured it out, but we'll know soon enough. Tell that parking fella to get us a porter. I'm not walking into this place lookin' like some country mouse draggin' her bags behind her.'

'Can you call a porter for us, please,' I say obediently, stepping out of the car and surrendering my keys. Moments later I am wishing that I carried our luggage myself. It's easy, I've done it every other night; Grandma's medium and large suitcase counterbalance nicely, and I just hook my old doctor's bag, which does more frequent duty as an overnight case, on my arm. It has never occurred to me before that our luggage is the last word in scruffy.

'This it?' asks the porter, nodding to the three cases. I nod, watching his face for any sign of derision. My bag and Grandma's suitcases sit sheepishly on the plush carpeted surface of his brass trolley – which is infinitely more luxurious than my car. But slower. The porter has to push his trolley at a rattling run to keep up with Grandma as she sweeps into Bally's lobby and heads straight for an eighty foot long reception desk manned by a platoon of clerks.

'Good God,' I say, ogling and following her slowly. The room we have entered is actually a cave so large that if I squint I can see the far end, but only just. And above me are incredibly high ceilings, high enough to offset the impression of claustrophobia common to rooms without windows, even the largest of rooms. Acres of patterned dark carpet cover the floor, and the place reverberates with colour, predominantly crimson, black, gold, and flesh. Everywhere there are people, a bewildering array of people, and lined up in between and among the people are slot machines – hefty, colourful machines ranked and ordered like the soldiers of a vast and powerful army. It is overwhelming.

'C'mon,' says Grandma. 'Tenth floor overlooking the city. We got to hurry up and get changed, 'cause we're due for a feed in ten minutes.'

Dinner, at one a.m. . . . in a haze of weariness I follow Grandma and the bellboy up to our suite.

My hair is twisted up and fastened to the back of my neck with a fake tortoiseshell clasp. It is the most elegant gesture I can make to glittering bejewelled Bally's, and I make it knowing that if I wore my hair like this in the hospital then at least one patient would tell me I should wear it this way more often. The compliment would glow in me until a hospital administrator would suggest cautiously that I adopt a neater, less tumbling hairstyle. Already I can feel tendrils falling, plastering to the damp area at the back of my neck where I wiped a washcloth during a hasty freshen up. A spit bath, Grandma calls it. Her spit bath is over, and she exudes the scent of a flowery bath oil provided by the hotel in tiny travel-sized bottles. Wearing a full-length purple chiffon evening dress and matching purple glass beads, she shimmers with excitement. In my wrinkled khaki skirt I am fit only to mind her train and carry her pocketbook, because Grandma's evening bag, looking like a purple ostrich egg pressed to her hip, can hold no more than a few thousand dollars without popping open.

'You look beautiful, Grandma. What a stunning dress.'

'Thomas bought it for me fifty-five years ago 'cause he fancied me showin' some bosom at The Elway Club. I've kept my figure good, don't you think?' She preens and puffs out her chest. 'Did no harm that for years I fretted 'bout getting what food we did have into the boys rather'n me.'

My doctor side is a practising pessimist. It's no good telling the physician inside me that Grandma is in amazingly good shape for an eighty-five year old woman; the physician knows that already. What preoccupies the doctor is the deterioration, no matter how defiant, of a human body. Grandma has shrunk since my grandfather made her a gift of this dress. Fabric scissored from the hem has been added to the neckline, helping to hide the layers of papery skin which sag into her bosom. And Maude Suche originally wore sky high heels with this dress, but she worries about her brittle ankles now – a concern the doctor shares – so she slips her feet into crepe-soled purple lace-ups.

'It really is a fine dress, Grandma, and you and the dress do each other credit. Do you wear it to remind you of Thomas Suche?'

'No.' It is a decisive syllable, allowing no room for doubt. 'I wear it to remind me of *Li'l Maude*. I could never fit her down the front of this dress without a little bit of silver showin'. Every time I sneezed the handle'd pop up into plain sight. Now she's gone I don't got to worry about that.'

A variety of restaurants rings the cave that is Bally's gambling arena. There are buffets and places to buy pizza by the slice, ice cream parlours, Mexican cocktail bars, and seafood restaurants. Grandma ignores them all. Her instruction to Herbert Prune was that he make a reservation in the nicest restaurant available, and by that she means the most expensive; she wants his pockets to hurt from digging. Allowing her nose to guide us, Grandma circles the gambling den until we find a restaurant which looks more like a library. It is a serious eating establishment with plenty of dark wood, white linen, and a vaguely English 'clubby' feel about it.

'You got a reservation for me, I reckon,' Grandma says, puffing out her chest at the *maître d'*. 'Herb Prune should've called and made me a reservation.'

'Yes, Madam,' the man replies, smiling a smile that is unusually cordial for one-thirty a.m. 'For you and your granddaughter, Mrs Gunslinger-Suche, I believe. It is very interesting to meet someone with your surname. And what a lovely dress.'

'Thank you,' says Grandma. 'But the name is just Maude Suche.'

'Oh, you needn't abbreviate your surname on my account. I'm perfectly *au fait* with double-barrelled names, Mrs Gunslinger-Suche. Please follow me.'

Grandma frowns at the *maître d'*s back but obeys,

stepping slowly and deliberately. She sinks into her velvet covered seat like a coronet being lowered on to a noble brow.

Seated at the restaurant's inmost table, we are still less than one hundred feet from the slot machines.

'I've been directed to tell you, Mrs Gunslinger-Suche, that the gentleman called Herbert Prune is responsible for the bill this evening. He wishes you to have your heart's desire at his expense. Enjoy your meal.' He offers us big brown leather menus which handle in the unwieldy way of newspapers.

'Maude Gunslinger-Suche!' Grandma grimaces at me from the high perch of her velvet banquette. It puts her directly at my eye level.

'Gunslinger Grandma! I think I'll be dining on salmon, grilled, with a dill hollandaise. For what do you hanker?'

'A good hunka beef, if they got it. You ever hear of Kobi beef? That's the best money can buy. Fifty dollars a pound, and that was fifty years ago. Kobis are cattle fed nothing but best grain, and each cow is massaged by hand every day for *hours* until the fat breaks down and the beef gets good marbling. How'd you like to eat somethin' that's lived better than you have, huh? Some of the swanky gals I babysit for get chunky in the winter, then come spring they go to the salon and have their fat massaged! Big bucks, I can tell you. Anyway, I'm gonna order me a eight ounce fillet steak. How 'bout we have some soup first – I'm fond of that French Onion. You want some wine?'

'I would love some wine.'

'Good. We ain't payin', so we'll order the kinda wine

Thomas would've. It's gotta have dust on the bottle and dirt inside, and I want the wine fella to carry it like a plate of Holy Communion.' Grandma half rises to flap her lustrous red nails at a man in a tailcoat, then she eases back into her seat. 'He's the Smelly A. He'll fetch us a wine menu.'

Smelly A, smelly A. Smelly A? 'You mean the *sommelier*.'

'Don't get uppity with me, Doctor. That's what I said.'

We order a wine that makes the *sommelier*'s eyes pop. He asks carefully if I would like to change my entrée so as to be able fully to appreciate the red wine, and that's how I end up eating beef, a big slab with its own silver sauceboat of *sauce béarnaise*. The vegetables are served separately – white asparagus, tiny rose-coloured potatoes, broccoli like perfect bonsai trees, baby carrots – all exquisitely steamed and offered up individually by a waiter wielding a large silver fork and spoon. Though the menu is not creative, this is festive food, cooked superbly.

'Stop yawnin',' Grandma orders. 'You yawn your way through a night shift at the hospital? I wouldn't let a doctor who yawned get *near* me. Yawning's real unprofessional.' She chews open-mouthed at me in rebuke, and the rare red meat on view would further inspire Dante to write about hell.

'I don't have to be professional right now. I'm not on duty, and if I *were* on duty I would probably be eating a candy bar instead of gourmet food. I miss out on eating well, Grandma. I seldom have time to cook or chew in this leisurely fashion. But it's not because I'm a doctor. Probably the first decade of any serious career would leave me little time to do the things I really want to do.'

'Huh.' Grandma swallows her last bite ostentatiously and points at me with the tines of her fork. 'When's the last time I saw you drink a glass of wine?'

'You know I don't, not very often. I never know when I might be called in. Wine makes me tired, and if I'm already tired it makes my hands shake. See?' I hold my napkin up in my right hand so that we can watch the linen shiver. 'Hands that shake do little for a doctor's credibility.'

'Betcha lawyers drink whenever they feel like it.'

'You may be right, but I'm not a lawyer, so I'll just enjoy more wine right now while I know I can.'

'You finish the wine. I gotta order coffee so we can see if there's any money in it. You know money? That's what I call those little bubbles stickin' to the side of my coffee cup. Sometimes I have money, and sometimes I don't. Once the waiter pours my coffee, then I'll know whether to make my first bet a hundred dollars or a thousand. Should we start on the poker or the roulette? Or do you wanna play the twenty-five dollar slots?'

'What I *want*, Grandma, is to go to bed so we can get up early and drive to the western-most edge of California. I really need to see what the beach looks like. And the Pacific. But if you're determined to gamble, then I'll stay awake to see you lose your first thousand dollars. It shouldn't take too long. In fact, I bet – no pun intended – I can stay awake the whole hour it takes you to lose all your money.'

'What'd you have to say that for?'

I look at her levelly and know my face reveals nothing. But I feel shame at trying to spoil her pleasure. The money from *Li'l Maude* is not my money – I don't expect it to be. And yet I can't help feeling irritated about the use she plans for her thirty thousand dollars. That money would make an enormous dent in my medical school loans, or fund a research assistant at the National Cancer Institute – something *useful*. Given how hawkishly Grandma has always watched over money, she could have the millionaire feeling she seeks simply by spending a fraction of the amount in her pocketbook. But it's her choice, and I guess I must remember that even if I can't justify it; how she spends *her* cash is *her* choice. The kind of money resting snug in her handbag is beyond my mental grasp in size and sacrifice.

Grandma stares at me, irked, and I stare back until her shoulders stiffen and retreat, anticipating the approach of the waiter. We sit in silence while Grandma's brew is poured. No tiny bubbles crowd the side of her cup – she has plain filtered coffee. But I have cappuccino, and there is so much froth on the surface that I cannot see the liquid.

'Your "money" don't count,' Grandma says. She sounds vexed. 'My "money" don't exist. It's a bad sign – we're gonna leave here without our shirts.'

'No,' and I smile lopsidedly at her, '*you* might leave here without your shirt. The only money I have is in the bank, safe and sound to pay off med school loans. If I gambled and lost, it wouldn't be a shirt I'd lose, it'd be a labcoat, and that's too expensive for my tastes. All you lose is wild money, Mrs Gunslinger-Suche. Let's sign the bill and find the nearest roulette table. Or poker. Your choice.' Your money.

'Thomas got lucky at poker first time I was in Reno. Maybe I oughtta go for poker first, in the spirit of this trip. But then again, I kinda fancy roulette.'

It could be any time of day or night in this immense gambling cave. Outside it might be a shy grey early morning or a blazing bright late afternoon, but inside Bally's you would never know. I have yet to see a clock. And time-specific foods, like scrambled eggs, pancakes, and three-course dinners are available twenty-four hours a day. As are cocktails, beer and wine. It is the ultimate in environmental manipulation.

Grandma walks with her hand on the fat pocketbook I carry for her, and she pats this as we approach the roulette table. People here wear more elegant clothes than in the slot machine section; men are in dinner jackets while most of the women wear long dresses and sparkling jewellery. Grandma's long red talons have lots of company here, but to really fit in, she needs a diamond ring the size of a golf ball. 'Folks here look like they come by the millionaire feeling without even tryin'!' Grandma's whisper is awed. 'Did you see that gal just put a loada chips on numer 39? That was a thousand bucks! Look there! That little pile of chips on 39 is a thousand smackers. They're spinnin' the wheel now, watch!'

Around the table all eyes follow a tiny silver ball which flies round and round under the rim of the roulette wheel. The fervour of the onlookers' stares seems inversely proportional to the amount of money wagered. Grandma has bet nothing but her gaze is more concentrated than perfume, while the woman who settled a thousand dollars on number 39 only looks up occasionally from her diamond-crusty watch. A soft collective murmur rises from the roulette crowd as the ball settles into a slot marked sixteen. No one put any chips on that number. Again, the crowd murmurs as a long wooden rake sweeps across the table, collecting all the chips for the casino.

We watch for fifteen minutes, fascinated, until Grandma whispers, 'Don't reckon this game appeals to me. The bucks float away too easy. Let's try poker.'

We watch poker – the elegant strain of silent players trying to beat the dealer – and this also fails to win Grandma's favour. She tugs on my arm to bend my ear. 'Every Tuesday night back in Maryland the gals and me dump out our purses and play poker for small change –'

'Shhh,' demands the croupier, glaring at Grandma.

'This ain't a church,' she shoots back, though she hooks her arm through mine and leads a retreat towards the neon slot machines. 'Just nickels and dimes, that's all we play for. Sometimes I win a coupla bucks, which is plenty exciting for me. Lookee there, a quarter! Somebody dropped a quarter.' Grandma unhooks her arm and steps forward, ready to bend and pick it up. She fails to see a woman zooming in, her fingers outstretched like the talons of a hawk diving on a fieldmouse.

'Mine!' calls the woman. She is Asian, more tiny than Grandma, and agitated.

'No,' says Grandma, looking very fierce, 'mine. Go find your own quarter. You saw me see that coin, then *you* wanted it for yourself. You didn't drop it! It ain't yours!'

The two women face off against each other, like cats ready to scratch. 'Mine,' insists the woman, snatching the coin from between my grandmother's fingers and shaking it in the air. Her face goes pink with rage and triumph. Grandma stares at the disputed coin for a moment, then she springs, dazzling the enemy with a blood red turbo-charged flash of fingernails. With one hand Grandma rips the quarter from the woman's fingers, and with the other she punches her in the shoulder. Skipping backwards, Grandma grasps me by the arm and scoots away.

'I showed her,' she says, panting. 'That bitch. This quarter's gonna be real lucky for me, I can feel it. There was no money in my coffee cup,' she crows, 'but I made my own luck!'

'It seems to me that you always have, Grandma.' I don't turn to her as I speak, because my eyes are sweeping all approaches for the co-claimant to the quarter. I swivel, scanning behind us, and am stopped by the curious expression on Grandma's face. She looks down at the quarter in her palm, turning it over and over, heads and tails, heads and tails.

'No, I don't make my own luck. What I'm good at is makin' my own *way*. You know, I can't spend a dime of this money from *Li'l Maude*. Not a dime. I just can't.' She looks frustrated and purple and downcast.

'We haven't found the right game for you, Grandma, that's all. Let's try the craps table, or find a poker game with a pleasant dealer. And look at all the slots.'

'No, I'm not gonna. I'm done here.' She draws herself

up to her full height. 'How much do you reckon folks got to put in a twenty-five dollar slot machine every time they play that one-arm bandit? Just to pull that handle. How much? It's not twenty-five bucks, it's *seventy-five*! I been watchin', and it's all come back to me, one coin for each little fruit window. To get three cherries you gotta dish out three tokens. Too rich for my blood. I'm feelin' the millionaire feel just by walking round with this money in my pocketbook – I know I *could* play, if I *wanted.* That's the difference, Doctor. This's how a queen feels.' Grandma squeezes my arm and smiles up at me a complicated smile of relief and rebellion. Opening her pregnant handbag, she whips out ten one-hundred dollar bills and waves them at me. Here in Reno, by the twenty-five dollar slot machines which cost seventy-five dollars to play, no one even looks twice at a thousand dollars. Except for me. I am unschooled in fiscal insouciance.

Grandma crunches the bills in her fist, making a small ball of money. 'Here,' she says.

'What?'

'It's for your budge. You oughtta have a little somethin' in your bosom to fall back on. And it'll give you a millionaire feeling like I got, knowin' you *could* spend it if you wanted.'

I can feel the amazement on my face. Grandma stares up at me and watches while my eyes go back and forth between her and the wad in my fist. I am suffused with gratitude and money glory.

'Now. I gotta get to the cashier and get five nickels for my lucky quarter. I got no problem spending money I *found*, so I'm gonna have one fifteen-cent pull at the nickel slots, and then we're goin' to bed.'

While Grandma changes her quarter for nickels, I walk to the nearest nickel slot machine and study it. Sevens, lemons, cherries . . . I notice my right hand floating up to pat my budge, to feel how inflated my chest feels with money, and I quell the impulse to do it again. This particular trick is Grandma's, and I remember how it embarrassed and irritated me when I was young. But I can't stop my hand, it rises of its own volition.

'I got 'em!' Holding five drab nickels, Grandma appears at my shoulder. Neither one of us really looks at the tiny frail figure who appears at the slot machine next to us, hitching herself up on the stool so she can pull the machine's arm in comfort.

'One . . . two . . . three,' Grandma says, dropping the nickels into the slots. 'C'mon, Lady Luck! Maude needs new shoes!' Almost hyperventilating with excitement, Grandma plays the machine. I stand back, my arms folded tight against my body to help prop it up as a wave of fatigue hits me powerfully. After days of hard driving and a near sleepless night at Arches National Park, my body is ready to give out. And right now it's nearly three o'clock in the morning. Thank God Grandma is ready for bed.

Her back is to me as she watches the spinning of the slot wheels. And then I hear the screech and see Grandma's body start to shake.

'AHHHHHHH! YAAAAH!'

The physician's beeper goes off in my head like a siren. *A heart attack! Get an epinephrine IV! An epinephrine IV or even sodium bicarb, it's in the car first aid kit! You should have made room for the defibrillators, you fool! For God's sake, Grandma is having a heart attack! Move!*

Shut up, says the granddaughter in me. My hand is on my grandmother's back, and I know the noise isn't coming from her. Grandma is bouncing up and down on her stool with her face in her hands. The noise comes from Grandma's neighbour, the co-claimant to the quarter.

'Three sevens,' the woman screeches. 'AHYEEEYAH! What you win, what win?'

Grandma is chuckling too hard to speak. Down by her knees the slot machine has vomited out an uncountably vast number of nickels. You could stir the nickels with a spoon then stand the spoon upright in the pile. It's an amazing mound of nickels.

'I might be here a while,' says Grandma, turning to me with the remnants of her chuckles. Then she picks out five nickels and offers them to her neighbour. 'Here,' says Grandma. 'These are for you. I won them with *my* quarter.'

The woman stares haughtily at Grandma's palm before turning back to her own slot machine. 'Stick up your nose. I win my own, win more!' The words are a battle cry, and they fall on the ears of Maude Orpwood Suche, who might otherwise have scooped up her winnings and put them in a cut glass vase in the middle of her coffee table to remind her everlastingly of Reno, Nevada.

Grandma is nothing if not a warrior, and her battles have never been ordinary.

• • •

'Wake up, darn it. You okay?' She leans over me and breathes whiskey fumes in my hair. 'Wake up, for corn's sake what does it take?'

Coming out of my stupor I notice first that the weight of Grandma's pocketbook on my stomach is gone. Though I crossed my arms through the handles for safety, her pocketbook is gone. Thirty thousand dollars. I can't believe I went to sleep watching over thirty thousand dollars. 'Where . . . where,' I fumble verbally.

'When I saw you'd gone to sleep on this sofa I came and got my bag,' Grandma tells me. 'Don't have a spell.' She is buoyant with happiness, and all I can do is blink at her.

'I played for three hours on one quarter I picked off the rug! That's how to gamble! I lasted longer than Emily Chen who tried to steal my quarter in the first place – she's out five bucks tonight, and I'm dead even. I've had my fun, now let's get some coffee into you, because we're headed for the beach. Right now. It's time to see how far West we can go.'

San Gregorio Beach, California

The car can drive no further West. We've reached cliffs, and the beach is down below though I can't see the sand. Or the Pacific. I can't see the Pacific at the beach, and the reason why is mist. Just five miles inland the sun hung brightly in a hot blue sky, and redwood trees, like big cousins to the pine trees of Maryland, stood tall. Five miles ago I had hopes for this coast, for the beach, for putting down roots into this dry Western soil. But here only beige cliffs stand out against the fog.

'I'm not getting out of the car,' I tell Grandma. 'You can, if you want to. But I will not.'

'Jeezle peezle,' she says, peering into my face. ''Course you're getting out of the car. Don't be a fool.'

I glare at her, knowing how unreasonable I'm being. I'm so tired and dismayed, and rationally I know tears are likely but not very helpful, while irrationally I want to cry until my face turns red and my tear ducts run dry. I am a doctor, and the only sickness I fear for myself is homesickness. I know no cure except home. Forcing myself to reach for the door handle, I step outside on to the cliffs above San Gregorio Beach and look down into the mist.

Bending over at the waist, Grandma jerks hard on her shoelaces, making them as tight as possible for the jagged trail down the cliffs on to the sand, then she reaches for my arm and we begin a slow descent. I'm pleased that I can worry about Grandma slipping; the anxiety is a welcome distraction.

On the sand, fifty feet below the car, the temperature is ten degrees colder than the air above. ''Cause of the mist, I reckon,' Grandma says. 'Back in 1949 Thomas and the boys and me hit the sands for the first time in San Diego. The Pacific didn't look like this down in Southern California.'

I can feel the chill of the water from here, in the slight breeze which lifts off the water and brings the scent of cold salt to my nose. Because I grew up on the Chesapeake Bay and possess the discerning nose of a Bay woman, I can smell that the water temperature hovers around sixty degrees fahrenheit – an autumnal water temperature in Maryland. If blue crabs were indigenous to this part of the world, they would be sluggish in the cool depths. I know how they would feel.

'Wanna take a walk?' asks Grandma, clutching her elbows.

'No.' I remove my sweater and hold it while she threads her thin old arms through my long sleeves. 'I need a nap. I can't even think about this place until I've had another hour's sleep. I'll run back up to the car. Have a nice walk, Grandma.'

I can feel her eyes on me as I climb back up the cliffs. Once at the car, though, I take a blanket from the trunk and walk back down to the beach to sleep on the sand. It's eleven o'clock in the morning, and the sun has to rise out of this fog sometime. I'm sure the surprise of it will wake me.

But it doesn't.

When I wake myself up, throwing the blanket off my arms with the violence of a sleeping person impatient with the standards of climate control, my watch says two o'clock. I'm hot, and my hair is stiff with salt spray. Above me the sky is palest grey blue, and behind and beneath me is the beige of sand and cliffs. The Pacific rolls in front of me, unshrouded and dark, and it has enticed Grandma close. Motionless, she sits on damp sand about twenty feet closer to the water, and between her and the surf froth hulks a black mound of resilient fishy flesh. I can smell it from here, just as it can smell me; I know by how its head moves.

It's a sea lion. Just sitting on the beach with Grandma and me, and though I want to edge closer, I'm anxious about frightening it. Barely breathing I stare at the sea lion, who occasionally turns, with a dense liquid ripple around its shoulders, to watch Grandma and me. When at last it slides back into the rising tide, I stand up to see it go, and then, rubbing my stiff neck, I walk to Grandma.

'Hello. I feel much better for my nap. Not optimistic, exactly, but more tolerant.'

She doesn't turn her head to look at me.

'Are you all right, Grandma? Maybe you should have a nap, too.'

Shaking her head without speaking, she turns to me and I see that the fog over the water went into her cloudy wet eyes. Oh, Grandma.

'I guess', she says wretchedly, 'you come to a point where you can't run away from yourself no more. Only thing worse than a young fool is an old fool. And what's worse'n both is a forever fool. That's me. I came on this trip to look at my mistakes, the ones I made with Thomas, but they don't matter a drop of rain to a flood. Thomas was my punishment, along with everything that happened after. It hurts so bad to be a fool. Try not to do that, make a real big try. I'll feel better if I know bein' a fool helped you out. Nerf made those four bullets with four people in mind, I know he did. He knew I'd never use 'em, but it was revenge and escape made him think of it. They were for Thomas and Timola, and Nerf and me. All because I was too weak to listen to myself.'

Her gaze never wavers from the spot where the sea lion disappeared. 'I *should* have married Nerf Fleishman. I loved him, and he loved me. Everything that happened after I made the wrong choice is my fault, 'cause *I* let other folks make *my* choices. I got to face that.'

Because I don't know what to say I dig my fingertips into the sand. I am a water person, and the impulse to make dribble castles and moulds of my hands and toes does not desert me in times of trouble. If anything, the impulse is harder to ignore. Scraping wet sand together, I fit a hillock between the arches of my feet. And then it seems that my grandmother is waiting for me, expecting something of me.

'I'll be coming home in two years' time, Grandma, once I've learned what *I* want to know. Would you like to ride cross country with me, West to East? You don't have to tell me right now. It's a standing invitation. Regrets only.'

She holds her hand out to me and I pull her up so that we can walk along the shore. As we walk the fog rolls back in and the rising water pushes us up closer to the cliffs, but the sand feels good under my feet, and the smell of the ocean revitalises me. When we turn back for the car, Grandma speaks after a long silence, and though it seems like a *non sequitur*, it isn't.

'No regrets.'